VALLEY
OF THE GUN

Center Point
Large Print

Also by Ralph Cotton and available from
Center Point Large Print:

Jackpot Ridge

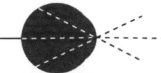

**This Large Print Book carries the
Seal of Approval of N.A.V.H.**

VALLEY
OF THE GUN

Ralph Cotton

CENTER POINT LARGE PRINT
THORNDIKE, MAINE

This Center Point Large Print edition is published
in the year 2013 by arrangement with NAL Signet,
a member of Penguin Group (USA) Inc.

The text of this Large Print edition is unabridged.
In other aspects, this book may
vary from the original edition.
Printed in the United States of America
on permanent paper.
Set in 16-point Times New Roman type.

ISBN: 978-1-61173-727-1

Library of Congress Cataloging-in-Publication Data

Cotton, Ralph W.
Valley of the gun / Ralph Cotton. — Center Point Large Print edition.
pages cm
ISBN 978-1-61173-727-1 (Library binding : alk. paper)
1. Large type books. I. Title.
PS3553.O766V35 2013
813´.54—dc23

2012049269

For Mary Lynn . . . of course

PART 1

Chapter 1

Whiskey Bend
The Badlands, Arizona Territory

Afternoon shadows stretched long across the rocky land as Arizona Ranger Sam Burrack walked into Whiskey Bend from the south, dust-covered, leading his copper black-point dun by its slack reins. When he saw the tall figure wearing a black duster step out into the empty street forty yards in front of him, he knew what to expect. He stopped for only a second, long enough to flip the reins up over the dun's saddle and give the tired horse a push, sending it out of the way.

Staring straight ahead, he slowly drew his big Colt from its holster and walked on, his thumb over the gun's hammer. He didn't stop again until he stood thirty feet from the gunman, facing him. He took note of the man's riding duster gathered back behind the long custom-made Simpson-Barre .45-caliber pistol holstered on his right hip.

The gunman, Lightning Wade Hornady, had stayed behind while the other five riders left Whiskey Bend only a moment earlier. The dust of the five riders still loomed in the air on the far end of the wide street. Seeing the gunman reach for something in his vest pocket, Sam tightened his thumb over the gun hammer, ready to cock it on the upswing. Yet he held back, seeing the man raise a gold watch by its braided horsehair fob and hold it in his right hand.

"Pardon me, young man, whilst I wind my watch," Hornady said, cool, confident, opening the lid on the shiny timepiece and glancing down at it. "If I don't wind it while I'm thinking about it, I fear I'll spend the entire evening under an air of uncertainty." He grinned around a long cigar clamped between his teeth. Smoke wafted from beneath his thick mustache. "I hope you don't mind, *Marshal?*"

"I'm in no hurry," the Ranger said flatly. If this cordial manner was the way Lightning Hornady wanted to play it, he would accommodate him. *But only up to a point,* Sam cautioned himself. Correcting the gunman he said, "It's *Ranger* . . . Arizona Territory Ranger Samuel Burrack."

The gunman looked bemused; he stopped winding the watch, his left thumb and finger still clutching its stem.

"Oh, I see," he said. "Then you would be the young fellow who caused such a stir, killing Junior Lake and his whole gang back in—"

"I would be," Sam said, cutting Hornady short, staring into his eyes, yet managing to pay attention to the gunman's hands.

"I have to say, I am taken aback, Ranger,"

Hornady said, his left hand taking the watch now, his right hand dropping easily down his side, hanging near the big custom Simpson-Barre revolver. "When they asked me to stay behind and kill you, I didn't realize what an important fellow you are."

Sam didn't reply right away. Instead, he watched the gunman's left hand closely as it slipped the watch back into his vest and lingered there. The Ranger found it interesting that the gunman had held the watch in his right hand and used his left hand to wind it.

Wade Hornady opened and closed his right fingers near his gun butt, his left hand clasping the lapel on his duster. He chuckled behind his long cigar.

"Why have you been dogging our trail so fiercely, Ranger?" he asked. "Don't you have plenty of other innocent citizens to harass and aggravate?"

"You and your pals robbed the bank in Goble day before yesterday," said the Ranger. "That's why I'm dogging you."

Hornady's right hand appeared ready to grab for his holstered revolver. But Sam had already seen enough to know the move wasn't coming from the right hand. Lightning Hornady was only drawing his attention to the custom revolver.

Watch for the left, Sam cautioned himself.

Hornady shrugged, gave his confident grin.

"It was only a small pissant of a bank, nothing worth getting excited over—certainly not worth getting yourself killed over, is it?"

This journeyman gunman played his part well, Sam noted, so well that the Ranger decided if he waited long enough and gave this gunman enough room, the odds were good that Lightning Hornady might get an edge and kill him right here where he stood.

Sam continued to stare at him, revealing nothing.

"Well, *is it?*" Hornady asked again.

Without reply, without warning, the Ranger cocked the big Colt on the upswing, just as he'd planned to all along, and put a bullet through the unprepared gunman's chest. The Colt bucked in the Ranger's hand; the single explosion resounded along the street and out across the hill line.

Wade Hornady flew backward, his cigar abandoned in midair, appearing suspended there for a moment as he slid on the rough dirt street behind a settling mist of blood. As the cigar fell to the ground and the downed gunslinger came to a halt, Sam turned from side to side, crouched, fanning the smoking Colt toward any window or darkened doorway that could offer cover for any of Hornady's cohorts.

Once satisfied that Hornady had truly been left alone to kill him, Sam lowered the big Colt an inch and walked forward toward the prone gunman. Hornady struggled for the belly gun inside his duster as his bootheels scooted him backward in the blood-splattered dirt. He stopped and stared up as Sam loomed over him.

Sam reached down, brushed Hornady's bloody hand aside and jerked a smaller custom Simpson-Barre revolver from a belly rig. He looked it over, admiring the ornate engraving covering its entire barrel and frame. Evening sunlight glinted soft on the gun's ivory grips.

"Some gun," Sam said quietly. He shoved the adorned revolver into his gun belt, then drew his long-barreled revolver from its holster and let it hang from his left hand. He stared down at the bleeding gunman as townsfolk began easing back into sight and gathering a few safe yards away.

"We—we were still talking," Hornady said in a strained voice. He stared up at Sam in disbelief.

"You were," Sam said quietly. "I was all through."

Hornady looked at the gaping hole in his chest; blood surged.

"You shoot a man down . . . just like that?" Hornady rasped in an air of moral outrage, a stunned expression on his pale, tortured face.

"Yep, just like that," Sam said matter-of-factly. He stooped beside the bleeding gunman and studied the wound closely. "Dad Orwick must think highly of you, leaving you all by yourself here."

"I always work . . . better alone," the outlaw

said, gasping for breath. "Until now, that is," he added, looking down at his bloody wound. "Looks like you've done me in."

"My bullet missed your heart, Lightning," Sam said. "You've got a good chance of living through this."

Hornady looked surprised at hearing the Ranger call him by his trail name.

"You—you know who I am?" he said.

"Yep, everybody's heard of Lightning Wade Hornady," Sam replied.

"Let me get this straight," Hornady rasped, and coughed, raising a bloody finger. "You know who I am, and still, you just . . . walk up and shoot me?" He appeared to have a hard time making sense of it.

"You want a doctor?" Sam asked without replying. "There's a good one here, if we can catch him sober this hour of the day." He untied a bandanna from around Hornady's neck, wadded it, laid it on his bloody chest and placed the gunman's hand on it.

"Catch him *sober?*" Hornady coughed and shook his head. "No, thanks. If the drunken son of a bitch don't kill me . . . I'll go off to rot in Yuma Prison. *Huh-uh* . . . not for me."

"Suit yourself," said the Ranger. "Thought I'd ask." He reached into Hornady's boot well and pulled out a large knife in a rawhide sheath, with knuckle dusters shielding its handle. He looked the knife over, shook his head and shoved both it and Hornady's big custom revolver down in his gun belt beside the gunslinger's smaller revolver before turning to walk away.

Hornady glowered, looking at his two custom revolvers and his big boot knife wedged behind the Ranger's gun belt.

"Wait. . . . I changed my mind," he said, seeing the gathered townsfolk moving in closer. "I do want a doctor . . . drunk or sober. I don't want to die . . . not until I see you lying dead somewhere, Ranger . . . buzzards scooping out your brains." His words ended in a bloody cough.

"That's the spirit," Sam said flatly. He turned to an older man wearing a long gray beard who had walked up and looked down at Hornady's wound. Seeing a tin star on the bearded man's chest, Sam asked, "Are you the sheriff?"

"Yes, I am," the man said, turning a glance at the Ranger, then back to the wounded gunman. "I'm Grayson DeShay, volunteer sheriff, for the time being anyway." He shook his head slowly and added, "And I know who the two of you are. This one with his belly bleeding is Lightning Wade Hornady. You're Samuel Burrack, the Ranger who passes through here now and again, I'm told."

"You're right on both counts," Sam said. "I apologize for not coming to find you first, Sheriff. But this man was gunning for me as soon as I walked into town."

"I understand, Ranger," said Sheriff DeShay. "Anyway, I wasn't sheriff here your last time through. I decided it wise to hang back out of the way, for fear of you shooting me, thinking I was one of his pards."

"I understand, Sheriff," Sam said. "That was wise thinking."

Hornady gave a sour expression.

"Well, ain't this just wonderful? The two of you *understand* each other so well," he said in his cynical, pain-filled voice.

"Lightning here wants a doctor," Sam said to the sheriff, ignoring the bitter wounded outlaw's remark.

"An undertaker might serve him better," the volunteer sheriff replied. "What do you want me to do with him if he lives?" he asked. "What'd he do anyhow?"

"Bank robbery," Sam said.

"Him and the bunch he rode in with?" DeShay asked.

"Yep," said the Ranger. "He's with Fannin Orwick's Redemption Riders. Ever heard of them?"

"*Dad* Orwick? You bet I have," said Deshay. "I saw him once in Carson. That was years ago, though. The old bull's got more wives and kids scattered across these badland hills than you could squeeze into two freight cars. Calls his whole brood the Family of the Lord—which

16

reveals how highly he thinks of himself, I expect."

"That's him all right," Sam said. "He robs banks to support his *family*. I need to get on their trail while it's still warm. I'd like you to hold him until a posse gets here from Goble. If the posse doesn't make it, turn him over to the circuit jail wagon when it makes its rounds."

"I'll do that, Ranger," said DeShay, "only I didn't see Dad Orwick riding with the bunch who came through here."

"You wouldn't if Orwick played it right," Sam said. "I saw where three horses split off the trail a mile out. I expect he and a couple of his gunmen circled town. They'll take up with the others farther along." He nodded toward a line of hills in the distance.

"Shit," Hornady grumbled to himself with contempt. "These two pecker heads wouldn't recognize *Dad* if he walked up and kicked them in the sack."

DeShay ignored Hornady's grumbling and gazed out with the Ranger.

"It makes sense he'd do that," he replied.

Sam turned to DeShay, lifted the two Simpson-Barre revolvers from behind his gun belt and handed them to him. "You can sell these guns to help pay for this one's keep here."

"You can't sell my guns," Hornady shouted in spite of his pain. "I've got money . . . I'll pay for my jailing . . . I can afford my keep."

17

"Do what best suits you, Sheriff," Sam said. "Any money he has on him is most likely stolen."

"Obliged, Ranger," said DeShay. He hefted the two custom-made revolvers in his hands and looked them over closely. "I might want to keep these for myself." He gave Hornady a flat grin.

"What about my knife, Ranger?" Hornady asked with a scornful tone. "I expect you thieving sons a' bitches will steal it too, huh?"

"Shut up," Sheriff DeShay warned, giving Hornady a stiff kick in his side. Hornady let out a deep, painful moan and grasped his chest.

Sam pulled Hornady's knife and its rawhide sheath from behind his belt and handed it to the sheriff.

"If you'd waited a second longer, you'd have seen me give it to him and saved yourself a kick in the ribs," Sam said.

"I'll see you in hell, Ranger—*in hell,* I tell you!"

"Another word out of you and I'll tell Dr. Lanahan to stitch your mouth shut," DeShay said down to Hornady. "If he's drunk enough, he'll likely do it and have himself a good laugh about it."

Hornady coughed blood and closed his eyes as the Ranger walked away. When Sam picked up the reins to the black-point dun, he turned to the sheriff and said, "If you need me, I'll be at the livery barn getting this dun fed and tended before I move on."

"Obliged, Ranger," said DeShay. "I'll be along and let you know how he's doing, if Doc don't miss a lick and cut him in half." He grinned fiercely down at Hornady, then turned to two townsmen standing nearby and gestured down at the hapless outlaw. "You fellows get him up and carry him over to Doc Lanahan's for me." He turned to another townsman and said, "Gainer, go fetch the doc from the saloon. Tell him to set his bottle down. He's got a patient needing him."

"This is his drinking time. What if he won't come?" asked Ted Gainer, a tall, serious-looking man with a thick, wide mustache and watery eyes.

"He'll come. He heard the gunshot," DeShay said confidently. "He always comes, even if his path ain't always in a straight line."

Ted Gainer turned toward the saloon a block away, where a crowd of onlookers jammed the open batwing doors, some of the more curious of them already stepping down from the boardwalk and walking forward.

"Tell him I'll get some coffee boiling," DeShay called out in an afterthought. He grinned down at Hornady as the two townsmen stooped to pick him up. "That'll help him clear away some of the dancing squirrels and pin whistles before he goes to cutting and stitching on Lightning Wade here."

Hornady moaned at the prospect and closed his eyes.

The two townsmen laughed as they raised

Hornady by his shoulders and bootheels and walked away along the dirt street with him hanging limp between them. But Hornady saw nothing funny about it. He cursed to himself and let his mind drift away into a dark tunnel of unconsciousness, blood dripping steadily from his wound.

"That blasted Ranger," he murmured in a weak and trailing voice. "Just when everything's going my way. . . ."

Chapter 2

A few minutes had passed before Dr. Howard Lanahan stepped into his office. He stopped and stood in the open doorway of the surgery room, steadying himself with a hand on either side of the doorframe. He stared at the two men. His bleary red eyes ran along Lightning Wade Hornady, who lay prone and bleeding on a surgery gurney; then he looked Sheriff DeShay up and down, DeShay standing close beside the gurney.

"Which one of you three gentlemen wants to be my patient?" the big doctor asked, his voice clear but thick.

"Holy God," Hornady moaned, hearing the doctor's query, knowing he and the sheriff were the only ones there.

"Jesus, Doc," said DeShay with slight chuckle, "*he* is." He gestured a hand down at the bloody Hornady. "Are you going to be able to—?"

"That was a little joke, Sheriff," the big, red-faced doctor said, cutting DeShay off. "Of course I'm perfectly able to do my job. Sometimes I just like to lighten the air a little before dabbling these fingers in a man's guts."

He grinned, taking off his battered derby hat as he stepped over to the gurney and looked down at Hornady. He deftly spun his derby toward a tall corner hat rack, but it missed the rack altogether and sailed out an open window.

Sheriff DeShay saw the doctor's error but wasn't going to mention it. He continued to stare at the doctor.

"I set a pot of coffee to boil when we got here, Doc," he said. "It ought to be ready by now. Why don't I get you a cup? You can drink it before you get started." He turned and headed for the kitchen in the rear of the clapboard house.

"A sterling idea, Sheriff. Bring the pot," Dr. Lanahan replied to DeShay over his shoulder as the sheriff's boots resounded along the hallway. "That is, if my patient here doesn't mind me sipping whilst I work." He stared down at Hornady with a leering grin and squeezed the wounded outlaw's thigh. "I'm tempted to ask which leg we're removing today, but I have a hunch you don't appreciate my keen sense of humor."

"That's it. I'm out . . . of here!" Hornady struggled to raise himself up onto his elbows, but the doctor eased him back down. Blood surged up between the doctor's fingers.

"Now, now, take it easy," Lanahan said. "There's nothing for you to get all excited about. From the looks of this wound, you'll most likely leave here in a box anyway."

The doctor peeled off his swallow-tailed coat and rolled up his shirtsleeves. He reached to a shelf, took down a bottle of clear liquid and picked up a folded white cloth.

Hornady watched the doctor pour a few drops of chloroform liquid onto the cloth.

"Is that what you use to knock me out?" Hornady asked in a weak voice.

"Yep, unless you'd prefer a sound blow from a blackthorn shillelagh I keep under my desk," Dr. Lanahan said. He took a deep breath and held it.

Hornady started to ask, "Is there any danger in this stuff making a man *mumph*—" But his words stopped short. His eyes flew open wide. He caught the bittersweet taste and scent of the vapory liquid press down over his nose and mouth.

"Sweet dreams," Dr. Lanahan said, holding the cloth firmly over Hornady's face. The wounded outlaw's whole body gave one stiff jerk, then fell limp. His eyes rolled up in their sockets and seemed to stick there.

From the doorway behind the doctor, Sheriff DeShay stood staring, coffeepot and empty mug in hand. He walked to the gurney, setting the pot down on a small table, and looked at Hornady's eyes.

"Is he all right, Doc?" he asked.

"That's a hell of a question, Sheriff," said Dr. Lanahan. "I could damn near read a book through the hole in his chest." He closed Hornady's eyes, then took the coffee mug and held it for DeShay to fill. "Other than that and losing enough blood to fill an ox bladder, he seems chipper enough." He stifled a belch and sipped the strong, hot coffee, making an ill face as he swallowed.

"What's wrong, Doc?" DeShay asked.

"I hate putting so much effort into drinking just to stop short and sober up all at once," the doctor said. He sighed, took another sip and shook his head. "It's a waste of both good whiskey and human endeavor."

"Are you going to be needing my help doing any of this?" DeShay asked quietly.

"What you're asking me is, am I sober enough?" the doctor said flatly. "My answer is, what choice do I have? You see any other doctors running around here, drunk or sober? Either I fix him up or we get out the shovels and wax. Now step back and give me room to drink my coffee." The doctor sipped and paused. "Better yet, get out of here. I work better without being watched."

DeShay only nodded. He reached behind his back and took out a pair of handcuffs. Using both hands, he took off Hornady's right boot and let it fall to the floor. Then he cuffed the unconscious outlaw's ankle to a gurney rail and jerked it a little, testing it.

Dr. Lanahan raised both hands above Hornady's bloody chest and turned them back and forth. "I'd wash them first," he murmured to himself, wiggling his fingers, inspecting them, "but I'm only going to get them bloody anyway." To DeShay he said over his shoulder as if in afterthought, "Where will you be in case I need to send somebody for you?"

"I'm going to the livery barn to see the Ranger—talk to him before he leaves town," said DeShay, already heading for the front door.

Crossing an empty side street on his way to the livery barn, DeShay spotted the lone figure slip from the shadows ahead of him and stalk toward the rear door of the barn, a rifle in his hands. When the man turned to check the street behind him, DeShay sidled quickly out of sight around a corner of a shack and watched. The figure continued on, then stopped and crouched behind a stack of building lumber, and DeShay took the opportunity to move forward himself.

The gunman's attention was so concentrated on the livery door that he neither heard nor saw the sheriff until DeShay stopped ten feet behind him and stood with Hornady's big Simpson-Barre pistol raised and aimed.

"Lay that long iron down easy-like and raise your hands," DeShay said quietly.

Hearing the voice behind him, the gunman tensed, looking ready to spin and fire.

Seeing what the gunman had in mind, DeShay cocked the big Simpson-Barre, making sure the man heard it.

"That'll be the worst idea you've had all day," he said. "Drop the gun. The next sound you hear won't be me telling you again."

"Take it easy, DeShay," the gunman said, recognizing the sheriff's voice. "Look, I'm laying it down. There we go."

DeShay watched him set the rifle atop a pile of boards.

"That's part of it," DeShay said. "Now turn around, *slow.* Let me get a look at you."

The gunman raised his gloved hands chest high. Turning, he gave a sheepish grin.

"It's me, Albert Hirsh," he said. "Looks like you caught me fair and square, Sheriff. I was about to relieve myself right back here behind this stack of planks." He gave a shrug. "I know what you're thinking—you're thinking I'm too damned ornery to walk to the jake. And you're right. I don't blame you for thinking it. It's nothing but ornery and inconsiderate, a man pissing wherever he pleases these days when there's facilities aplenty in every direction—"

"Shut up, Hirsh," DeShay said, cutting him off. "I saw what you were setting up to do here, you bushwhacking turd."

"*Bushwhack?* No, Sheriff, you've got me all wrong," the gunman said. "Improper personal habits, yes, I admit to. But bushwhack a man? *Huh-uh,* that's not my way."

DeShay stared at him, the big custom revolver cocked and pointed at his chest.

"Where's the rest of Dad Orwick's men, the ones you rode in with earlier?" he asked.

"Oh, they've all gone on, Sheriff," said Hirsh. "They sent me back to check on Lightning. We heard a shot after we rode out and when Hornady never caught up with us . . ." He let his words trail.

"So you figured something was amiss," DeShay said flatly.

"Pretty much," said Hirsh, giving him an innocent look. "Were we wrong thinking it?"

"Lightning Wade Hornady got a bullet shot through him right after you and your pals left town," DeShay said. "An Arizona Ranger shot him down." He cocked his head slightly to the side. "But why is it I feel like you already knew all this?"

Hirsh shrugged again, his hands still chest high.

"That I can't tell you," he said, "although I

always said you're sharper than a briar when it comes to the knowing of things right off the top of your head. It must come from some deep inborn well of insightfulness would be my only explanation."

"A deep well of *insight* . . . I see," DeShay said as if considering it. "Let me tell you something else that keeps running through my mind. I can't help thinking you and your pals had a good laugh after riding out of here, thinking how you'd robbed the bank over in Goble and ridden straight to Whiskey Bend"—his expression darkened— "to *my town,* with a posse licking at your heels! And how do I hear about it? I hear about it when a Ranger rides in and shoots down one of your pards in the middle of *my* street!"

"Easy, Sheriff. Nobody meant you any dis- respect," said Hirsh, seeing the sheriff's gun hand tighten around Hornady's big custom revolver. "Anyway, I wasn't the one in charge, else I would have straightaway called you to the side. You and Dad being friendly as you are, I would have told you we'd been out on a spree. You can believe that."

"Who was in charge?" DeShay asked.

"Arvin Peck," said Hirsh. "Right before Dad and his *segundos* split off from the rest of us, he told Peck to get us through Whiskey Bend and on up the trail."

"And my name wasn't mentioned, in any way?"

DeShay said. He rubbed his thumb and fingers together in the universal sign of greed.

"Not that I heard, Sheriff," said Hirsh, "and that's the gospel truth, so help me."

"You're lying, Hirsh," said DeShay.

Hirsh looked confused.

"I am?" he said. His eyes widened, seeing DeShay's gun hand tighten, along with the look on the bearded sheriff's face. "What part's not true?" he asked, as if genuinely confused.

"The part about nobody mentioning me," DeShay said. "Nobody pulls a robbery and comes riding to my town afterward. Not unless they're taking care of me. It's a matter of respect."

Hirsh looked relieved, knowing what part of his story he had to recount.

"Okay, you're right—that part was a lie," he said. "But the rest really *was* the gospel truth. The last words out of Dad's mouth before he and his *segundos* cut out were 'Peck, you see to it you take care of Sheriff DeShay.'"

"But he didn't," DeShay said.

"I know and it's a terrible thing when folks can't be counted on to do what they're supposed to. I'd apologize if I thought it meant anything to you." He studied the sheriff's cold stare and asked meekly, "Would it?"

"No, it wouldn't," said DeShay.

Seeing the tip of the custom revolver rise from pointing at his chest and level on his face, Hirsh swallowed a hard knot in his throat.

"Can I say something?" he asked.

"Make it quick," said DeShay.

"I see that's Lightning Wade's gun you're training on me. I just want to caution you that it *does* have a hair trigger, in case you haven't already shot it and found that out for yourself. I say this because if you don't really intend to shoot me, I wouldn't want it going off by accident. You see what I mean?"

"I do," said the sheriff. "But you needn't worry about an accident."

Hirsh swallowed another hard knot.

"Meaning . . ."

"Meaning just what you think it means," said DeShay.

The big custom revolver bucked in his hand. Hirsh's forehead pitched back at a sharp angle, forcing him hard against the pile of building planks. A large red mist exploded from the back of his head as he collapsed to the ground, dead, and sat slumped against the stack of lumber.

"You're right about this hair trigger," DeShay said, looking down at the smoking revolver in his hand. "I'll have to be careful about that." He noted the rich, distinctive sound of the big gun, the deep after-ring of high-quality steel. *Very nice gun.*

Looking out across the top of the stacked lumber, he saw the Ranger appear at the edge of the livery barn door.

"Ranger, it's me, Sheriff DeShay," he called out. "I flushed us out an ambusher among these boards."

Recognizing DeShay in the waning evening light, Sam walked forward, rifle ready in hand, and stared down at the dead outlaw. He looked at the rifle lying atop the lumber where Hirsh had dropped it.

"Do you know him?" Sam asked.

"His name is Albert Hirsh—was anyway," said DeShay, staring down with the Ranger. "He's one of Dad Orwick's gunmen who was here earlier." As he spoke he opened the Simpson-Barre, flipped out the spent round and replaced it. Smoke still curled from the long barrel.

"He was laying for me," Sam said, seeing the location, the proximity to the rear barn door.

"That's the way I made it," DeShay said quietly. "I could've been wrong. . . ."

Sam shook his head a little.

"You weren't wrong," he said. "I'm obliged. Lucky for me you spotted him."

DeShay dismissed the matter with a nod. He snapped the cylinder shut and stuck the big revolver down behind his belt.

"Orwick has two kinds of men riding with him," he said. "There's gunmen like this one he calls his *company,* and there's another group he calls his *disciples.*" He looked at Sam. "All in all they make up the Redemption Riders. Pardon me for mentioning it, if you already knew."

"I didn't know," Sam said. He looked DeShay up and down. "I appreciate anything you can tell me about Orwick and his Redemption Riders."

DeShay thought he saw a questioning look in the Ranger's eyes.

"Before I say another word, let me tell you why I know so much about him and his men, Ranger," he said.

"I'm listening," Sam said.

Deshay took a breath and let it out slowly.

"All right, I know Dad Orwick," he said, then quickly corrected himself. "That's not to say we're friends or anything of the sort. But him and his men rode through here shortly after I volunteered to wear this badge. We developed sort of a live-and-let-live attitude for each other."

Sam just stared and listened.

"Now, don't go getting the wrong idea, Ranger," DeShay continued. "I'm not in cahoots with him and his thievery. But so long as he breaks no law in my town, I don't crowd him any. He rides through, sometimes takes up supplies for his families, then rides on. It's all respectablelike." He shrugged and added with a slight grin, "Even the merchants here welcome him. With all his wives and offspring, it's like feeding an army."

"Not to mention his gunmen and bank robbers," Sam said flatly, giving the sheriff a look.

31

"I didn't have to tell you, Ranger," said DeShay "I could have kept it to myself. You'd never been any the wiser."

"I know you didn't have to tell me," said Sam, "and that brings me to wonder why you did."

"Because I'm a lawman, just like you," said DeShay. "I don't want you thinking otherwise. But look where my town is." He gestured toward the distant hills and vast stretches of desert land. "We're far from everything and everybody. I have to do what's best to keep this town on its feet. Making a fight with a man like Dad Orwick is a good way to put us out of business and get myself killed."

"Easier to just get along and look the other way when you have to," Sam said.

"That's right," DeShay said defensively. "If him and his men ever broke the law here in Whiskey Bend, I'd be all over them—Orwick knows that. But that has never been the case."

"And if it came down to choosing sides, him or the law . . . ?" Sam asked, leaving the question hanging.

DeShay nodded at the dead man on the ground.

"You tell me, Ranger," he said. "Which side was I on?"

Sam only nodded.

"I want you to know," said DeShay, "this man trying to ambush you in my town changes things. As far as I'm concerned, I'll ride with you after the rest of the bunch—give them the message that I won't allow that sort of thing here."

"Sheriff, I'm obliged for your offer and for saving me from an ambush," Sam said evenly. "But I'll be riding after them alone." He half turned to walk back to the barn.

"Oh? Why's that?" said DeShay. "Is this the thanks I get for trying to be honest with you?"

"No," Sam said. "I'll be riding *alone* because that's how I ride." He walked away as the sheriff stared after him.

"I'm a lawman same as you, Ranger," DeShay pointed out.

"I never said otherwise," Sam replied without looking back at the sheriff. This was neither the time nor the place to argue the matter, he told himself.

"All right, then," DeShay called out. "I'll ride with the posse from Goble when they get here. I've no doubt they'll welcome my help."

"Do what suits you," Sam called back. "Tell them to watch for me. I'll be on the trail in front of them."

Chapter 3

It was dark by the time the Ranger finished attending to the black-point dun and led the big copper-colored horse out of the livery barn, his riding duster draped over the saddle. As he stopped and put on the duster, the dun chuffed and blew and stamped a hoof as if in protest of the ensuing ride. Cradling the horse's head in the crook of his arm, Sam patted its jaw with a gloved hand.

"I know it's been a long day, fellow," he said quietly. "But you're fed and rubbed and rested." He paused with a thin, wry smile. "I wish I could say the same for myself," he added, realizing that he hadn't been off his feet since he'd walked into Whiskey Bend.

The big dun sawed his head a little as if trying not to give in too easily. But he settled at the Ranger's touch, liking the feel of his hand, the soothing tone of his voice.

"Anyway, that's all I've got for you right now," Sam said with a firm final pat.

He stepped into his stirrup and swung himself up into his saddle. Drawing his Winchester from its boot, he checked it out of habit and held it with its butt propped up from his thigh. Beneath him the dun moved forward and sidelong, high-stepping, ready to go now that his grousing had somehow been reckoned and assuaged.

"That's all you wanted, a little appreciation?" Sam said as if in surprise. He gathered his reins, collected the horse and with a tap of his knees set the animal into an easy gallop, knowing it would take the better part of the night to shorten the gap between himself and Dad Orwick's men.

Once out of Whiskey Bend, Sam let the dun set its own pace, riding across a stretch of sandy flatlands leading to the black hill line standing in the grainy purple distance. By the time the dun had started up into the rising hills, a waxing three-quarter moon lit the night, outlining the black ribbon of trail where it snaked up the hillside's rugged barren face.

The dun slowed its own pace at points where the trail fell blackened behind stands of boulders and shadowy stretches of pine and brush. But then, as if knowing what the Ranger expected of it, the horse kicked up its pace as the trail cleared and the moonlight returned.

So far so good, Sam told himself, grateful to have the moon and starlight on his side.

He rode on.

Nearing dawn, at a fork in the trail, the Ranger stopped the horse and stepped down. In the grainy light he lowered himself on one knee and checked the hoofprints in the trail dust, seeing the four riders had taken a trail leading upward and in the direction of Silvery Hills, or *Colinas Plateadas* as the Mexicans had called the mining town since as far back as the days of Spanish rule.

Another good break, he reminded himself. The town lay at the top end of the narrow trail. Sam knew he was looking at the only way in and the only way out of Silvery Hills, unless Orwick's gunmen wanted to risk their and their horses' lives on one of the countless game paths that criss-crossed the steep, treacherous landscape. He had no reason to think they would do that. But he did have reason to believe their only possible motive for riding up to Silvery Hills would be to rob the mine payroll.

Yep, he decided, reminding himself it was nearing the first of the month—payday for the hard-rock silver miners. Robbing the mine payroll with a posse on their trail was exactly the sort of brazen thing a bunch like Orwick's men would do, he thought. Besides, if he was wrong, they would still have to come down this same trail. Either way, as he knew he couldn't get to the Silvery Hills mines quick enough to stop anything, the best thing for him to do would be to stake out a position somewhere high along the trail and lie in wait. He was certain he wouldn't get Dad Orwick himself, but he would settle for four of Orwick's gunmen.

"And I know just the spot," he murmured to

himself, gazing into the grainy darkness ahead. Beside him the dun piqued its ears and raised its muzzle, as if looking out with him. The Ranger stood and patted the horse's jaw. Then he stepped back up into his saddle and put the animal forward at the same easy gallop.

When he reined the dun down to a halt again, a sliver of daylight had seeped up and wreathed the eastern horizon. He stepped down from the horse, but this time he didn't bother stooping to look at the hoofprints. He could see them well enough to know that nothing had changed.

"Let's find you a good spot. It'll be daylight soon enough," he said quietly to the dun, guiding the horse off the trail onto a steep, winding game path that led deep into the rocky hillside.

An hour later, after eating a breakfast of dried elk sliced from a shank he had packed inside his saddlebags, Sam washed his meal down with tepid water from his canteen and waited. Lying behind the cover of rock he'd strategically chosen overlooking the trail from Silvery Hills, he pressed his ear to the back of his gloved hand on the ground at the first sound of distant rifle fire.

Here we go. . . .

He soon felt the slight tremor of distant hoofbeats moving down the trail toward him. He had no doubt the sound belonged to Orwick's men. Who else would be leaving the town in such a hurry, guns blazing, this time of morning?

He looked up at the rocky hillside to make a quick check on the dun where he'd picketed it, thirty yards away, tucked partially out of sight from his angle, yet impossible to see from the trail below. Under Sam's gaze, the dun raised its muzzle and stared back at him, a sprig of thin pale greenery hanging from its jaws.

Safe and sound. Good. . . .

As soon as he was finished with Dad Orwick and his miscreants, he'd take the dun back to the badlands Ranger outpost and give him a good rest. He'd pick up his Appaloosa stallion, Black Pot, at the outpost and ride on to wherever his next assignment led him.

But first things first, he reminded himself, feeling the tremor of hoofbeats beneath him growing closer—starting to hear them now, the thundering roar of them resounding down the rock-lined trail. He rose in a crouch, dusted his chest with a gloved hand and picked up his Winchester rifle from against the rock where he'd stood it.

Had he continued to look toward the dun a moment longer, he might have seen the lone figure move forward silently through the rocky terrain and raise a hand to the horse's muzzle to keep it settled. But the horse wasn't having it. The edgy animal jerked its muzzle away from the offered hand, gave a warning chuff and stamped a hoof on the rocky ground. The lone figure dropped instantly out of sight even as the Ranger heard the dun and looked in its direction, this time swinging his rifle around with him.

But just as soon as Sam turned, he realized he was too late. He saw the white flash of a rifle shot as he felt the bullet punch through his duster and slice across his right shoulder. The bullet threw him off balance for only a second, but in that second he felt his boot slide backward in the loose dirt and slip off the rocky ledge where he'd taken position.

As a second shot whistled past him, he felt himself falling, tumbling over rock. His Winchester flew from his hand as he grasped for something, anything to stop his downward plunge. But he found nothing. Instead, he landed hard, ten feet down the steep hillside on another ledge in a shower of dust and loose dirt. As soon as he hit the ledge, he tumbled again, this time jolting to a halt against a sunken boulder, the side of his head taking the impact.

He felt the likeness of a cannon explosion somewhere inside his skull, and in spite of all his efforts to fend off an encroaching darkness, he sensed it surround him, knowing there was nothing he could do but surrender to it. A ringing silence overcame him; he felt his eyes close as he fell slack and sank farther and farther down into that swirling, eerie darkness.

When he batted his eyes open a moment later —how much later he had no idea—the world revealed itself to him through a gray, watery veil. He saw a shadowy figure standing over him, and watched the tip of a rifle barrel push aside his duster lapel to better see the badge on his chest.

Addled and half-conscious, Sam nevertheless realized that wearing a badge in this wild, lawless stretch of badlands could go one of two ways: it could save his life or it could cost him his life.

The Colt . . . , he thought, trying in vain to focus on the figure standing over him. But as his weak hand managed to slowly crawl to the holstered gun on his hip and drag it out, he felt a boot clamp down on his wrist. At least he'd tried, he thought, feeling himself drift away again into an eerie darkness as he heard the rifle hammer cock above him.

You don't go down this easy, he heard his inner voice say. Yet he turned loose of the thought as he felt the darkness close in again. This time something told him to relax, to give in to it, that everything was as it should be. There was peace here. This was how a lawman died. This was what he'd known was coming all along. He pictured himself growing smaller in the world around him, leaving . . . leaving.

This wasn't so bad, he told himself, nothing at all as he imagined dying would be. . . .

Seeing the Ranger's eyes close, the lone figure

standing over him rolled Sam's head back and forth with the toe of a scuffed boot, making sure he was unconscious.

"Arizona Ranger . . . ," a quiet voice said. The figure studied the badge and poked it with the tip of the still-smoking rifle barrel. With a sigh the figure added, "What will I do with you until Dad Orwick gets here?"

The tall figure looked out along the trail coming down from Silvery Hills, realizing that after hearing the rifle fire, whoever was riding away from the mines wouldn't come down this trail at all. They would most likely break away from one another and take their chances, coaxing their horses off the narrow path and down on the steep, treacherous hillsides.

"So much for my element of surprise," the voice said. The figure stooped, picked up Sam's Colt and held it in a gloved hand. "You've messed up everything for me, Ranger."

Then the figure reached up, took off a wide-brimmed plainsman-style hat and shook out a long gathered reel of hair. The hair fell in a gentle sway, reaching below shoulder level.

A hand slipped out of its glove and adjusted the long, glistening hair back from a strong yet delicate woman's face. Pale blue eyes flashed catlike in the direction of the hoofbeats that had already fallen silent.

"Congratulations, Ranger," the voice said softly,

wryly, gazing down at Sam. "You just managed to save Dad Orwick's life."

On the trail, Deacon Jamison and long rider Burt Tally had jerked their horses to a halt in unison, both outlaw and churchman hearing the gunshot on the trail below them. Four more riders came to a quick halt behind them and sat staring from their saddles, their rifles already in hand.

A boyish churchman who'd been given the name Young Ezekiel by Dad Orwick himself sidled his horse up closer to Deacon Jamison. He led a string of ten stolen mine horses on a long rope behind him.

"What do you make of it, Deacon?" he asked under his breath.

The deacon, a large man whose broad shoulders strained against the seams of his black wool coat, only shook his head slowly as he stared down the trail.

"Let us pray it's not Dad returning onto our trail and running into the posse from Goble," he said. He stroked his long black beard with his free hand.

Burt Tally smiled and looked at Vincent Callahan, another gunman recently riding with Dad Orwick's company.

"Whilst you're praying, tell the old bearded man upstairs I said *mucho gracias* that at least we're the ones carrying the mine payroll," Tally said, reaching a hand back and patting the bulging canvas bag tied down behind his saddle.

"Don't speak mockingly of the Lord in my presence," Deacon Jamison said in a sharp tone, his thick hand wrapped around the stock of the rifle on his lap. "I won't stand for your blasphemy."

"Easy, Deacon. Don't get your drawers in a knot," said Tally, his thumb quickly cocking the rifle on his lap even though Jamison had only given his warning. "You're already behind in the game." He raised his rifle an inch and pointed it toward the burly churchman, letting him see he had the drop on him. "Learn to cock up first, then make your demands. It'll keep you from meeting Jesus before you've a mind to."

But the deacon only stared angrily, not backing down any more than he had to.

"I'll take your advice and be better prepared next time," he said. "Now, be warned that I will hear no more of you speaking offensively toward the Lord." He raised his hand from his uncocked rifle and pointed a thick finger for emphasis.

The churchman, Young Ezekiel, drew his horse even closer beside Jamison. The string of horses bunched up behind him.

"Nor will I," he said solemnly.

Tally looked the two up and down and chuffed with contempt.

"Riddle me this, gentle souls," he said. "How

can I be guilty of offending someone or something that I don't have the slightest belief in?"

"Mark my words, Tally, you will come to believe," Jamison said gruffly, "lest you forfeit your soul to everlasting hell."

"I might do just that," said Tally. "But I bet I'll have more friends than you where you're headed—"

"Why, you filthy, sinful heathen!" Jamison shouted.

"Cut it off, both of yas," said a stoic gunman named Frank Bannis, who lunged his horse forward and stopped between the two as he gazed in the direction of the rifle fire. "I'm sick of you two talking all that religious malarkey."

"*Malarkey?* How dare—!" Jamison began, but his words were cut short as Bannis' Colt streaked up from his holster, cocked and jammed into the churchman's thick chest.

"One more word," Bannis hissed, "I'll make no threats—I'll kill you quick."

The churchman shut up; so did Burt Tally. Tension fell over the riders.

After a second, Bannis lowered his Colt but held it in hand, the barrel slightly tipped toward Deacon Jamison.

"Young Ezekiel," he said in a cool, even tone, "unstring them horses and get them going."

The men sat and watched as the young churchman loosened the rope down the line and shooed all the horses away.

"What're we going to do, Frank?" an older gunman named Morton Kerr asked quietly as the horses looped along the trail and veered off and down into the rocky hillside.

Bannis reached a hand out toward Burt Tally for the canvas bag behind his saddle.

"Give me the money, Burt," he said. "We're breaking off here and going down through the rocks. We're not going to risk running into that posse in close quarters."

"What about the water hole?" Burt asked. "These horses will need watering."

"Stay away from the water hole." He looked at the two churchmen and said, "Deacon, one of you *zealots* take a spot high up and watch over that water hole." He gave a thin, sarcastic smile and added, "Kill any *godless heathen* you see come near it. You do enjoy killing *godless heathens,* don't you?"

The older churchman only glared at him.

"Now give me that money, Burt, like I told you to," said Bannis.

Tally reached back, untied the money bag and brought it around toward Bannis. As he did so, he shot the riders a look.

Cautiously he said, "Frank, why is it you're going to carry the money? Was I doing it wrong?" He gave a weak grin.

"I'm not carrying it," Frank said. "We're divvying it up. Everybody's taking part of it down these hillsides. That way if we lose a man or two, we've still got most of our booty." He looked around at the group. "Anybody object?"

"No," said Kerr, "it's the only thing that makes sense. I've seen more than a couple good men go down on these rocks and never rise back up."

"What about those two heathens Hornady and Hirsh?" Deacon Jamison asked.

"What about them?" Bannis said, already opening the canvas bag on his lap.

"What will they think when they come up this mining trail and don't find us riding down it?" Jamison asked.

What will they think? Bannis stared at him, a stack of money in his hand.

"I don't read minds, Deacon," he said. "Like as not that's what the rifle fire was about. Maybe the posse caught up to one of them—maybe both—and shot them down."

Deacon thought about it; he passed Young Ezekiel a glance. Then he turned back to Frank Bannis.

"Dad isn't going to like it, us splitting up his money this way." Even as he spoke, Deacon Jamison caught the bundle of cash Frank pitched to him.

"You be sure and tell him all about it, Deacon," Bannis said. "Hell, tell him I forced you to do it, if you're afraid to tell him the truth."

"Dad knows that I fear nothing but the hand of

God," Jamison returned quickly. He hefted the cash in his big hand, considering it. Maybe this was the best thing to do under the circumstances. This, rather than let all of the money out of his sight. "And you're right. I will be telling him this was all your idea—that Young Ezekiel and I had little choice but to go along with it."

"You do that, Deacon," Bannis said, pitching a similar bundle of cash to Haywood Cummins. "Now both of yas get scooting down this hillside. Get above that water hole. We meet back up at the Munny Caves."

Jamison fumed but jerked his horse around as he jammed the cash inside his black coat. Beside him Young Ezekiel did the same.

"Yeah, and don't let the devil bite you in the ass on your way down," Burt Tally laughed, taunting the two churchmen as they coaxed their horses off the trail and down the slope of loose gravel and rock.

"You can't keep your mouth shut to the deacon, can you, Tally?" Frank Bannis said as the churchmen rode farther down the steep hillside.

"When it comes to these religious zealots, I expect not," Tally said, pushing his hat brim up, watching the two riders stir dust on the hillside. "I can't help picking at them, same as I can't help picking at a rattlesnake when I come upon one."

"Wonder why that is," Frank said, taking out another bundle of cash, tossing it to Kerr.

Tally only chuffed and shook his head.

"Hell if I know," he said. He thought about it and added, "My old man was a preacher for a time. I expect I saw how phony it is. He was railed out of three churches for not keeping his hands off the brethrens' wives. They was touchy as hell about their womenfolk."

"Is that a fact?" Bannis pitched him a bundle of cash. "Dad Orwick has solved that," he said. "He takes the brethrens' wives and marries them himself." He grinned. Closing the canvas bag, he rolled it up with a large amount of cash still tucked away and stuffed it inside his duster. "Must keep down a lot of bickering that way." He grinned.

"I wish my old man had thought of it," said Tally. "It would've saved me and my brothers from peeling lots of tar and feathers off his back."

"We ready to ride?" Bannis asked, seeing the distant reminiscing look coming onto Tally's face.

"What? Oh yeah, sure enough!" said Tally, snapping out of it.

"Split up, then," said Bannis. He nudged his horse forward off the trail onto the hillside. "See you at the shack, quick as you can get there. You don't show up, I'll figure you're dead. I come across you somewhere after that, you *will be*."

"*Adios*, Frank," said Tally. "I'll be there. I'm too damn tough to kill."

The three split off, their paths widening farther apart down onto the rocky hillside.

Chapter 4

The Ranger awoke slowly to the beat of a bass drum pounding mercilessly inside his head. He ached all over from the fall he'd taken. His duster and shirt had been removed; he glanced sidelong at his right shoulder and saw a bandage covering the bullet graze. In his half-conscious state, he looked around and noted that he was indoors, lying on a wooden-framed bed against a plank wall. Yet above him he saw no ceiling, only the sky, blue and clear with a curl of smoke drifting on a light breeze. He looked across the room at a burning hearth. He smelled coffee boiling. But surrounding the hearth he saw trees, brush and rock reaching up a rugged hillside.

Looking down from the cot, he saw a rough pine-plank floor beneath him. The floor wavered unsteadily for a moment. Sam closed his eyes tight and wondered if he was still sleeping— sleeping to the insistent beat of the drum. Reopening his eyes, he tried to raise his hand to his head, but his effort stopped short as he felt the bite of handcuffs holding him locked to the bed frame.

What was this . . . where was he? He shook his cuffed wrist, testing the handcuffs. Then he turned his face quickly toward the sound of the voice and saw the figure in the long riding duster walking toward him, rifle in hand.

"I see you're awake," a husky but feminine voice said. The sound of bootheels clacked as the tall figure stepped onto the plank floor, moving closer.

A woman? Sam batted his eyes, trying to still the drumbeat and clear his addled brain.

"Yes, a woman," the husky voice said, as if she were reading his thoughts through the questioning look on his face. "I'm glad you're waking up. I was getting worried. I thought I'd killed you."

"You shot me?" Sam asked.

"I'm afraid I did," the tall woman admitted, stopping, standing over him, adjusting the rifle over into the cradle of her arm. "I didn't see your badge until it was too late. I thought you were waiting for Dad Orwick and his men."

"I was," Sam replied, having to put more effort than usual into speaking clearly.

"I mean I thought you were one of them," she corrected, "a guard he left behind or something— that is, until I saw your badge. Then it was too late."

Sam let out a breath.

"I was waiting for his men," he said, his mind beginning to clear some. "They robbed the bank in Goble."

"For his men?" the woman said. "I was waiting for Orwick himself."

"Then you were going to be disappointed," Sam said. "Orwick already split off from the rest of them."

"That snake," she said. "He's good at disappearing at the right time."

Sam raised his free hand and rubbed his temple, trying to still the drumbeat and collect whatever sense he could make of the conversation. He held his cuffed hand up as far as he could and looked at it, recognizing the handcuffs to be his own, the ones he kept inside his saddlebags.

"Is there a reason why you've got me cuffed to this bed frame?" he asked drily.

"There was," she said. "There's not now. Sorry. I was afraid you'd wake up and realize I shot you before I had time to explain why." As she spoke, she reached inside her duster pocket and took out the key to the handcuffs.

When she unlocked the cuffs, she handed them to him. Sam rubbed his wrist, feeling pain in his grazed shoulder. He looked to the far edge of the fallen shack and saw his copper dun and another horse reined to a lone standing timber.

"Obliged," he said, sitting up stiffly on the side of the bed. "And thanks for bandaging my shoulder," he added.

"Don't mention it, Ranger," she said. "It was the least I could do." Sam noted a calm, almost icy detachment to her words, her demeanor. "I'm thankful I didn't kill you," she said, as if to keep

51

from appearing to not really care much one way or the other if she did. "Especially now that I know you're after the same prey as I am."

Sam gave her a curious look.

"The same *prey?*" he said. "That sounds like you're a bounty hunter."

"Oh, does it?" she said. "Well, I'm not," she added. "Maybe *prey* wasn't the right word. I should have simply said we're after the same man." She offered a slight smile that revealed very little. "You no doubt want him dead or alive. I want him dead, nothing short of dead."

Sam only stared at her. He watched her reach a hand up and shove the wide-brimmed plainsman hat back off her head. The hat hung below her shoulders on its rawhide string. With the hat off, Sam could more clearly see her face. She was finely featured, with faint streaks of silver in her pulled-back hair.

"You want him dead?" Sam asked. "What did he do to you that has you intent on killing him?"

"He married me," the woman said flatly.

Sam tried not to sound too surprised. He wanted to hear more, but he could already tell that with this woman, he would have to listen, not pry.

"He married lots of women from what I've heard," Sam said.

"Yes," the woman said, "and as with me, most of those marriages were performed against the bride's will."

Sam continued to stare coolly, knowing she had more to say, and knowing she would get it said, in her own time.

"It's a long story, Ranger," she said with a slight sigh, cutting a glance toward the coffeepot hanging over the hearth fire. "Could you stand some coffee—get your head cleared the rest of the way?"

"I could stand some," Sam said. He started to stand on shaky legs. His hand went carefully to the large, throbbing lump atop his head.

"No, sit still, Ranger," she said. "I'll get it for you. Take it easy and get yourself rested up. You took a hard fall."

"My horse . . . ?" he said, looking out across the narrow clearing on the hillside.

"I took care of everything," the woman said. "It was the least I could do." She gave a thin but authentic smile. "I'm Matilda . . . Matilda Rourke," she said. "Please call me Mattie."

"Arizona Territory Ranger, Samuel Burrack, Miss Mattie," Sam said.

"I meant Mattie without the *Miss*," she said.

"Yes, ma'am," Sam said.

He sank back down on the side of the bed, watching her turn and step over to the hearth. He noticed the long tail of hair hanging down her back to her waist, shiny dark hair laced with streaks of silver.

"I was afraid that's who you were, Ranger

53

Burrack," she said over her shoulder. "I've heard of you. I know you ride these trails."

"Didn't you expect someone would be on their trail soon enough?" he asked.

"Yes," she said. "But I expected it to be a posse. And I didn't except it to be so soon. That's why I thought you were one of them—maybe even Dad himself."

"You were married to the man and you wouldn't be able to see I wasn't him?" Sam asked curiously. He watched her pour coffee into a cup and walk to him with it, her rifle still cradled in her arm. She was older than him, eight, ten years, maybe more, he estimated. Yet he saw the stride of a younger woman—a confident, self-assured woman.

"I'm afraid I don't see as well I used to," she said. She pushed a strand of silver-streaked hair back from her cheek as she handed the coffee cup down to him. "I bought a pair of spectacles, but I'm not used to them yet. I'd left them in my saddlebags." She lowered her voice and her eyes. "I'm sorry," she said in a near whisper. "Had I been wearing them I would have seen you weren't Dad."

Sam noted the bandaged graze on his shoulder.

"On the other hand," he said, "if you'd thought I was one of his men, maybe I can count myself fortunate you weren't wearing them."

It took her a second to catch his irony.

"Oh yes, come to think of it," she said as his meaning became clear to her. "I am quite a good shot with this." She gave a nurturing lift of the rifle in the crook of her arm.

Sam sipped the steaming coffee. He wanted to know more about this woman. Were there things she could tell him about the man he was tracking? Of course there were. But it was more than that, he told himself. There was something about the woman herself. . . .

"Just being married to Dad Orwick was enough to make you want to kill him?" he asked. He eyed her inconspicuously. Behind her duster, she wore battered, snug buckskins. A tall skinning knife stood in a fringed sheath crosswise across her flat belly. Atop an open collar button a brown linsey-woolsey shirt revealed the upper edge of faded red long johns beneath it.

She reached a scuffed boot toe out and dragged a weathered wooden chair closer to the bed. She pulled Sam's bullet-torn shirt from the chairback and pitched it over onto the bed beside him. Sam nodded his thanks and looked back at her.

"Killing him's the least of what I first wanted to do," she said, sitting down. "When I managed to break away from his family, I lay awake nights imagining some of the most awful, torturous things I could conjure up—" She stopped short and turned an ear toward the hillside.

Sam froze in the process of lifting the cup of

coffee to his lips, and the two stared at each other.

"Did you hear that?" Mattie Rourke asked in a hushed voice, half rising catlike from the chair.

Sam only nodded, reaching down, setting the coffee cup on the plank floor. He picked up his boots standing at the edge of the bed.

"Riders," he said, "coming from down trail—ten minutes, maybe sooner."

She stood and held on to her rifle with both hands.

Sam stiffly pulled on his boots and looked all around for his gun belt, shaking the last of the cobwebs from inside his head, noting the drum-beat had slowed considerably.

"The posse from Goble?" she asked him, still whispering.

"Let's hope so," Sam said. He pushed himself up from the edge of the bed and pulled his shirt on over his bandaged shoulder. He gave Mattie a questioning look.

"Your gun belt and duster are on your horse," she said, nodding to where the horses stood staring back at them.

Sam stumbled a little as he started to take a step. But Mattie caught him, steadied him, looped his arm across her shoulders and walked on.

"I'm all right," Sam said, even though he didn't resist her help. He shook his head as if to clear it entirely.

"I know you are, but just in case," she said, walking him toward the horses.

"We'll get atop the trail over them," Sam said, feeling weak now that he was up and moving. He realized he wasn't back to himself yet.

The woman looked at him as she stopped beside his copper-colored dun. She considered what he'd said, with the look of one who was not used to following another's direction. She resented his assumed authority, but she calmed herself, took a patient breath and let it go.

"Yes, you're right, Ranger," she said quietly. "That's what we should do." She helped guide his boot into the stirrup as he raised it. Then she kept close, her hands up, spread, ready to help, even as he swung himself up into the saddle on his own and settled onto it.

The eight-man posse from Goble wound its way up the switchback hill trail. Ten yards ahead of the other riders, a buckskin-clad man named Dee Ragland scouted the trail for the hoofprints left behind by Dad Orwick's gunmen. Riding slowly, Ragland bent low down the side of his horse, examining the dirt. Now and then he held up a gloved hand to bring the others to a halt.

"Good God Almighty, must we constantly be stopping like this!" said Kerwin Stone, the bank president from Goble, as once again he and the riders around him jerked their horses to a halt.

"What does he think we're going to do, ride up there and stomp these horses all around so he can't see the prints?"

Beside him, the sheriff of Goble, Fred Hall, let out an exasperated breath. He looked at Stone, then at Sheriff Clayton DeShay, who had thrown in with the posse as it came through Whiskey Bend.

"I have to say I don't understand Dee's reasoning myself, but he's known for his tracking skills—and he is part Indian."

"Part Indian indeed," Stone grumbled. "He's an idiot. There is no rationale to us having to ride so far behind, and keep stopping every time it strikes his fancy. What possible purpose does it serve?"

"I agree this is taking too damn long. I'm going up to talk to him," said Sheriff Hall. "But you and Sheriff DeShay hold everybody back until I hear what he has to say."

"We don't need to be *held back* like we're a bunch of damned fools, Sheriff," said a black teamster named Morgan Almond, one of the riders crowded up around the banker.

Almond spit and ran a hand across his dust-caked lips. "You need to knock Ragland in the head so's we can ride on and catch these robbers. If we're not going to catch them, I'd as soon go back to Whiskey Bend and load my wagon."

"He's got a point, Sheriff," said a well-known hired gunman named Arlis Fletcher. "Speaking

58

strictly for myself, I had no money in that bank. I'd like to either get on with this or go home." The gunman wore a bearskin coat in spite of the warming day. A dusty black derby perched jauntily to one side of his head. A brace of holstered Colts rested on his hips. He gave a flat smile beneath a fine-trimmed mustache and patted the chest of his thick coat. "Fact is, I'm near out of rye."

Sheriff Hall looked at the men, then at DeShay. The posse was getting edgy. It wouldn't last much longer.

"Everybody settle down. I'll be right back," he said, turning his horse forward and riding away toward the trail scout. As he approached Ragland, the scout waved his hand back and forth furiously, trying to stop him. But Sheriff Hall rode on.

"Damn it, Sheriff, stay back!" said Ragland as Hall slid his horse to a halt a few feet away. "I can't have these prints disturbed, not if I'm going to be able to figure anything out about them."

"Aw, hell, Ragland," the sheriff said in disgust, "why all this stopping and starting? What is it you're finding out anyway that's so damned helpful?"

Ragland held a hand up toward him with a scorching stare.

"We've got six riders, Sheriff," he said. "And following those six, we've one rider alone—I'm supposing that to be Ranger Burrack."

Looking down at the mass of hoofprints in the dirt, Sheriff Hall shook his head as if not believing the scout.

"How the hell can you read that one rider is following six others in a mess of prints such as this?" he asked.

"It's not hard if I can keep you and those knotheads far enough back," Ragland said.

"Watch your mouth, Ragland," Hall warned.

Ragland ignored the sheriff's caution, pointing down at the tangle of prints in the dirt.

"See how this one set of prints laps over the others?" he said.

"Damn it, Ragland, of course one set is always going to overlap. That doesn't tell you nothing," said Hall.

"Not from here," Ragland said. "But look back between here and the posse. See how that one set of prints stays on top, forms its own trail if you stare at them close enough?"

Hall squinted and stared back along the trail toward the waiting riders. After a moment, he made out a line of ghostlike prints that stood out, faintly, unbroken above the jumble of prints beneath them.

"Jesus . . . ," he said.

"I told you," said Ragland. "Look long enough at the stride, you'll see this lone rider is moving at a faster gallop than the ones he's trailing."

"Jesus . . . ," Hall repeated, truly impressed.

"I'm a lawman. How the hell do you know—?"

"Indian blood." Ragland cut him off, patting himself on the chest.

"Horse dribble," said Hall. But seeing the banker and the others encroach their horses a step closer, he shouted out at them, "Stay the hell back, Stone. You're messing up this man's tracking!"

Smiling to himself, Ragland turned his horse forward on the trail. But before he could go ten feet, he saw two figures rise into sight among the rocks above them.

"There we are, Sheriff," he said, pointing up at the Ranger and the woman who stood looking down at them, the Ranger with a hand raised in a show of peace.

But Hall, looking up, taken by surprise, jerked his Colt from its holster. Sensing his panic, Hall's horse reared with him. Startled, the sheriff let his cocked Colt fly from his hand, strike the ground and fire wildly near the already spooked horse's hooves. Hall flew from his saddle, his foot twisted and stuck in the stirrup.

Ragland sat staring in disbelief as the sheriff's horse spun and bolted back toward the rest of the posse, the hapless sheriff bouncing, screaming and spinning along in the dirt beside it.

Chapter 5

By the time Sam and Mattie Rourke had led their horses down through the rocks and stepped out onto the trail, the posse had gathered at a large rock and had Sheriff Hall sitting, leaned back against it. Sam looked down the trail at the gathered posse, then back at the scout, who had waited for him and the woman.

"Ragland," the Ranger said as his only greeting.

"Ranger," Ragland replied. He looked at the woman.

"Mattie," Sam said, "this is Dee Ragland, a scout I've known for some time. Ragland, this is Mattie Rourke," he added.

Ragland touched his hat brim and said, "Ma'am." Then he nodded toward the tracks on the trail and said to Sam, "I figure that's you on top."

"You figured right," said Sam. "What got into that one?" He nodded toward Sheriff Hall as the three turned and started walking along the trail toward the others.

"Beats me," said Ragland. "I pointed you two out, and he went plumb nuts for a second."

"A second is all it takes out here," said Sam.

"Lucky we've got your pal Sheriff DeShay with

us," said the scout. "He can take over from here."

"I expect he can at that," said Sam. "Only he's no pal of mine. I met him coming through Whiskey Bend. First time I ever laid eyes on him."

"Huh," said Ragland. "He made it sound like you asked him to stay behind and wait for us, so we could be careful not to run upon you." He looked at Sam. "You didn't tell him that?"

"Yes, I did, in a way," Sam said. He decided not to say any more about it right now. With the sheriff from Goble down, it would have to be DeShay who led the posse from here. Sam's rule was to work alone; he didn't want to break it.

They walked on in silence.

"Holy Mother Luck . . . !" Mattie said quietly, seeing what a mess the horse had made of Sheriff Hall as they drew closer.

Hall's hat lay on the ground beside him, its brim ripped almost off the crown. His left boot was missing, appearing to have been pulled off when he was dragged. His right boot had been cut off his swollen foot, and his foot was propped up on a small rock, already turning the color of fruit gone bad. A white piece of ankle bone shone through broken skin. Both sides of his face were scraped and swollen; he held a wet bandanna to his broken nose. Even his hands were scraped and bloody.

"I ought to shoot that cayuse where he stands," Hall said in a strained and broken voice.

"Hell, it weren't the horse's fault," said the black teamster. "You spooked before he did. He was just doing what a horse does—"

"Damn it, Almond," said Hall, cutting him off, "I know what a horse *does*." He lowered the bandanna from his face. "Look at me now." He gestured toward his broken foot. "I can't lead a posse the shape I'm in."

"That's for damned sure," said Arlis Fletcher with a flat smile beneath his thin mustache. "I'd say this outing is about to wind itself down." He stood up and slapped dust from his bearskin coat. He turned with the others as Sam, the woman and Dee Ragland walked up.

Hall appeared embarrassed as he acknowledged the Ranger and shook his ragged bloody head.

"Ranger, I don't know what come over me. I never panicked like that in my life."

"You don't owe me an explanation," Sam said, stooping down beside him. "Looks like they're going to have to get you back to Whiskey Bend, have the doctor there set that foot."

"I know," said Hall, "I wish I could stay on here, but damn, this is a bad one." He looked up at the woman standing beside Sam. "Who's your lady friend?"

Sam started to introduce Mattie to the sheriff, but before he could, Arlis Fletcher stepped close to her and eyed her up and down.

"Say, I know this one," he said. "She was in

town the day before the robbery. I saw her talking to Lightning Wade secretlike beside the mercantile store."

The men turned their eyes to Mattie. Fletcher's hand instinctively moved closer to his holstered Colt. Sam saw Mattie's hand drift near the big knife sheathed across her belly. Noting how close Fletcher had put himself to the woman, Sam edged himself between the two and eyed the gunman up and down the same way Fletcher had just eyed Mattie.

"Show some manners, mister," Sam said to Fletcher in a low warning tone. As he spoke, his hand slowly drew his own big Colt and held it loosely at his side.

Fletcher settled a little and took a step back, knowing that at any second the Ranger's Colt would take a hard swipe at his jaw.

"There's my manners," said Fletcher, spreading his hands slightly. "Now ask her, see if she denies it."

"I'm not asking her anything," Sam said.

"Ranger," said Hall quietly, "she was in my town, talking to a man before he took part in a bank robbery—I've got a right to ask."

Sam started to object, but Mattie stopped him.

"It's all right, Ranger," she said. "Sheriff, I *was* talking to Lighting Wade in your town," she said. "I've known Wade for a long time."

"Oh?" said Hall. "What was you talking about?"

"It wasn't about robbing the bank," Mattie said. "You've got my word on that."

"Your word, huh?" Fletcher said. He gave a sly, nasty grin, again looking her up and down.

"You heard her the first time," Sam said, not liking the gunman's accusing tone. "Keep acting the way you're acting, you better have an empty shirt pocket."

"The hell is that supposed to mean?" Fletcher asked, backing another step as the Ranger eased forward.

Well aware of the Ranger's reputation for swinging a gun barrel, Sheriff Hall cut in, "Meaning he's fixing to knock your damned teeth out, you fool. Now shut up before I tell him to go ahead and—"

"I'd like to see him try," said Fletcher, suddenly taking a stand, his feet spread shoulder-width apart. He threw back the bearskin coat, revealing his tied-down Colt .45.

"No, you would *not,* Fletcher," the pain-racked sheriff barked hoarsely. "Now stand the hell down and shut the hell up."

The gunman took the sheriff's command seriously. He withdrew another step, keeping his eyes on the Ranger's big Colt.

"Anything you say, Sheriff," he replied, letting his shaggy coat fall over his gun.

Sam took a step back also, sensing that was the end of it.

"I still haven't heard what you and Lightning Wade were talking about, ma'am," the injured sheriff said to Mattie, wincing in pain as he spoke.

Instead of answering, Mattie looked at the Ranger, who took the matter upon himself.

"She said it wasn't about robbing the bank, Sheriff," he said.

"And you vouch for her, Ranger Burrack?" Hall asked.

"Here's what I vouch for," Sam said. He raised his sombrero and showed the large lump on his head, the wide purple bruise reaching down below his hairline. "She shot me—winged me, thinking I was one of Dad Orwick's men. Her shot grazed my shoulder and I fell off a cliff. If she hadn't raised me up and taken care of me, I'd likely be dead now." He gave Mattie a look.

"That don't make her right, Ranger," Hall said.

"To me it does," Sam said. "If she was with Orwick's bunch, a bullet through my head would have kept these questions from ever being asked." He stared at the injured sheriff.

"All right, I'll go with that, if it suits you," Hall said.

"Now, wait just one minute, Sheriff!" Kerwin Stone cut in sharply. "Shouldn't she at least be questioned?"

The sheriff gave the banker a sour expression.

"She just was, Stone," he said. "Weren't you paying attention?" Before Stone could reply, Hall turned to Clayton DeShay and said, "Good thing you came along with us, Sheriff DeShay. It looks like you'll be leading this posse."

"Whoa," said DeShay in surprise. "I've got to get back to Whiskey Bend. That's my first responsibility."

"Then why'd you come along with us to begin with?" Hall asked pointedly.

Sam watched and listened. Knowing that DeShay had used his name in joining Hall and the posse, he was curious himself as to why the sheriff of Whiskey Bend had come along. But it seemed DeShay didn't want to discuss anything.

"Pardon me, Sheriff Hall," he said quickly. "Of course I'll lead your posse. I wasn't expecting to be asked, is all."

"I don't like this one bit," Stone cut in again.

"Then you tell us what the hell you do like, banker," Hall said in a heated tone. "You want to lead this posse yourself, go right ahead on."

"What about this man?" Stone said, pointing a thick soft finger at Sam. "He's a duly sworn—"

"I don't lead posses," Sam said, cutting him off. "I'm riding on ahead. If you want my opinion, you go back to your bank, Mr. Stone. Let this posse and me plan on how to take down Orwick and his men—bring your money back."

"Nothing suits me more than getting back to my office, Ranger," Stone said. "But I need assurances that the money is coming back."

"If I can get within gunshot of it, it'll come back," Sam said matter-of-factly.

Arlis Fletcher chuffed aloud, not attempting to hide his contempt for the Ranger's words.

"If bold talk is all it takes, I'd say you've got Orwick and his gang whipped already," he said.

Sam ignored the brash gunfighter.

"Go home, Mr. Stone," Sam told the banker. "I won't lead the posse, but I'll work with it any way I can." He looked at Mattie and nodded toward their horses standing behind them.

"Then by thunder," said Stone, "I will stay out here, lead them myself!"

"No, you won't," Hall said in a heated voice. "I'm the sheriff, and I'll say who leads the posse." He looked at DeShay. "It's up to you, *Sheriff*. You rode along to help . . . Well, it's time to help." He gestured toward the others. "Tell them what you want done."

Surprisingly, DeShay turned to Sam.

"What's your take on it, Ranger?" he asked. "You've been on their trail longest."

Sam nodded and looked at Ragland.

"I know you saw where the gang split up a ways back," he said. "I've got a hunch that's where Orwick and some top hands cut away there. The other men rode up this trail and robbed the mine payroll."

"The mine payroll!" Stone cut in. "What on earth brought you to this speculation?"

"I heard gunfire from up the trail earlier, and this trail ends at the mines," Sam said. "There's no other reason for them to go up there."

"For God's sake," Stone said, "my bank's money is on the line and all you can come up with are wild hunches?"

"Damn it, Stone!" Hall growled, staring up at him. "Let everybody alone—let them do their jobs."

"Ragland here showed us where they split up," DeShay said to Sam and Ragland, considering things. "What you're saying makes sense."

Sam nodded and said, "If it's true, you can bet that wherever Orwick went, the bank money went with him."

Sheriff Hall shook his head and chastised himself.

"I should have figured that out myself," he said under his breath.

"Like I said, it's only a *hunch,* Sheriff," Sam repeated for Hall's sake. He gave Kerwin Stone a cold look, then turned his eyes back to DeShay and Ragland. "But it's the best we've got right now."

"I agree," DeShay said. "What's our best move from here, Ranger?"

"Ragland here is the best tracker among us," Sam said. "It might be wise for you and your men to ride back where the ones split off, let Ragland keep you on their trail. Whoever is up this mine trail has heard enough gunfire that they've broken up and gone down the hillsides every direction."

DeShay picked up on the Ranger's line of thought.

"So, Dad and his top men already planned to circle below these hills and meet up with these others down on the trail to Ol' Mex."

"There it is," Sam said. "It's a hunch, but it's the only thing that makes sense to me." He looked at Ragland. "I've tracked my bunch this far. You ride back and get this posse onto the others' trail. Maybe we can squeeze them in between us and get this thing done."

"I'll put us right up their shirttails," Ragland said to DeShay. "You've got my word."

"I know you will," DeShay said. "I've already seen your work." He looked at Arlis Fletcher and said, "I figure if you're not as quick with your gun as you are with your mouth, you'd already be dead. Can you take orders from me?"

"Why, yes, sir, Mr. *Sheriff of Whiskey Bend*," Fletcher said, belligerent and defiant to a flaw.

DeShay ignored his sarcasm and looked Morgan Almond up and down.

"Will you be sticking with me?" he asked.

"I come along to catch these thieves," Almond said. "It ain't in me to leave a job unfinished." He jiggled a battered Spencer rifle hanging in his hand. "I hit most what I aim at, rifle or six-shooter." He patted a big six-shooter holstered on his right hip.

DeShay nodded. In a no-nonsense tone he said to Almond, Fletcher and Ragland, "It'll only be the four of us. I don't want anybody else."

The three nodded.

Sam looked at two townsmen who had remained a few feet back from the others.

"Do you two men mind escorting Sheriff Hall and Mr. Stone back to Whiskey Bend? Somebody's got to do it," he said.

DeShay realized his mistake, turning the two men down in front of the others, yet he could tell they'd both had their fill of this manhunt.

"I was just getting ready to ask you both to do that," he said to the two. He shot the Ranger a glance of thanks.

The two men looked at each other as if a prayer had been answered.

"We don't mind at all, Sheriff," one said as the other nodded in agreement. "If that's what you need us to do, we are right here for you."

"Obliged," DeShay said, leaving the two men their dignity. Getting Sheriff Hall back to town was a legitimate task. "Then it's all settled," he added. He turned to Sam and said between the two of them, "Obliged, Ranger. I've got it from here." He gave Sam a look and said, "See you when we get this settled."

Sam nodded and turned to Mattie and the

horses. When they'd swung up onto their horses and ridden a few yards up the trail, she shot a glance at the Ranger.

"You took my side," she said, sounding a little surprised.

Sam just looked at her.

"I'm not used to that," she said, "someone speaking up for me, that is." She gave him a faint smile. "It felt strange."

"I only told the truth," Sam said. He turned his eyes forward to the trail.

"I know," she said, also looking ahead. A moment passed before she said, "But you didn't mention that I'd been married to Dad Orwick."

"I didn't?" Sam said without turning to her. "It must've slipped my mind." He nudged the copper dun's pace up and rode on. The woman nodded to herself and rode along beside him.

Chapter 6

In the falling shadows of evening, the Ranger stopped the copper black-point dun on the higher trail up to the mines. He stepped the horse wide of the hoofprints that turned off the trail, plunging down a steep labyrinth of cliffs, brush tangles and land-stuck boulders. Just off the edge of the narrow trail, he saw the hoofprints spread out.

"That's about what we figured," he said, his

eyes following the prints until they disappeared from sight.

Beside him Mattie Rourke looked back and forth, keeping a taut hand on her reins as if her horse might attempt to follow its predecessors on its own.

"Are we going down there?" she asked, keeping herself from sounding reluctant.

Sam looked out at the waning sunlight on the western sky, judging the time of day and the distance to the stretch of flatlands below.

"No," he said, "not this late. It'll be dark before we get to the bottom. We don't want to break a horse's leg."

She backed her horse as the Ranger backed his. Turning on the narrow trail, they put the animals forward again at a walk, searching the upside of the rugged slope for a spot to conceal a campsite. Sam saw the questioning look on Mattie's face as she gazed at a huge boulder standing thirty yards above the trail.

"We could have company overnight," he said. "The mine has guards they send out on their own. They wouldn't know us from Orwick's riders in the dark."

"I understand," Mattie said. "It's better we see them first if they come this way in the night." She followed close behind as Sam turned the dun from the trail up along a thin path leading around the large boulder.

When they stopped behind the boulder, a small

clearing lay before them completely sheltered from both the trails below and above. Stepping down from their saddles, they led the horses across the small clearing to a thick stand of brush. As soon as they had dropped their saddles from the horses' backs, Sam dragged a thick length of deadfall pine over beneath the large boulder, covered it with dried brush and twigs and built a small, sheltered fire. Mattie started wiping down both horses while he poured water from a canteen into a coffeepot, threw in a handful of ground coffee from a tin in his saddlebags and set the pot to boil. Then Sam poured canteen water into his sombrero and watered the horses.

Sam stood and shook out his sombrero and nodded up the dark trail running beneath them.

"There's a good runoff pool up ahead," he said, concerning the horses. "We'll water them better come morning. There's no cover there. We'll want to get in early and get out and on our way."

"To avoid the mine guards?" Mattie asked.

"Yep," Sam said. "Men can get skittish and contrary when they're man-hunting. Sometimes the hardest part of catching outlaws is avoiding other folks who are out to do the same thing."

The two sat down in the low firelight, drank hot coffee and ate strips of dried elk heated and softened over the short flames on the tip of the Ranger's knife.

As they ate, Sam noted the look on Mattie's

face. She appeared to be wrestling with whether or not to tell him something. Sam didn't press her; if she wanted to tell him, she would, but if she didn't want to tell him, he had a notion that no amount of questioning would pry it from her. Finally she seemed to come to a decision. Sam watched her set her cup down and wipe her fingertips across her lips.

"I know where Dad Orwick is going," she said quietly.

"Oh . . . ?" Sam looked at her. He might have asked why she was telling him now. Why not earlier? But he wasn't going to. It had something to do with him standing up for her with the posse, he thought. His action had gained her trust. Whatever the case, any information she gave him, he was grateful.

"He has been setting up a new compound for his family in the Mexican hills above San Paulo," she said softly, "in a place called *Valle del Fusil.*"

"Valley of the Gun," Sam said.

Mattie gazed away from him, into the low flames as if speaking of Orwick conjured up old and terrible memories for her.

"Lightning Wade told me Dad's been gathering in all of his wives and children there for the past year," she said. "He has always found Mexico to be more *tolerant* of how he lives—" Her voice took on a wry tone as she spoke. "He saw they let the Mormon Saints colonize there, so he decided to do the same. He figures the land will swallow up him and his followers."

"Is that where you were prepared to go kill him, if that's what it took?" Sam asked.

She sighed and looked off across the darkness for a moment, then back at the fire.

"Yes, that's where I was going if I missed my chance on the trails," she said. "To be honest, once I saw you were all right, I was planning to cut out from you during the night and get back on his trail. Going into his compound in the valley would be my last resort."

"I'm obliged you told me," Sam said. "I've never been to the Valley of the Gun, but I know the hills above San Paulo. It's good hiding grounds. I can start searching out his compound once I get over there."

"Dad has a way of being hard to find when it suits him," Mattie said. "I was there back when he first discovered the place years ago. By now he's probably forgot I was ever there." She paused for a moment. "What I'm saying is, I'll take you there if you don't mind crossing the border."

"I don't mind crossing," he said. "Seems I spend more time in Ol' Mex of late than I do in Nogales." He sipped his coffee and added, "So this means you've changed your mind about cutting out in the night?"

"Yes," she said quietly.

"What changed your mind?" he asked just as

quietly. "Because if it was me speaking up to the posse . . . I was only—"

"I said I'll take you there," she said. "Let's leave it at that for now."

"Yes, ma'am," Sam said with a faint smile.

He watched the woman set her cup aside, wrap herself in a blanket and lean back against a rock. He sipped the last of his coffee, stood up, draping his blanket over his shoulder and slung coffee grounds from his tin cup.

"I'll just let you get some sleep now," he said. "Let the fire burn on out if you like. Nobody's likely to see us up in here."

"Where are you going?" she asked.

"I'm going up atop the boulder," Sam said. "With this half-moon waxing, I'll be able to see a long ways in every direction."

She looked across the clearing in the darkness where he'd left his saddle near the copper dun.

"You're going to sleep on a rock, nothing to lay your head on?" she asked, in a concerned, almost motherly tone. "At least fold your duster for a pillow. Your head must still be hurting from the fall."

"I'm lots better," Sam said. "Anyway, I don't want to sleep too sound. I might miss something."

Mattie watched him touch his sombrero brim toward her and walk away.

"Good night, Ranger," she said under her breath, feeling the weariness of the day close in around her.

Even as the Ranger stepped out of the small circle of firelight, under her blanket she eased her rifle up against her and closed her eyes with her finger inside the trigger guard and her thumb over the hammer. In spite of the long, hard day that lay behind her and the weariness she'd felt only a moment earlier, when she closed her eyes, sleep didn't come easily.

The Ranger's coffee? Yes, partly . . . , she told herself.

But the fact was, it had been years since sleep came easily to her. Anytime she fell asleep too soon or too sound, in minutes she would awake with a start, like someone dreaming of falling off the edge of a great precipice. Only in her case, it was not falling that terrorized her. It was the face of Dad Orwick hovering above her. She drew up inside her blanket and clutched the rifle tighter just thinking about it.

In such short, tortured dreams she became a child again, and before her mind mercifully released her from sleep, once again she witnessed, heard and felt the pain of that broken child as clearly as ever.

"Anyway, I don't want to sleep too sound. I might miss something," the Ranger had said. If only that could be her case, she thought, feeling herself give in only grudgingly, ready to stave off sleep at any point should the old dream return to haunt her. *Careful, careful,* she warned herself,

drifting warily, hearing the crackling of the fire grow more distant in the darkness. . . .

And in what seemed like only a moment, her sleep was over as the Ranger stooped beside her and nudged her shoulder with his fingertips. Her eyes opened instantly and darted all around. Already alert, like some creature of the wilds, gauging the safety of its terrain. She stiffened at his touch; her eyes fixed onto his, questioning, anticipating his intent.

"What do you want?" she asked in a harsh, threatening voice. The warning growl of a she-panther, Sam thought. He noted the shape of the rifle beneath her blanket.

She saw him stand up—a black silhouette against the purple sky, his rifle cradled in the crook of his arm.

"Time to go," he said softly.

"Oh . . . yes," she said, catching herself, her voice going softer as sleep cleared from her mind and recollection came upon her. She looked at the smoldering coals barely glowing in the campfire. She saw Sam's gloved hand extended down to her and she took it and rose, keeping the blanket around her.

The Ranger reached out a boot and crushed the already struggling coals. He rubbed the fire site around in the dirt as it gave up its last waning puffs of smoke.

"No coffee this morning," he said. "If all's clear

at the water hole, we can stop after sunup and build a breakfast fire up in the rocks."

She only nodded, dropping her blanket on her saddle lying on the ground. In the grainy light of a half-moon, she adjusted the rifle into the crook of her arm and looked at the Ranger.

"Old habits," she offered, even though he had made no mention of her sleeping with the gun.

"I understand," he said.

She stared at him. No, he did not understand, she told herself.

With no more on the matter, Sam turned and walked to their horses. The copper dun chuffed under its breath as he walked closer. He pitched the saddle blanket, then the saddle atop the dun's back. Cinching the saddle, he shoved his rifle into its boot and led both horses over to where Mattie stood tying her rolled blanket behind her saddle on the ground.

She stepped over to her horse, saddle in hand. Sam watched in silence as she readied the animal for the trail. Feeling his eyes on her, she wondered if she had cried out in her sleep. She would not ask, of course. Instead, she cinched the horse and took the reins from Sam.

"Ready when you are," she said.

The Ranger noted a tightness in her voice, but he let it go.

"We'll walk them down to the trail," he said, turning, leading the copper dun behind him.

• • •

Dawn lay in a long, thin glow beneath the dark eastern horizon as the two reached the water hole. While the animals drank their fill, Sam sank six canteens into the water and stepped back from the edge while they filled. Without speaking, he reached out, touched Mattie's arm and motioned for her to move away from the water's edge.

As she stepped back beside him, he nodded toward the water, the shine of moonlight on its glassy surface rippling slowly now, disturbed by the horses' muzzles. A reflection of the moon wavered on the slightest ripple.

"You're easier seen against the water," he whispered.

She nodded without reply.

Sam looked around on the ground for any sign of hoofprints. He understood that Orwick's men might have bypassed the water hole, having split away from one another on the hillside. But it struck him as stranger that the guards from the mines had not been here. They would have had time by now, and they would have most certainly followed the robbers down here from the mine trail. *Unless something had prevented them from following,* he thought.

Whatever the case, this was not the time or place to consider it, he decided—not here with darkness their only cover.

He stepped forward, stooped and capped the

canteens without raising them from the water. When the canteens were all capped, he lifted them at all once by their straps, keeping them close to the surface until they had shed their excess water quietly.

Mattie watched as he stood and hooked all six canteens to the dun's side for the time being. Stepping back from the water's edge, he handed her the reins to her horse, turned and stepped up into his saddle. In a moment the water hole lay behind them and they were headed back into the cover of rock along the stretch of flatlands.

As they rode along at an easy gallop, Sam sidled up close, reached over and hooked three of the canteens onto her saddle horn.

"In case we get separated," he said.

Mattie nodded as they rode on.

As daylight seeped over the horizon, they stopped amid a cluster of larger boulders and built a fire of brush and twigs. They made coffee and ate more heated elk from their knife blades.

While they ate, Mattie looked at the Ranger from above her steaming cup of coffee.

"When I told you I wanted to kill Dad Orwick, you didn't have much to say about it," she said.

"That's right," Sam said. He sipped his coffee, waiting.

She shrugged and said, "I found that a little odd. You being a lawman, I thought you would have had something to say about it."

"You mean try to talk you out of it?" Sam asked.

"Some lawmen would have tried," she said.

"Yep, some would," Sam said. He gave her a curious second glance. "Is that what you want . . . someone to talk you out of killing him?"

"No," she said firmly, "I'm just speculating."

The Ranger sipped his coffee.

"Whatever happened between you and Dad Orwick happened a long time ago, the way you told it," he said. "I figure you've had all the time you need to make up your mind whether or not to kill him."

"That's true. I have," she said.

Sam shrugged and said, "No point in me reopening the issue. If you've made it right in your mind, who am I to question it?"

She cocked her head curiously.

"See?" she said. "That doesn't sound like something a lawman would say."

"If it was somebody besides a man like Orwick, I might try to talk you out of it—for *your* sake, not his," he added. "But there're lawmen, bankers, posses all out to kill him. They post bounties that anyone is free to claim. I can't say much in his defense when so many have legally demanded his blood. Had you said you were after him for bounty, I wouldn't have said anything to try to stop you. Because your reasons are personal, that makes them no less justified, in my book. Is what he's done to others any worse than what he's done to you?"

"No," she said. "What he's done to them is *nothing* compared to what he did to me. Not only to me, but to many other women." Her expression turned dark. "We were none of us much more than children when he bought us, when he *married* us."

"Bought you?" Sam asked, hoping she'd keep talking, get some of it out of her system.

"Bought, traded for . . . swapped back and forth like breeding stock," she said. "That's all any of us were to Dad Orwick and his disciples. All of it in the name of his self-concocted religion— his powerful *'mandates from God.' "*

Sam listened as she acquainted him with her life as a child and as a young woman under the rule of a madman. He was determined he would listen for as long as it took.

Yet, before she had spoken much further on her life with Dad Orwick, they both fell silent and swung around, guns up and ready to fire, as a strange horse peeped around the edge of the boulder and blew out a breath, giving them a curious look.

"Stay here," Sam said to Mattie as he rose in a crouch, seeing no bit, bridle or reins on the horse's muzzle. He stalked forward slowly until he saw the horse step into sight, bareback, and dusty from the trail.

"What is it, Ranger?" Mattie whispered.

"Beats me," Sam said. He stepped forward and rubbed the horse's muzzle. He looked toward the boulder and said, "Let's climb up and take a look."

Chapter 7

The two climbed up to the top edge of the boulder and scooted forward on their bellies until they were able to get a good look out along the hill-side to their right. Strewn out on a path, weaving toward them through rocks, brush and boulders, nine more bareback horses strolled along as if following the first horse, now standing over beside the Ranger's dun and Mattie's dapple gray.

"Wild horses? Mustangs?" Mattie whispered.

"I don't think so," Sam whispered in reply. "They look too well fed and curried." He studied the hillside for a long while, still puzzled. "We're going to have to see what they're doing here, though. Anything out of the ordinary is cause for concern."

"I don't think we'll have to round them up," Mattie whispered. "It looks like they're coming right to us."

"Another good reason to think they're not wild," Sam said quietly. "They scented us from a mile away. They wouldn't come looking for us if they were wild." He glanced back over his shoulder in the direction of the water hole, trying to figure it out.

"They're horses that have been turned loose, spooked or something," Mattie said, her voice less of a whisper now.

"I've got it," Sam said, still looking back toward the water hole. "It's water they're after. They came to our scent because they're tame. They're used to people and our smell."

"But where are they from?" Mattie asked.

"I don't know," Sam said, moving back toward the boulder's edge. "Let's go down and ask them."

Sam slid over the edge of the boulder and took a footing on a thin, protruding crevice halfway down its side. Stopping, he turned and held a hand up toward Mattie. But she ignored his hand and slid down, took a foothold on the crevice for only a second, then jumped the remaining few feet to the ground.

Sam jumped down behind her and walked toward the gathered horses, Mattie right beside him.

"No brands," he said, looking the horses over. He touched a gloved hand to the nearest horse's side. He gave the animal a rub and saw no signs of the horse shying back from his gesture. Turning his back to the horse's shoulder, he stooped and raised its shod hoof between his knees and looked at it. "No shoe markings. . . ."

He set the hoof down and looked all around as the horses gathered around him and Mattie curiously. He gave a gentle but firm shove to get one of the horses' noses away from the canteens hanging from the dun's saddle horn.

"They're thirsty," Mattie said, rubbing a horse's sweaty, dirt-streaked neck.

"Yes, they are," Sam said. As he spoke he stepped over and took down a coiled rope he carried at his saddle horn and let out a couple of loops. "Somebody must've woken up this morning and found their corral empty. There's a good chance someone is looking for these fellows right now."

"What are you doing?" she asked, seeing the Ranger make a loop around the muzzle of the horse who'd arrived first. He led it closer to another horse.

"Stringing a couple of them," Sam said. "We'll take them to the water hole, get them watered."

"But you didn't want to be there in broad daylight with no cover," Mattie reminded him.

"That's right. I didn't, not if I could keep from it," Sam replied, continuing to string the second horse. "Right now I can't help it. These horses will get themselves in trouble out here on their own. There's a stage relay station just north of the border. We'll leave them corralled there for whoever they belong to."

"It'll cost us time," Mattie said, stepping in, helping him string the horses together.

"I know," he said. "If you want to ride on ahead, I'll catch up to you along the trail."

"No, I'll stick," she said, looping the rope around the third horse's muzzle. "Fact is, if we're going back to the water, I might manage to wash up some, if it's all the same—if we have time, that is?"

"We'll make time. It'll take a few minutes for me to water these cayuses," Sam said. He watched her add the horse to the string.

"Three will do it?" she said. "We've got more rope."

"Three's enough," said Sam. "We've got the leader and these two to boot. The others will follow the string." As he spoke, he looked across the hillside. "There could be others straggling behind, but they'll follow as they show up."

Sam took the remaining rope coil in his hand and swung up into his saddle. Turning his dun, he gave a slight pull on the rope, coaxing the first horse around beside him.

"They're tired enough, they won't be hard to handle," Mattie said, seeing the other two strung horses fall in line behind their leader. She stepped up into her saddle and swung her dapple around beside the Ranger.

Giving his dun a nudge forward, Sam saw her give him a curious look.

"What?" he said.

"You," she said, nudging the dapple forward

with him, the lead string horse walking along between them. "You have a peculiar streak."

"Do I?" Sam said. He looked himself over idly like a man searching for a bug on his shirt.

"Yes, you do," Mattie said. "I see it whether you see it or not."

"Circumstance changes its mind pretty quick where I live," he said. "I've learned it's best to change right along with it when I can. Most things happen as they should, whether we see it or not." He gave a slight shrug. "Anyway, horses need water, whatever the circumstances." The hard line of his face softened a little beneath his dark beard stubble.

"I know," she said, glancing back, seeing the loose horses plodding right along behind the three on the lead rope. She let out a tense breath and relaxed a little in her saddle.

It's all right, she reassured herself. The Ranger was a good man, she had come to realize. She could trust him. She felt safe with him, safer than she'd felt in a long time, she thought.

Safe . . . , she told herself, liking the thought of it, liking even the sound of the word, and she allowed herself to relax a little more.

She would kill Dad Orwick when the time came to do so; she had no doubt about that. She turned and looked at the Ranger as they rode along. And when it came time, she was certain the Ranger would do nothing to try to stop her.

Why would he? Every word she'd told him about Orwick was the truth.

As soon as the two had arrived at the water hole, Mattie galloped a few yards farther and stopped her dapple gray behind a waist-high stand of rocks. She dropped her horse's reins and crouched low enough to keep from being seen while she shed her boots and clothes and stepped down into the tepid water.

Sam watched her guardedly until she was out of sight, and then he shifted his attention to the winding trail and the rocky hillsides in every direction. While the horses drank, he stepped back and forth along the water's edge, his rifle cradled in the crook of his left arm.

So far so good. . . .

But no sooner had the Ranger thought it than he spotted a buckboard wagon racing toward the water hole at the head of a rising stream of dust. Not wanting to call out to Mattie and hear his echo resound along the hill line, he stooped and quickly hitched the lead rope around a stand of brush.

In the water behind the low rocks, Mattie heard the sound of the Ranger galloping toward her. She hurried out of the water and grabbed her clothes. Disregarding the wet long johns she'd washed and left lying atop a flat rock, she wiggled into her trousers, her wet hair hanging down her shoulders. She had reached for her shirt when the Ranger swung his dun around the low rocks and saw her clutch the shirt to her bosom, turning away from him.

Sam quickly tried to divert his gaze, but when she turned away, he stared, almost stunned for a moment, at the long, deep whip scars that criss-crossed her pale back from her neck down beneath the waist of her trousers.

My God. . . . The Ranger caught himself and turned away quickly.

"Sorry, Mattie," he said, forcing his eyes away from the terrible scars, knowing they were a secret she would not want shared. "There's a wagon coming. Get dressed. Hurry."

"I'm hurrying," she said, throwing her shirt around herself. She began buttoning it as she looked over her shoulder at him.

The Ranger saw a look on her face that he could not discern. Was it shame, rage, a plea for pity? All those things? He wasn't sure, and she looked past him and out toward the buckboard too quick for him to determine.

"Since you're here, stay here," Sam said, seeing how soon the wagon would be upon them. "Stay down and keep me covered if I need it."

Mattie finished buttoning her shirt and snatched her rifle up from against a short rock.

"I've got you covered," she said.

Without another word, Sam turned the dun and

raced back the few yards to where the horses stood drinking. He swung down from his saddle and gave the dun a shove on its rump.

In the wagon seat, two men saw the Ranger take a stand as his dun moved out of the line of fire. They watched the Ranger's big Colt come up from his holster, in no hurry, but they noted that he cocked it as he held it down his thigh.

"Swing around, Bud," the man in the seat beside the driver said. "Put me clear and close. I've got him." As he spoke he jerked a long-barreled shotgun up with both hands, slammed its butt against his shoulder and started to cock its hammer, taking aim.

But as the wagon driver swung the buckboard around sideways to the Ranger, Sam's big Colt came up level and fired.

The man's eyes flew open wide, seeing the Colt buck in a cloud of smoke—hearing the shot explode, feeling the hard hammering jar as the bullet struck the low side panel of the wagon seat, only an inch from his behind.

The long-barreled shotgun flew from the man's hands, spun in the air and hit the ground butt first. A blast of blue-orange flame erupted from its barrel.

The Ranger reached a hand up and opened the lapel of his riding duster as he took aim, smoke curling up the Colt's barrel.

"The next one's going to take some meat with it," he called matter-of-factly.

"Whoa! Don't shoot!" the man called out, throwing his hands up, rising from his seat a few inches, still feeling the impact of the bullet in the wooden side panel. "I think I'm hit!"

"Jesus, Breely, he's a lawman!" the driver said, jerking the buckboard to a sudden halt, one hand holding the team of horses' reins, the other raised chest high in submission, away from a holstered Remington on his hip.

"I see that *now,*" said the passenger. He stood up into a crouch, both hands raised. "I'm shot here," he called out to the Ranger.

"No, you're not. It just feels like it," Sam said, stepping forward, the smoking Colt still in hand, pointed up, raised at his elbow.

"Damn it, I know when I'm shot!" the passenger insisted.

"Go on and check yourself," Sam said, stopping close enough for both men to see his badge.

As the passenger felt around all over his buttocks, the driver set the buckboard brake handle, hitched the reins around it and stood up. He leaned and looked the other man's butt over good and shook his head.

"You're not shot anywhere, Breely," he said, sounding embarrassed. "Stop feeling your ass."

The passenger looked at both hands and, seeing no blood, appeared relieved. "Why'd you shoot me anyway, Ranger?" he said.

"You were getting ready to shoot me," Sam

said. "Besides, I didn't shoot you. I shot a hole in the wagon seat, just to settle you down."

The wagon driver chuckled under his breath.

"You sure did that, Ranger," he said. "Can I step down from here?"

"Yes," Sam said. "But stay away from that six-shooter."

"You got it, Ranger," said the driver. "I'm Ollie Haines. This is Dan'l Breely with the sore bottom."

"You think this is funny?" Breely growled. He idly reached a hand back and kneaded his stinging rear end.

"No, I don't," Haines said. "I felt it all the way over on my side. So I know it hurts. But it's over and nobody's dead. Be grateful for what you got."

"You be grateful," said Breely. "I'm most likely looking at a bad bruise out of this."

Ollie Haines only shook his head and turned back to the Ranger.

"Anyway, those are our horses. We come to get them," he said, gesturing over at the horses. "They stayed a jump ahead of us all night and morning."

The animals had flinched and turned quickly at the sound of the gunshot. But now they had gone back to their water as if nothing had happened.

"What are they doing out here?" Sam asked.

As he spoke he raised a hand and motioned for Mattie to come over from behind the short rocks and join him. Both men looked at her as she swung up into her saddle and rode toward them.

"We work for the mines, up there," Haines said, nodding to the high hill line. "We were put upon by bandits. They stole our payroll and rode off with all the guards' horses. They led them a few miles out and turned them loose, I reckon. We found their lead rope a few miles back on the high trail. The sons a' bitches thought of everything."

"Yep, I'd say they did," Sam replied. He stopped in front of the team of horses and rubbed one on its muzzle. Mattie brought her horse to a halt and stepped down beside the Ranger. Both men eyed her appreciatively, her wet silver-streaked hair clinging to the front of her drenched shirt.

"This is Miss Matilda Rourke," Sam said. He turned to Mattie and said, "These men work for the mine."

Mattie looked them up and down, her rifle in hand.

"Ma'am," the two said in unison, peeling their hats from their heads.

"Looks like this team could use watering too," Sam said. He started to touch his gloved hand to the horse's nose again. But the animal stiffened at his touch and collapsed to the ground, almost taking the other horse with it.

The Ranger looked stunned, but only for a split second. He took a step back as the sound of a rifle shot resounded from high atop a hillside.

"Down!" he shouted at Mattie, even as he hurled himself against her and took her to the ground under him. Beside them a bullet thumped into the hard dirt. The sound of the shot followed a second behind it. Sam rolled with the woman pressed against him, until he heard Dan Breely let out a deep, hard grunt and fall to the ground. Sam rose, dragging Mattie with him, taking cover on the other side of the buckboard, where Ollie Haines already lay crouched against the front wheel.

"The sons a' bitches left a man staked over this watering hole," he said in a trembling voice. "Now they've killed ol' Dan'l."

Sam and Mattie gave each other a look, both knowing how lucky they'd been to stay away from the water hole in daylight. Whoever was up there had seen the buckboard coming and decided to wait until everybody was gathered here.

Mattie's horse had spooked and galloped away. The string stirred and chuffed for a second, but went back to their drinking.

Sam noted the rifle Mattie still managed to clutch to her bosom as another bullet thumped against the other side of the wagon.

"Can you cover me here?" he asked.

"You're going up after him?" she asked.

"Yes," Sam said. "If not, he'll sit up there and

pick us to pieces. I just need you to keep him busy—throw him off."

"You're covered," she said. As she spoke, her eyes went up to a drift of rifle smoke and her fingers raised the long-distance sights on her rifle. "I'll do more than keep him busy. If I get a glimpse of him, he's dead."

"Here I go," Sam said, seeing the dun standing over by the water's edge, milling restlessly. He patted a hand on her shoulder, turned and raced toward the dun. Mattie braced the rifle against the front corner of the wagon and took aim in the direction of the smoke.

Chapter 8

A shot thumped into the ground as the Ranger leaped atop the dun and raced across the short stretch of flatlands in the cover of rocks. No sooner had the shot resounded than Mattie began a vicious string of return fire. When the firing slowed, another shot from up the hillside whistled past Sam's head. He rode the dun dangerously fast up a narrow path in the direction of the shooter, seeing the fresh drift of smoke.

A third shot from above him ricocheted off a rock and spun away. But this time instead of hearing Mattie lay down a barrage of return fire, Sam heard only one single shot from the buckboard. Yet this shot sounded prolonged, more important somehow than the shots preceding it. The sound of it seemed to stretch all the way from the buckboard to the hillside, echoing off rock as if it could have come from either direction. He glanced back down toward the buckboard and saw Mattie stand up for a second and wave a hand back and forth slowly before lowering herself back down out of sight.

"She hit him?" the Ranger said aloud to himself. He looked up toward the drifting smoke. *She must have. . . .* If the shooter wasn't hit, why wasn't he firing?

Sam deliberately slowed the dun and continued on, but not without caution. Even if the shooter was hit bad or dead, there could still be another shooter, just waiting for him to slow down enough or stop long enough to present a good target.

Nice and easy, he warned himself, keeping the dun at a slower but steady pace until higher up the trail he submerged both the horse and himself in the cover of boulders.

At a level where he'd judged the shooter to be perched on a cliff, he stopped the dun, stepped down from the saddle and let the reins fall to the dirt. In a silence broken only by the low whir of a breeze across the rocks, he slipped around a corner of stone. Colt drawn and ready, he moved along a narrow ledge with nothing beneath him but an airy drop onto the tops of spiky scrub pines and hard rock three hundred feet below.

He turned at the next rounded edge of a boulder and he felt relieved as he came upon the ledge where the shooter lay facedown in a puddle of fresh dark blood. Looking around warily, seeing only a horse in a small clearing back away from the ledge, Sam stepped forward and noted the gaping exit hole in the back of the shooter's bloody head.

Standing over the body, Sam reached out with the toe of his boot and rolled the dead ambusher over onto his back.

"You're no more than a kid," he whispered, a look of surprise on his face. He stared at the bullet hole in the young man's forehead just above his left eye. The dead man's hat lay nearby with a bullet hole just above its brim. *What were you doing riding with outlaws like these?*

He had to remind himself that Dad Orwick had more than just outlaws riding with him. He had disciples, churchmen, perhaps even members of his flock of all ages, doing his bidding. On the ground he saw a small ornament, a silver wagon wheel on the end of a horsehair watch fob. He picked it up and looked around at boot prints interspersed with a small, round indentation.

A peg leg? Could be, he told himself, sticking the silver wheel trinket into his vest pocket. At any rate, the shooter hadn't been here alone.

Sam shook his head and considered whether or

not to tell Mattie how young this shooter was. After a moment of staring at the dead boy lying at his feet, he shook his head, reached down and took the shooter by his shoulders. Still feeling warmth through the young man's shirt, he dragged the body into a stand of brush.

No, he thought, he wasn't going to mention the shooter's age to Mattie unless she asked, and why would she ask? It served no purpose, he decided, letting out a breath. She had killed the shooter who was out to kill them. Let that be the end of it.

He walked to the standing horse and led it around a thin path to where his dun stood waiting. When he searched the dead man's saddlebags and found nothing of any importance, he stepped atop his copper dun. Leading the shooter's horse behind him, he took his time descending the steep trail to the stretch of flatlands, then moved at a gallop. He slowed down as he neared the buckboard where Mattie stood watching, the hand above her eyes acting as a visor. Ollie Haines stood beside her, having stripped the harness and reins from the dead team horse and backed the wagon away from it.

"I got him, didn't I?" Mattie called out confidently as the Ranger drew nearer.

"You sure did," Sam said, slowing his horse and the horse beside him. "Good shooting," he said, not wanting to think any more about how young the shooter was.

"I told you if I got a glimpse of him, he'd be dead," Mattie said.

"You sure did," Sam said again, stopping, swinging down from his saddle. He held the dead shooter's horse toward Haines as Haines turned from the buckboard and walked over to him.

"Obliged, Ranger," said Haines, taking the horse and looking it up and down. "This one will do." He dropped the horse's saddle and led the animal to the buckboard, standing it beside the other team horse.

"We're getting up out of here. You need to do the same," Sam called out to him. He saw Breely's body lying on the buckboard, a blanket tucked around it. "Any minute this place could turn hot again."

"I'm ready to roll!" Haines said, Sam's words causing him to cut a wary glance up along the hill line. "Soon as I tie this string behind my wagon, I'm cutting out of here."

"We'll stay here and cover you until you're up out of sight in the hills," Sam called out to him.

"Much obliged, Ranger," Haines called out in reply, his voice sounding worried.

Sam and Mattie watched him work quickly while they both kept their eyes on the hillside in the direction where Sam had found the young ambusher.

"Did you see any sign of another rifleman up there?" Mattie asked, scanning the hillside.

"No, I think it was only the one shooter," said Sam, keeping his words guarded. "But this is still a bad place to be in broad daylight. It looks like Dad Orwick is big on leaving gunmen behind to cover his tail."

"He's always been that way," Mattie said reflectively. She looked at Sam as he watched the upper hill line. "It could be like this the whole way," she said with a slight warning. "A gunman waiting where you're least expecting it."

"I'm always expecting it," Sam replied. He turned his eyes to hers. "A place as open as this, I'd be expecting it even if I wasn't trailing somebody." He looked her up and down. "Are you all right?" he asked, sensing something pressing on her mind.

"I'm fine," she said, but Sam didn't believe her. He kept his eyes on hers until she had to look away for a second. When she looked back at him, she asked, "The gunman . . . did my shot kill him right away? I mean, did he suffer?"

There it is.

"No," Sam said firmly, "he never knew what hit him." He looked away toward the hills again. He let out a breath. Instinctively, some inner voice had warned him not to tell her about the young shooter. He was thankful now that he'd heeded that warning.

"I know he's not the first man you ever shot," he said, making a wry reference to his bullet-grazed shoulder. "Is he the first man you ever killed?"

"Maybe," she said guardedly.

" 'Maybe'? " Sam's eyes turned back to hers.

"I mean, *yes,*" she corrected herself. "I've thought so long and hard, imagining how it would feel killing Dad Orwick. . . ." She let her words trail. Sam saw the pale, ill look on her face, now that her first taste of killing had set in.

Oh yes, he thought, he was glad he hadn't said much about the ambusher.

"The way you're feeling right now," Sam said, softening his tone of voice, "that's how you'll feel every time."

"Really?" she said.

"Yes, really," said Sam. "It never *feels* any different . . . If you're lucky, you just won't think about it as much." The two studied each other's faces for a moment, then turned their eyes back to the hillsides until they heard Haines call out behind them.

"I'm gone here," he said, having climbed quickly into the buckboard, let off the brake handle and settled onto the hard wooden seat. "Anything you want me to tell the guards at the mines, Ranger?"

"Tell them to watch for me if they're still riding out searching for the robbers," Sam called out.

"I doubt they'll be riding out after this long," Haines replied. "The boss might set a bounty on them. Send out Gayle Warden or some other big gun. Otherwise these thieves can pat themselves on the back for this one."

Mattie and the Ranger continued to watch the cliffs and hillsides as the buckboard and the string of horses moved away in a rise of dust. When the wagon disappeared behind the first tall stand of rocks, Mattie let her grip relax on her rifle stock.

"Who's Gayle Warden?" she asked Sam.

"He's a bounty hunter who does a lot of work for mining companies, railroads and such," the Ranger replied. "They hire him because he's familiar with Old Mex. He made a name for himself killing a few loudmouth gunmen over in Sonora and Mexico City—they call him the Iron Warden there."

Mattie shook her head slowly as they both walked to their horses and took up their reins. All that remained of the buckboard and horses was a drifting cloud of dust. On the ground lay the dead team horse, a simmering feast for the creatures of prey. Overhead, two buzzards had already begun circling wide and slow.

"Bounty hunters, lawmen, posses, mining guards," she said, stepping up into her saddle. "This world you live in is something a person must see for herself in order to believe it."

"Some folks see it and still don't believe it," Sam replied quietly, "times when it spills off the badlands and into their civilized world." He gave another look around. "Let's get off these flatlands," he said.

In his saddle, he nudged the dun toward the short rocks at the water's edge where Mattie had washed her long johns and left them on the ground. Without stopping, the woman veered her horse over to the rocks, reached down from her saddle and picked up the wet undergarments. She draped them out over the dapple's rump to dry as they rode on.

Higher along a rocky hillside, the Ranger picked up a single set of hoofprints and the two of them followed the prints the rest of the afternoon. When they stopped and gazed at a small, weathered shack sitting in a clearing ahead of them, Sam sniffed the air closely.

"Over here," he whispered to Mattie.

She followed him without a sound. They reined their horses off the thin path and out of sight behind a stand of thick, mature pines that stood like ancient columns between heaven and earth. As they stepped down from their saddles silently, Sam drew his big Colt and cocked it down his side.

"What is it?" Mattie whispered.

"Cooking smoke," Sam whispered in reply.

"I don't see it," Mattie said, glancing all around.

"Because it's gone," Sam said. "Somebody cooked up some rattlesnake, then put the fire out."

Mattie sniffed the air closely. A look of recognition came to her face.

"Now I smell it," she said.

Sam nodded and said, "Stay here with the horses. I'll move in close and see if they're still there."

"Be careful—" she said, catching herself but stopping a second too late.

Be careful? Sam just looked her up and down.

"You know what I mean," she whispered.

"I'll try," Sam said in a lowered voice.

He crept through the pines toward the shack in a crouch, his six-gun in hand. Circling the small clearing, he stepped out and approached the shack from the side, keeping himself unseen. He tested the plank porch before putting all his weight on it. Once he determined it was all right, he moved to an open window and peeped inside for any sign of life.

He saw no fire in the small hearth, only a bed of waning red coals. But he did see a tin skillet of rattlesnake meat lying on a wooden table. A blackened coffeepot sat in the hearth coals. The aroma of snake meat and coffee wafted faintly— just as he'd thought, he told himself, easing silently to the open front door. Nobody left coffee and a skillet of snake meat to go to waste.

Stepping inside the door, Sam walked to the rear window and glanced out, noticing a fatigued horse tied to a pine sapling at the edge of the clearing. No sooner had he seen the horse than he heard the creaking of a roof plank and glanced up at it.

Here he is, Sam told himself.

He eased closer to the skillet on the table, picked it up and shoved it onto a low, glowing bed of ashes, his eyes upturned, listening. With his gloved hand, he reached into the skillet, picked up a small gray-white chunk of back meat and put it in his mouth.

Chewing slowly as if to keep from being heard, he waited in a tense silence until he heard the roof creak again, footsteps moving diagonally upward toward the center. Then he stopped chewing and fired three quick shots almost straight up, stair-stepping each shot higher toward the roof's peak.

"*Aiiii!* Son of a bitch!" a voice cried out in pain.

With his Colt raised, Sam followed a loud thumping sound down the roof with the tip of his smoking barrel. Where the noise stopped, he fired again. This time he heard the man fall off the edge of the roof and land heavily on the ground outside the rear window.

Stepping over to the window, Sam began chewing again, the big bull rattler not being the most tender he'd ever eaten. He looked down on the ground at the bloody man, who was struggling toward a fumbled rifle a few feet away.

"Don't try for it," Sam warned him, his Colt ready to fire again. "You're shot bad as it is."

The wounded man stopped reaching for the rifle and rolled onto his bloody side. He stared up at the Ranger with clenched teeth, his mouth bleeding.

"Damn you to hell, look at me!" he shouted. "Shot straight up! Blown off the *got-damn* roof!" He clutched at the inside of his upper thigh, where a stream of heavy blood spewed between his fingers. "I hate to even guess where that bullet went." Seeing Sam chew the snake meat, he sobbed pitifully, "I've carried that rattler all day, looking to sup on it."

"It won't go uneaten, I promise," Sam said as if offering the man consolation.

"I swear to God, if this ain't the awfulest damn mess I've ever seen!" the man raged and sobbed. He looked down his chest at another bullet hole pumping dark blood with each beat of his slowing heart. "What did you shoot me for anyway?" He jerked his shirt open and let a broken bundle of stolen money spill out onto the dirt.

"I think you know," Sam said. "What's your name?"

"Burt Tally," the wounded man mustered.

"Where are all your pards meeting up, Burt Tally?" Sam asked.

Tally took on a stubborn look, but only for a second.

"Aw, to hell with it," he said with a bloody cough. He swiped a handful of bloody money up into his fist and let it fall wistfully onto him. "I don't owe them nothing." He relaxed the side of his face down onto the dirt. His voice turned shallow, weaker. "They're all meeting at Munny's."

"Where's that?" Sam asked. Seeing the man succumb to death, he said louder, "Where is that?"

"I know where it's at," Mattie said from the open door behind him.

Sam swung around at the sound of her voice. Catching himself, he lowered his Colt.

"You should have waited outside," he said.

"Sorry," she said. "But I do know Munny Caves. They're caves Dad's men have been using for years."

Sam lowered his Colt into its holster.

"Hungry?" he asked.

"Starving," Mattie said, stepping over to the skillet warming on the bed of coals. She picked up the skillet and set it on the table.

With no chairs, the two sat on the edges of the rickety table and converged on the warm meat with their fingers. They ate until the snake meat sated their hunger. Then they found a battered tin cup and shared coffee, not bothering to go to their horses and get their own cups.

When they were finished, they sat resting for a moment, the Ranger's gloves off, lying across his knee. After a silent pause, Mattie sighed and pushed the tin skillet away from them.

"I know what you saw at the water hole today," she said quietly. "I hope that's not what you'll see every time you look at me. I don't want pity."

Sam only nodded, not knowing what to say. Finally he raised his eyes from the hearth and said, "It won't be what I see, Mattie. What I saw today will only remind me that you're a strong woman for what you've lived through. Strength is always to be looked at with respect, never with pity."

She gave him a faint, tired smile and said, "A strong woman, yes, but never a very good child bride. I fought that old devil every time he forced himself on me. The whippings always followed. I was one of his captive wives for twenty-three years. I bore seven children. All of them from unwelcome seed, yet they are my children nonetheless." She looked away again and said, "For a time I told myself I couldn't leave because my children were too young. . . ."

"I understand," Sam said. He saw her eyes glisten and fill, but her voice remained strong, as if willing itself so.

"But one day, young children or not, I knew I must leave, or else take my own life. Either way, my children would no longer know me. Either way, there would be other wives to look after them. I chose to live, Ranger." She paused, then said, "You're a man of the law. Did I do wrong?" Now she turned her eyes to him; a single tear spilled down her cheek.

Sam reached his hand over, rubbed the tear away with his thumb and cupped her cheek. He knew that as a lawman he had no say or right of judgment in such matters. But if he knew that something he said could offer her comfort, who was he to deny her that?

"Mattie, it's never wrong to choose living over dying." He brushed a strand of silver-gray hair back from her face. "That's what those seven children would tell you too."

She breathed deep and let her cheek relax against his hand, liking the warmth of it. She felt herself want to lean closer to him across the table. Sam sensed it and felt the same. Yet they both stopped themselves and straightened and stood up from the table's edges.

"All right, then," Sam said. He nodded toward the rear window. "I'm going to go drag him away from here. We'll spend the night here where there's a hearth to shield a fire. Tomorrow you can lead us to Munny Caves."

"It's a long ride from here. We'll need our rest," she said.

"I'll get his horse and ours and bring them inside," Sam said, turning toward the open door.

"Sam?" Mattie said.

He stopped and looked back at her.

"I should tell you. There's been no other man since Dad—I doubt there ever will be."

"I understand, Mattie," Sam said. They eyed each other closely before he turned away and walked out the door.

PART 2

Chapter 9

Inside Dr. Lanahan's large clapboard house in Whiskey Bend, Lightning Wade Hornady lay propped up against his pillow on a narrow bed in the corner of the small room he now shared with Sheriff Fred Hall from Goble. Hornady still wore an ankle cuff and a three-foot length of chain that held him to the bed frame. He was feeling better, stronger, yet he didn't want anyone to know it. He'd started making his escape plans the minute the doctor assured him he would most likely live, in spite of his wounds and his loss of blood. That was all Hornady had needed to hear.

He'd convinced himself that with another day or two of rest, he'd be able to break the single-rail bed frame as if it were made of matchsticks, climb out the window and make his getaway. Of course, now he had this son of a bitch to deal with, he thought to himself, drawing deep on a cigarette he'd rolled. He blew out a stream of smoke and stared at the back of a tall wicker-trimmed wheelchair facing the room's only window. A double-barreled shotgun stuck out from the side of the wheelchair.

"You know, Sheriff Hall," Hornady said matter-of-factly to the back of the wheelchair through a looming cloud of smoke, "I can't think one solitary thing says you have to stay here and do DeShay's job for him. I can see you're in pain here."

"Never you mind my pain, Wade Hornady," he heard Sheriff Hall say gruffly. The convalescing lawman sat in the wheelchair gazing out the window through bloodshot eyes. A wooden leg support held the sheriff's plaster-casted broken foot straight out in front of him. Above the cast, the sheriff's purple, swollen toes appeared to almost throb in pain.

Staring unseen from his bed, Hornady gave a thin, devilish grin.

"I'm only thinking of you, Sheriff," Hornady replied. "I know for a fact that a man always feels better at home in his own bed. I always say that's where true healing starts, and not a minute before."

"I know you'd like that, Hornady—you and me leaving here, heading back to Goble, just the two of us on the trail," Hall said to the wavy windowpanes in front of him. "But you'd do well to remind yourself that just as bad as you want to bash my head in and cut out—that's how bad I want to cock both hammers and blow your breakfast all over the wall."

"Whoa, you've got me all wrong, Sheriff," said Hornady, puffing his wrinkled cigarette, stifling a nasty laugh. As he spoke, he struggled to sit up on the side of the bed and looked down at the bandage on his chest, only a dot of dried blood in the center of it. "Getting shot has caused me to restudy my whole wasted life. I'm looking forward to making amends, walk the straight and narrow from now on—maybe try to show others the right path, so to speak."

"That's real good to hear," Hall said in a sarcastic tone. "Does making amends mean you'll be offering back the money that you sons a' bitches stole from our bank in Goble?"

"Oh, about that . . ." Hornady wasn't able to completely hide a slight chuckle in his voice. "All the time I've been an outlaw, I can't say I've ever supported any type of *return policy*. I've always believed a man keeps what he earns in this hard world, no matter how he's earned it."

Hall could take no more of it. He swung the wheelchair around recklessly and gave a hard roll toward Hornady's bed.

"You rotten, smirking bastard!" he shouted, trying to raise and aim the shotgun while the chair rolled on its own. "I'll show you *return policy!*" The sheriff's elevated casted foot led his charge.

Seeing the sheriff's foot coming at him, the shotgun pointed and the sheriff struggling to cock the hammers, Hornady grabbed the plaster cast between both hands and banged it up and down mercilessly on the wooden leg support. The sheriff's agonizing scream only encouraged

Hornady. He twisted Hall's broken foot back and forth with one hand and clamped his other hand down over the purple toes, bending them viciously. Hall screamed louder, but he held on to the shotgun.

Hornady glanced around in desperation for something, anything, to use as a weapon. Eyeing a rug beater leaning against the wall beside his bed, he yanked it up. Holding the broken foot with one hand, he began beating Hall's swollen toes savagely.

From the other room, Dr. Lanahan heard the rhythm of the pounding rug beater and the tortured screams of the sheriff. *What the hell?* He ran toward the door.

"Turn it loose! Turn it loose! I'll keep beating these toes till you do!" Lanahan heard Hornady shouting on the other side of the door.

The sheriff, unable to bear the pain and unable to cock the shotgun because of it, turned the gun loose. Hornady jumped at the opportunity, grabbing the gun barrel and yanking it from the sheriff's hands.

The doctor heard the gun blast just as he threw open the door and saw the wheelchair shooting backward across the room in a streak of smoke and blue-orange fire. The wheelchair crashed against the window ledge, flipped backward and hurled the bloody sheriff through the wavy glass panes and into the side yard.

"My, but didn't he leave in a hurry?" Hornady said.

"Oh Lord!" said the doctor, seeing the smoking double-barrel cocked and aimed at him.

"I hope you don't have to leave the same way," Hornady said with a grin.

"Don't shoot!" Lanahan said. *Of all days to be sober,* he chastised himself. "You don't have to kill me," he said.

"I know," Hornady said in a light, almost playful voice, "but I sort of want to, the way you've treated me, the callous remarks you made."

"That's just my style," Lanahan said. "Call it gaining my patients' confidence—getting their attention."

"Oh, right. Sort of like this shotgun does for me," Hornady said. He grinned and added, "Reach back and shut the door. Then get over here and get this blasted chain off me. I feel like a damn yard dog."

"If you're thinking about leaving, I've got to caution against it," the doctor said even as he did as he was told. "You're in no condition."

"Is that a fact?" said Hornady. "I've got to caution against you opening your mouth again, else your condition will be worse than mine."

Hornady watched as the big doctor stooped beside the bed and opened the ankle cuff with a key from his vest pocket.

"Hurry it up, Doc," he said, "before folks start

to notice there's a dead sheriff lying in your yard."

"Oh my, oh my," the doctor said in a shaky voice, trying to hurry.

"Buck up, Doctor," said Hornady. "What's become of that bold cavalier rascal that was you, making all the carefree jokes about cutting off the wrong leg and such?" His countenance turned dark as he added, "Jokes at *my expense, that is.*"

The cuff opened and fell to the floor.

"Please give thought to what will happen to the sick in this town if you kill me," Dr. Lanahan said, his voice trembling in fear.

"I will, I promise," said Hornady. "Whilst I do, you can be putting on my socks and boots for me." He gestured down toward the boots standing under the edge of the bed. "I never could think barefooted."

While the doctor kneeled and put on the outlaw's socks and boots, Hornady heard worried voices calling back and forth to one another outside on the dirt street.

"They're starting to form up, you know," the doctor said. "It's going to be hard for you to leave town."

Hornady ignored him and shrugged.

"Where'd DeShay put my guns? I'm not leaving here without them," he said.

"I—I expect he's wearing them," the frightened

doctor said, pulling Hornady's boot up onto his foot. "Either that or he's left them hanging in his office."

"We'll just have to go there first thing and see, Doc," Hornady said.

"Listen out there. The townsmen are arming themselves. They'll shoot you to pieces," the doctor said in a weak and fearful voice.

"Oh yes, I know," Hornady said with a cruel grin, "and you too if I'm holding you in front of me." He laughed at the sick look on the big doctor's face. "Looks like we're going to see just how much they really think of you."

Holding the shotgun on the doctor, Hornady picked up his shirt hanging from the bedpost and threw it on, leaving it unbuttoned as he gestured Lananan ahead of him out of the room and toward the front door.

"After you, good Doctor," he said. He took a firm hold on the doctor's shirt collar, the tip of the shotgun barrel jammed into the doctor's broad, soft back. "If you think of something snappy and fun to say, by all means, feel free."

"Pl-please!" was all the scared doctor could muster.

Hornady stopped at the front door long enough to grab a wide-brimmed straw hat from a coatrack and put it on.

As the two stepped onto the front porch, a townsman held up a stopping hand to the other townsmen stationed behind cover along the dirt street.

"Don't anybody shoot!" he said. "He's got the doctor."

"Hear that, Doc?" Hornady said as if surprised. "They must like you after all." He jammed the tip of the shotgun barrel against him and said, "Now tell them we're headed to the sheriff's office. Tell them to have a horse waiting when I come out."

The doctor did as he was told.

"Listen up, all of you," he called out along the street. "Let us through to the sheriff's office. The man wants his guns. And bring around a horse for him, *please.* He has me at an extreme disadvantage here."

"Turn the doctor loose," a voice called out.

Hornady shouted in loud reply, "Are you deaf, you son of a bitch? Do what he said or I'm going to kill him right here, blow his bloody brains all over—"

"Damn it, man!" the doctor screamed at the townsmen, cutting Wade Hornady short. "Do what he says . . . He'll kill me!"

"All right, Lightning," a man called out. "Come on, then. Nobody's going to shoot at you. Don't hurt our doctor."

Hornady chuckled as he nudged the doctor across the porch and down the wooden steps to the street.

"I have to say, Dr. Lanahan, I'm just a little bit

disappointed," he said, nudging the big doctor forward. "It might have been worth getting shot just to see them splatter you all over the street."

Townsmen moved along warily, eyeing the wounded gunman and the town doctor until the two stepped inside the sheriff's office and Hornady closed the thick wooden door behind them.

"This is a fine mess you've brought us, Stone," one of the townsmen said to the banker from Goble, who had ventured into the street and stood looking back and forth in bewilderment, a big Remington pistol hanging useless in his soft hand. "We've got *your* sheriff lying dead in *our* street, and our sheriff off searching for the men who robbed *your* bank."

Another man cut in, saying, "And our *doctor* held hostage by one of *your* bank robbers."

"Robbing my bank doesn't make him *my* bank robber," Kerwin Stone shouted. He looked at Dave Chapel and Wylin Jessup, the two men from Goble who had escorted him and Sheriff Hall back to Whiskey Bend for help.

"Gentlemen," he called out to the townsmen, "I don't think you'd appreciate me trying to tell you how to run your town." He turned to Chapel and Jessup as he shoved the big Remington down behind his waistband against his huge belly.

"Dave, Wylin, both of you. Let's get mounted *pronto,* and proceed forthwith back to Goble. We've been here far too long as it is."

"What about *our* doctor?" a townsman shouted, watching the three men hurry to a hitch rail and mount their horses.

"I'm confident you'll work it out," said Stone over his shoulder. "As you say, he's *your* doctor."

But as the three backed their horses and turned them hastily in the middle of the street, a rifle shot exploded from a window in the sheriff's office, lifted Kerwin Stone from his saddle and flung him down to the dirt.

"Whoa!" Dave Chapel shouted, seeing the banker fall. He and Jessup spurred their horses forward and veered into a nearby alley for cover.

"Nobody leaves here until after I leave here," Hornady called out through the window.

Inside the sheriff's office, Hornady levered a fresh round into the Winchester, backed away and laid the smoking rifle on a battered desk beside the double-barreled shotgun.

"You shot him!" the doctor said in surprise, even though he'd already seen what Hornady was capable of. "You shot the banker for no reason!"

"Any outlaw who needs a reason for shooting a banker is in the wrong business," Hornady said absently, searching the office until he spotted his small custom pistol hanging on a gun rack. He checked it and shoved it down into his belt. He looked all around for his larger revolver, but didn't see it.

"DeShay, you son of a bitch," he said gruffly, as if Clayton DeShay were standing there beside him. He jerked down a bandolier of rifle ammunition from the rack and slung it over his shoulder.

Leaving the shotgun where it lay, Hornady picked up the rifle, cocked it and stuck it in Lanahan's big belly.

"Turn around . . . out the door," he commanded. "Tell them all to get back. You better pray somebody brought me a horse."

Dr. Lanahan shoved the creaking door open and stepped out slowly onto the boardwalk. A hard nudge from behind sent him across the planks and down to the street.

"All of you get back and give us some room here," he called out. "Where's the horse he asked for?"

"Here it is," a man said, hurrying forward, leading a big bay, the horse all saddled and ready to ride.

"You get up on the saddle, Doc—remember, I'm right behind you," said Hornady.

As the townsmen watched in tense silence, the big doctor stepped up into the saddle. Hornady, feeling the pain in his wounded chest start to throb, swung up behind him, the pistol jammed into the doctor's pudgy back.

"Everybody stay put here until I reach the end of town, and the doctor lives," Hornady said, the rifle across his thighs. He moved the pistol up from the doctor's back and stuck it against the base of Lanahan's skull.

From the middle of the street where two men kneeled over, tending to the badly wounded banker, Stone cried, "For God's sake, please don't let him hurt the doctor."

"I like his attitude," Hornady said, batting his boots to the horse's sides and sending it galloping along the dirt street. The townsmen stood staring, guns in hand.

At the far edge of town, Hornady slowed the horse to a halt and turned it quarterwise in the street.

"Here's where you get off, Doctor," he said. He scooted back far enough for the big man to climb down. Then he smiled as he slid forward into the saddle and said, "*Adios*, now."

The doctor hurried along the street, still badly shaken by the whole experience. But before he'd gone twenty feet, three shots rang out from Hornady's small custom revolver, each bullet hitting Lanahan squarely in the back.

"I was only joking about not killing you, you big tub of guts," Hornady said as the horse circled in the street, stirring up a rise of dust. He looked back at the doctor and grinned. He spun the revolver expertly on his trigger finger, righted the restless horse and galloped away.

Chapter 10

Perched on a high, rocky ledge overlooking a narrow gully winding between two steep hill-sides, a rifleman named Dallas Burns levered a round into his rifle chamber. He watched closely as a single rider moved into sight on the trail a thou-sand feet below him.

"Rider coming," he said over his shoulder to another rifleman, this one resting on one knee beside a small fire.

The other rifleman, Stan Liles, stood up in a crouch with a cup of coffee in his gloved hand and eased over closer to the edge, beside Burns. He set his coffee down, stretched out a battered artillery telescope and raised it to his right eye.

After a moment of waiting in silence, Burns grew impatient.

"Well? Is it one of us or not?" he asked.

"Yep, it's Morton Kerr," said Liles, still staring through the telescope. "His horse looks like it's ready to fall over and give up the ghost any minute." He grinned and added, "Morton will be lucky if that cayuse makes it all the way up."

Dallas Burns chuffed and shook his head.

"Kerr never had any luck with horses," he said.

"All I ever saw him ride was rags and buzzard bait."

Searching back farther along the trail, Liles spotted another rider coming into sight.

"We got another one straggling in," he said. He stared through the scope for a moment longer, then said, "Looks like Deacon Jamison."

"Is Young Ezekiel with him?" Burns asked, laying his rifle across his knees now that he knew it was their own men.

"Nope, don't see him," said Liles.

"That's not good," said Burns. "This old bull and the kid always stick closer than grass in a pig turd."

"Not this time," said Liles. He lowered the telescope and rubbed both eyes.

"They must have had to split up for a while," Burns said, scooting back from the edge, getting up onto his feet and dusting the seat of his trousers. "We best go say who's coming."

"Dad ain't going to like the deacon showing up without the kid at his side," said Liles.

"He might not like it," said Burns, "but that's no skin off our butts, is it?"

"No, not at all," said Liles, collapsing the telescope, putting it away. "Truth be told, the kid and the deacon both make my skin crawl."

"Yeah, them and their cockeyed religion," Burns chuckled, staring out and down at the riders.

"It'll be a good half hour before Kerr gets up

here—even longer if he has to carry his horse," Liles said.

The two outlaws turned to a rope hanging down the hillside. Each in turn used the rope to help pull himself up a steep, dangerous path leading to where their horses stood waiting.

Untying his horse's reins, Liles stepped up into his saddle beside Burns, and the two turned their horses to a thin trail leading down to a narrow valley below.

"More truth to be told," he said. "I don't like the way Dad's been acting these past few months. Every time I'm around him, he's got the deacon or one of his top flunkies talking for him. I'm starting to wonder if he's lost his voice."

"I know why," said Burns. "He's doing it to remind us where our place is. He thinks of us outlaws like we're his damned servants. He doesn't like us, but he knows he needs us to keep his game afloat."

"Sort of like a mighty king and his underlings?" said Liles.

"Yep, that's how I take it," Burns said as their horses moved along at an easy gait.

"Religious folks always think they're better than us poor sinners," Liles said with a thin smile, "no matter how much they try to deny it."

"I know they can't help thinking it," said Burns. "But it sort of frosts my kernels to have a man turn his face away when I come into the room to report to him."

"Can I say something?" Liles asked, lowering his voice as if someone might hear him.

"I expect you can if your jaws are working," said Burns.

"I've noticed lately, lots of Dad's wives have been disappearing," said Liles.

Burns stared at him.

"I mean it," said Liles. "I've noticed the older ones are being weeded out up here and new ones are showing up over in Gun Valley."

Burns nodded and said, "All right, I've noticed that myself of late—just haven't mentioned it."

"What does it mean?" Liles asked.

"Hell, who knows?" said Burns. "The way Dad treats his women, I could see him using them up like laying hens and trading them off for some younger ones."

Liles appeared to consider it for a moment.

"There's a practice that could take hold and spread like wildfire," he said with a mindless grin.

"You're the one brought it up," said Burns. "I thought you were making serious conversation."

"I am serious," said Liles. His grin went away. "Trading them off, huh?"

Burns shrugged and said, "I'm just speculating. But don't think Dad wouldn't do it if it suited him. If we treated our horses like he treats women, we'd have to walk every place we go."

"You watch when we go to talk to him," said Liles, "see if he don't pass us right off to Cinders first thing."

"I don't have to watch," said Burns. "I already know he will. I can't recall the last time the man has looked me in the eye."

They rode on toward a tall, pointed black crevice at the bottom of a stone hillside. Out in front of the crevice stood a rifleman walking back and forth, watching them ride closer. To one side of the crevice, three horses were poised at a long wooden hitch rail.

"What's out there?" the rifleman asked as they rode in, slid their horses to a halt and swung down from their saddles.

"Two riders, Brother Bud," said Burns, "Morton Kerr and Deacon Jamison, coming up about twenty minutes apart."

"Thanks be to the Lord. It's about time everybody started showing up," said the rifleman, Brother Buddy Gentry. "I expect Young Ezekiel is with the deacon?"

"No," Burns said. He gave Gentry a look.

"Umm-umm," Gentry said, shaking his head, "and Dad already in a bad mood."

"Bad mood about what?" Liles asked.

"Never you mind about what. You two did your job. Now ride back and stay watching," he said dismissively. "We'll have more men straggling in. Make sure they're not being followed. I'll tell Dad what you said."

Burns and Liles looked at each other.

"I told you," Liles said to Burns under his breath.

"Where is Dad?" Burns asked, not to be put off. "I'd like to tell him myself." He started to take a step toward the dark crevice.

Brother Bud blocked his way, his rifle up across his chest.

"I'm following Dad's orders, Burns," Gentry said, adding in a low, even tone of warning, "You two will not want to put me to hard testing."

Hard testing?

Burns and Liles looked at each other again.

"Well, hell no, Brother Bud," Dallas Burns said with a dark chuckle. "I'd not put a man to *hard testing* unless I was all set to straightaway blow his head off." He gave Gentry a flat, cold stare, his hand near his holstered Colt.

"Let's go, Dallas," Liles said quietly, venturing a fingertip, poking Burns' forearm.

Burns rounded his arm away from Liles' finger and kept his stare on Gentry.

"I told you, Burns, it's my orders. Nobody comes in, not until Dad tells me otherwise," Gentry said.

"Let's go, Dallas," Liles repeated.

Burns released a tight breath, followed by a dark little chuckle.

"You can sure get under my skin sometimes, Brother Bud," he said, letting his gun hand uncoil at his side.

"Sorry," said Gentry, "but that's not my fault." He looked Burns up and down and said in a somber tone, "That comes from you not being saved—not knowing the word of the Lord."

"See? I tell him that all the time," Liles said, keeping himself from grinning. "Let's get riding, Dallas," he said to Burns. "Now that you know what your problem is, we'll see if you do anything to solve it."

The two turned and swung back up into their saddles.

Knowing Liles was only mocking him, Gentry said, "It wouldn't hurt neither of you to take to heed to the word of the Lord."

"Amen to that, Brother Bud," Liles said, touching his fingers to his hat brim. "We see any more of our men coming, we'll send them on through and watch their back trail."

The two turned their horses and rode away.

"Did he strike you as being drunk?" Burns asked. "I could have sworn I smelled whiskey."

"These fools always strike me as being drunk," said Liles. "As far as I'm concerned, it would be an improvement."

They rode on. Moments later, as they drew closer to the spot where they'd sat looking out over the trail, they both reined up sharp as they saw a big black blaze-faced horse step out onto the trail in front of them. Atop the horse sat Frank Bannis, a rifle standing straight up from his thigh.

"Jesus, Frank!" shouted Dallas Burns as his horse circled quickly before settling against the hard tug on its reins. "You need to announce yourself!" Beside Burns, Liles was having a hard time with his own spooked horse.

Bannis just stared at the two as they struggled with their horses and finally reined them down. Then he gave a flat smile.

"Anybody as skittish as you two must feel guilty about something," he said.

"We wasn't expecting you up here, is all," said Liles. "We saw Kerr and we saw Jamison. But you surprised the hell out of us."

"Yeah, how'd you get up here past us anyway?" Burns asked, looking a little embarrassed.

"Because I'm good, Dallas," Frank said. "How far back are Kerr and the deacon?"

"By now," said Burns, "Kerr should be topping the lower ridge. Jamison is a few minutes behind him. We saw that Young Ezekiel isn't with him."

"No?" said Bannis. "He should be. Last I seen them both I told them to set up above the water hole and take care of anybody on our trail."

"Maybe the kid will be along directly," said Burns.

"Could be his horse threw a shoe or something," offered Liles.

But Bannis was having none of it.

"The deacon would have lagged back with him, if that was the case," he said. He nodded in the direction of the crevice. "Is Dad back there?"

"If he is, you couldn't prove it by us," said Burns. "His Highness ain't talking to the likes of us these days."

Bannis stared at him, knowing this kind of talk could get his back skinned if Dad got word of it.

"Frank," said Liles, "Dallas don't mean nothing. We was just talking about how hard it is to see Dad straight up these days."

"Don't I know it?" Bannis said quietly. "But if I was you, I'd keep my mouth shut about it. Dad's up to something, and it's clear he doesn't want us meddling." He nudged his horse forward on the trail toward the crevice.

"Forget I said anything, huh, Frank?" said Burns.

"I already forgot it," Frank said back over his shoulder. "I won't even tell Dad that I slipped in past you."

"Obliged, Frank," Liles called out to him as he rode away.

As he neared the crevice, Frank Bannis saw the horses tied at the hitch rail, but he saw no sign of Brother Bud Gentry standing guard, walking back and forth in his usual manner anytime Dad Orwick was at Munny Caves. Ever cautious, Frank backed his horse and rode over to a stand of brush and rock. There, he stepped down from his saddle, tied his horse's reins to a rock spur and walked quietly to the cave entrance, his Colt out of its holster and cocked while he checked the thing out.

He moved silently into the black crevice and walked along seventy feet until he felt the narrow stone tunnel begin to widen into a cavern. Across the thirty-foot cavern, a torch stood burning in its stand on the jagged stone wall, casting shadowy light for him to see by. He walked over to the torch, took it down and held it in front of him.

Walking on into another narrow crevice opening that led into a wider tunnel lined with burning torches, he began to hear the sound of voices deeper inside the large cave. Gun still at the ready, he continued as the voices grew clearer. At a sharp turn in the tunnel, he stopped and stood back against the stone wall and listened.

"But, Dad, please!" said Brother Bud's sobbing voice. "You yourself drink. We all know it!"

Instead of hearing Dad Orwick reply, Frank Bannis identified the voice of Elder David Barcinder, Dad's second-in-command among the disciples.

"How dare you compare yourself, Gentry?" Barcinder's voice shouted angrily. "Your job was to guard and protect Dad! But instead you partook of strong drink, broke your pledge to God and shirked your duty to our leader."

"Dad, please, I'm begging you!" Gentry's voice pleaded.

Bannis heard Dad reply, yet the voice he listened to was not the usual deep, God-like voice of authority. The voice sounded low and shallow.

"You know what's expected of you, Brother Bud," Dad replied. "There's no mercy for you here."

What the hell . . . ? Dad?

As Bannis listened, he couldn't believe his ears. That wasn't the voice of Dad Orwick he'd come to recognize these two years of riding for him.

Lowering his torch, Bannis edged forward and peeped around the corner of the stone wall. Across the cavern he saw Gentry on his knees in front of a large, high-backed chair that served Dad Orwick like a throne. Only today Dad was not on his throne. Instead, Bannis saw the broad-shouldered silhouette standing back in the shadows on the grainy outer edges of the torchlights. He saw Dad's familiar wide flat-crowned hat, his long ankle-length riding duster.

"Dad, I know I did wrong," Gentry pleaded in a trembling voice. "But please don't kill me. I will never do anything like this again, I swear to—"

"Hold it," said Barcinder, cutting the pleading man off. He turned and looked in Bannis' direction.

"Who's there?" he demanded in a raised voice.

Bannis cursed himself silently and waited.

"Who's there?" Barcinder demanded again. "Come forward, make yourself known!" He took a cautious step toward the torchlit tunnel, a rifle raised in his hands.

Damn it. . . .

"Take it easy," Bannis called out. "It's me, Frank. Is everything all right here, Dad?" He stepped forward, looking past Barcinder and Gentry. But Frank saw the black silhouette duck out of the cavern and disappear down another tunnel. Boot-heels resounded from against the stone floor, moving farther away with each hastened click.

"What the hell?" Frank said, hurrying across the cavern floor. "Dad, wait. Damn it, it's me. I need to tell you—"

"Back off, Bannis," Elder Barcinder ordered in a threatening tone. "And watch your profanity when speaking to our leader."

"Go to hell, Barcinder," said Bannis. "You don't tell me what to do." His Colt cocked in his hand, he started to go on down the tunnel after Dad Orwick. But as he advanced, two disciples appeared out of the shadows, shotguns raised and ready.

"You are badly mistaken, Bannis," Elder Barcinder said as the two disciples moved closer into the cavern. "I do tell you what to do. Now drop your gun."

"Huh-uh, I don't *drop* guns," Bannis said, leveling his Colt at Barcinder's chest.

"One word and they will *smite you down* in fire," Barcinder warned.

"Yep, I expect they will, but you won't be seeing it," said Bannis, not giving an inch. "Now give them that word. Let's get this pony trotting."

"Frank, *please* don't let them kill me!" Gentry pleaded from his spot on the cavern floor.

"Shut up, Brother Bud," Bannis said in a tight, level tone. "I'm a little busy right now."

"You can't save him, Bannis," Barcinder said, "if that's what this is about. He's one of ours."

"I know that," Bannis replied. "I've got no say in you boys *smiting one another down* in the name of the Lord. But I came here to talk with Dad—tell him what's going on. Not to get you and these Bible-thumpers pointing guns at me, telling me what I can or can't do."

"Oh, so you'd have us believe you would die before you'd submit to my authority?" Barcinder said with a nasty, skeptical grin.

"Find out," Bannis said bluntly, his Colt leveled unwaveringly, ready to fire.

A tense silence passed. Finally Barcinder turned his icy stare to the two shotgun-wielding disciples.

"Lower your guns, brothers. Dad has left the cave now." He turned to Bannis as the two lowered and uncocked their shotguns.

"All right, Frank," he said. "Dad is headed out

now for Gun Valley. So feel free to report to me whatever you had to say to him."

"*El Valle del Fusil. . . .*" Bannis repeated the name in Spanish.

"Yes, Valley of the Gun." Barcinder gave him a resolved look.

Bannis lowered his Colt an inch and looked all around. Seeing the shotguns stay put, he let out a breath and lowered the Colt back down to his side, but he kept it cocked.

"I wanted to tell him that I split the mine payroll between me and the others instead of leaving it with one man, take a chance something happening to it," Bannis said. "It'll be showing up as the others ride in." As he spoke, he unbuttoned his shirt, took out a bundle of cash and tossed it to Elder Barcinder.

"You made a wise decision," said Barcinder. "Dad will be told about it."

"And I've got some bad news," said Bannis. "I wanted to tell it to Dad myself." He looked around, then continued. "I told Deacon Jamison and Young Ezekiel to set up an ambush above the water hole. Deacon is riding in right now, but there's no sign of Young Ezekiel with him." He stood staring at Barcinder to see how the news would be taken.

But the outlaw appeared unmoved. He only nodded and said, "Dad already knows. The two trail guards told us Deacon's riding in alone." He gave a thin smile. "So it turns out this whole gun standoff was completely for naught, wasn't it?"

"Still, I need to say it to Dad," said Bannis, "since I'm the one sent them."

Barcinder nodded again and said, "I know Dad will appreciate your sense of honor." He took a breath and said, "Now, are you all through?"

"Yes," said Bannis. "Where do I find myself some chuck around here?"

"We've got family wagons camped a mile farther along the trail," said Elder Barcinder. "My wives and some of Dad's are cooking for us. Once we're all fed, we'll be moving out ourselves."

"Obliged," said Bannis, realizing that must be where Dad was headed when he left here. Good enough; he'd look around for Dad when he got there.

Hearing Gentry sobbing on the stone floor, he looked down and saw the helpless man crawl toward him. The two men with shotguns moved in closer, watching Gentry's every move.

"Please don't let them kill me, Frank," Brother Bud Gentry said. "I fought the *demon liquor* as hard as I could. Sometimes I just fall victim to it." He tried to grab Bannis' trouser leg, but Bannis shook him loose.

"Can't help you, Brother Bud," said Bannis. "These are your *good brethren,* the ones you said you're *bound* to," he added coldly. "You knew

141

how they were when you threw in with them."
He turned and walked back the way he came in.
By the time he reached daylight at the front
crevice, he heard the muffled blasts of the
shotguns deep back in the earth.

"These loco sons a' bitches. . . ." He shook his
head, holstered his Colt and walked on. "And
they call *us* outlaws."

Chapter 11

Liles and Burns sat atop their horses in the middle
of the trail as Morton Kerr trudged the last few
yards uphill toward them. In the afternoon heat
he led his tired, sweaty horse behind him, the
animal on the verge of balking with every labored
step. When the older outlaw saw the two riders
staring at him, he turned the horse loose and
hurried ahead, both of his arms outstretched
toward the open canteen Liles held down for him.

"Boys . . . all I have thought about is water for
the last five miles," he rasped.

"You've got it now," Liles said, jiggling the
canteen.

Grabbing the canteen with shaky hands, Kerr
took a long, deep swig. Water spilled out of both
sides of his mouth and down the front of his
shirt. When he lowered the canteen, he saw Frank

Bannis riding toward them from the direction of the caves.

"I see Frank already made it here," he said when he'd lowered the canteen and run a hand across his wet lips.

"He just rode in a short while ago," said Burns as Frank approached the group, his rifle in hand. "Deacon Jamison is not far behind."

"Good," said Kerr, "I'm glad we all made it ahead of the law." He handed the canteen back to Liles and looked up at Frank, who had stopped and turned his horse quarterwise to the three of them.

"Howdy, Morton," said Bannis. "I expect you made it with no trouble?"

"No trouble at all, Frank," Kerr said. He patted his shirt where he carried the bundle of stolen payroll money. "This is one robbing spree that turned out pretty good, all things considered." He looked off in the direction of the cave farther along the trail. "Is Dad happy with how things went?"

"You can't prove it by me," Frank said. "Dad turned his back and walked away when I went to take him the money."

Kerr looked surprised.

"Ain't that a hell of a note?" he said. He glanced back and forth at the three men and saw something in the way they looked at one another. "All right, I smell something going sour around here. Somebody tell me what's going on." He stared up at Frank Bannis.

"Maybe it's nothing," Bannis said. "I just don't cotton to working with a man who won't face me."

"Ha, is that all?" said the older outlaw. As he spoke he reached into his shirt, took out the bundle of payroll money and pitched it up to Bannis. "I've been riding with Dad longer than any of yas. I ain't laid eyes on him in nearly a year. Dad gets some odd ways about him sometimes. I pay him no mind when he does."

Bannis caught the money, riffled it and shoved it inside his shirt.

"Something's not right," he said. "I can feel it in my bones."

"Ah, all these self-righteous bastards all think they're better than us," Burns said, dismissing the matter. "To hell with them. Don't let it bother you."

"I won't," said Frank, "after I look Dad in the eye and hear him tell me everything is square between us." He looked at Burns and Liles and asked, "How's the chuck down the trail?"

"It's good as it gets," said Burns. "One of Dad's older wives is in charge of the cooking. She cooks as good as a Mexican." He smiled. "Comes from Dad keeping her stashed below the border so long, I reckon."

"You mean Isabelle?" Bannis asked.

"Yeah, that's the one," said Burns. "She's one of his oldest wives, but she can outcook the whole bunch."

"Dad's no spring chicken himself," said Liles. "Maybe that's what's wrong. He's gotten old and sick and don't want none of us seeing it." He grinned. "Afraid we'll steal all them homely horsewhipped womenfolk of his."

"He needn't worry about me," said Burns. "I can find better-looking gals for under a half dollar any day of the week—not have to worry about giving them room and board either."

"Yeah, but you're not trying to squirt out a bunch of kids to take over the world," said Burns. "That takes stronger women than you can find for half a dollar. Right, Frank?"

Bannis only shrugged and looked away, not wanting to talk about it.

"Anyway, it's Dad's brethren he'd better worry about," said Liles. "They'd fall in love with a she-goat if they thought the *Lord* wanted them to start raising a herd for him."

"What do you say, Frank?" Burns asked. "You know more about these men than we do."

"I say I'm gone . . . I'm not going to sit here and talk religion with you two heathens on an empty stomach," Bannis chided. "Not when I could be eating my weight in chili peppers and beans." He turned his horse and nudged it away along the rocky trail.

"Damn, so could I," said Kerr, getting excited at the prospect of a hot meal. He looked around at his tired horse, then looked up at Liles. "Can I swap you horses until I get my belly full? I'll bring you something back if I can."

"Jesus, Morton," said Liles. He looked at the sweaty, worn-out horse standing behind Kerr, "you're awfully hard on horses." But he still swung down and handed Kerr the reins to his horse, taking the reins to Kerr's animal in exchange. "Don't wear him out," he said.

"Obliged, Liles," said Kerr. He hurriedly pulled himself up into the saddle atop Liles' strong-looking bay. "I'll treat him like he's my own." He turned the bay and hurried on to catch up with Bannis.

"Damn, I hope not," Liles called out, watching him ride away.

Three hundred yards along the winding trail, Frank Bannis slowed his horse and looked back when he heard Morton Kerr galloping toward him.

"Dang it, Frank," said the older outlaw, "didn't you hear me say I was hungry too?"

Frank nudged his horse forward again, this time with Kerr settling the bay and riding along beside him.

"I heard you," he said, looking straight ahead. "I knew you'd catch up if you wanted to. I told all of you, I didn't want to talk religion on an empty stomach."

"Hmmph," said Kerr, "long as I've known you, I've never seen you talking religion, *period,* empty stomach or not."

"You call that a bad trait?" Bannis said without looking around at him.

"No, sir, I call it a good trait," said Kerr. "But I'm curious why it is."

"Religion doesn't interest me," Bannis said, trying to let it go. "Anyways, we're outlaws. We ought to be talking about poker, or whores, something that makes sense," he added with a wry, tight grin.

"Come to think of it," said Kerr, "I never hear you talk much about whores or poker either."

"You know what they say, Morton," said Bannis. "A man who spends all his time talking about women and poker is a man who's most likely not getting much of the two."

"That's a damn lie," said Kerr, as if taking offense. "I get plenty of both—used to anyway. There's no harm in talking about it. Is there?"

"About whores and poker, no, I guess not," said Bannis. "But about religion, I don't know. What business have two hard cases like us got talking about God and the hereafter? We're never going to see either one."

Kerr only stared straight ahead without answering. Within a small valley coming into sight around a turn in the trail, they saw two big Conestoga-style wagons sitting back away from a large cook fire.

"It don't hurt to talk about it, though," said Kerr. "It's like politics. There's nothing more a man can do than spin your opinion." He paused, then looked Bannis up and down and said, "I figure you'd know lots about religion, being brought up by a bunch just like Orwick and his disciples."

Bannis stopped his horse, turned sideways in his saddle and stared at him.

"I was brought up by a good God-fearing Mormon family," he said. "My folks can't help that I turned out to be the way I am."

"Whoa, I meant nothing by it," Kerr said, raising a hand chest high. He stopped too; he withered a little under Bannis' stare, but managed to shrug and say, "All's I meant was it's the same religion as Orwick and his bunch, ain't it?"

"Hell no," said Bannis, "not even close."

He settled a little, let out a breath and turned back to the trail. "The Mormon Saints are a *real* religion." He gave his horse a tap of his heels. "This religion of Dad's is just something he thought up on his own—something that suits his own purpose."

"Some say all religions are the same thing," said Kerr, "that somebody had to sit down and figure every one of them up to begin with."

"You're a tough old nut, Morton," Bannis said.

148

He gave a short chuckle and added, "I can't say you're wrong, but I don't think you're right either. My point was, I didn't want to talk about religion, but here we are doing it anyway."

"So Dad's religion and yours are not so different after all?" he probed.

"I have no religion, and I don't believe in God," Bannis said firmly.

"I mean the way you were raised," Kerr said. "It's no different, when you think about it."

"It's a lot different," Bannis said. "My people were decent folks. They never held with bank robbing, or killing, or any of the things Dad and his bunch does."

"They lit out to Mexico the same way Dad's doing," Kerr threw in.

"Not for stealing and killing," said Bannis. "They had to come here because they were being denied their rights to practice their beliefs."

"Couldn't Dad say the same thing?" Kerr said. "He happens to believe in *stealing* to support his beliefs. But if he truly believes it's a mandate from God, why ain't it?" He gave a crooked grin.

"If we keep talking, I'm going to have to crack you in the head, ain't I, Morton?" Bannis said, only half joking.

Kerr let out a little laugh and the two rode on, seeing a tall older woman in a long gingham dress stand, looking toward them from beside the fire.

"There's Isabelle Orwick," said Bannis. "Reminds me so much of my own ma. . . ." He had to let his words trail. Then he said, "I have to say, if I had met a woman like her years back, I might have taken to religion and been a whole different man." He paused, then added, "Leastwise, I would have had something I might've thanked God for."

"Yeah, but you said you don't believe in God," Kerr pointed out.

"I don't," Bannis countered. "I'm just saying . . ."

He booted his horse up into a gallop and didn't stop or look around at Kerr as they both rode past a rifleman standing guard at the edge of the camp. Recognizing them, the guard waved them past and continued looking out in the direction of the high trail above the narrow valley.

When the two stopped and stepped down from their horses, Bannis took off his hat and walked to the fire. He smiled at Isabelle Orwick, as he always did, as she stepped forward with two tin pans in her hand for him and Kerr. But unlike other times, she did not return his smile. Instead, she ducked her face away from him and spoke over her shoulder.

"You two help yourselves," she said. "We only have beans and chopped pork, but we have plenty of that."

"Whoa, hold on, ma'am," said Bannis, recognizing that something was wrong and she was trying to hide it from him. He stepped around in front of her and said, "Look at me." When she did so reluctantly, he lifted her chin with his fingertips and saw her black, swollen eye.

Angrily he growled under his breath, "Dad, you rotten son of a—"

"No, Frank, wait. It wasn't Dad," Isabelle said, cutting him off. The expression on Frank's face suggested that he might fly into a murderous rage, something Isabelle had never seen in him before. Just the sight of it frightened her. "You have to understand that some things have changed here—"

"Who did this to you?" he growled, gripping her arm tight.

"Brother Phillip," she gasped, "but please let me explain. He had a right to do this."

But Bannis was having none of it.

"No son of a bitch has a right to do this—"

A voice cut him off again.

"See here, Bannis. Take your hands off her!" said Brother Phillip Kendrick, who had just stepped around the corner of the wagon, a long-stemmed pipe cradled in his hand. He stepped in close. "What the blazes is wrong with you anyway?"

Morton Kerr saw Kendrick make the mistake of putting his hand on Bannis to give him a shove. But it wouldn't have mattered, Kerr decided, seeing Bannis' Colt streak from his holster almost instinctively and make a vicious swipe across the unsuspecting man's jaw.

Phillip Kendrick's smoking pipe flew from his hand and soared into the wagon through its open tailgate.

"No, stop!" Isabelle pleaded with Frank Bannis, but Bannis was past reasoning. Even as the dazed churchman staggered backward from the blow, Bannis grabbed the front of his coat and struck him again, this time a backhanded blow that knocked out any consciousness still struggling to stay awake in Kendrick's addled brain. Yet the second blow didn't sate the outlaw's fury. He struck again, and again. Blood flew; teeth followed.

"Holy God, Frank, you're killing him," shouted Morton Kerr, seeing one deadly blow after another slash across Kendrick's face.

But Bannis didn't stop. When Kerr tried to grab him from behind, Bannis forcefully shook him off and continued the fatal beating. As Kerr landed on the ground, he saw Isabelle picking up a heavy iron skillet.

Uh-oh. . . . He watched wide-eyed as the woman hurried in behind Bannis, drew the big skillet back and swung it full, at arm's length. Kerr winced at the sight, and at the long, vibrating sound of the skillet ringing against the back of Bannis' head.

Kendrick fell from Bannis' grip and hit the ground like a bundle of rags. Bannis fell right atop him.

"Quick, get him out of here!" said Isabelle to Kerr, letting the skillet fall from her hand. She nodded toward the riflemen running from across the camp, having witnessed the merciless pistol-whipping. "Dad will kill him for doing this to one of his disciples."

She and Kerr began dragging Bannis toward his horse.

"And take him where?" Kerr asked as they started shoving Bannis up into his saddle.

"To Gun Valley," Isabelle said. "Hide him there. I'll bring you supplies when I can get away."

Kerr gave her a questioning look.

"This was my fault," she said, speaking quickly. "I should have told him right off. I'm Brother Phillip's wife now. He had a right to hit me. Dad unbound me and his older wives and bound us to his brethren."

"Wait," said Kerr. "Where will I hide him? This whole bunch is headed for Valley of the Gun."

"Go across the valley," she said, "to the old dugouts there." She raised Bannis' leg and pushed it over the saddle.

"I know where that's at," Kerr said. As he spoke he gave a hard shove and watched Bannis roll onto the saddle and slump forward onto the horse's neck.

"Hurry," she said. "I'll try to slow them down as much as I can."

Kerr glanced at the running rifleman and said, "Liles is going to have a conniption, me taking off with his horse."

"I'll explain it to him. Now go," Isabelle said, shoving him toward his horse.

Mounted, Kerr led Bannis, riding away at a hard gallop. The knocked-out gunman was lying limp, but managing to stay in his saddle. At the edge of the valley, Kerr rode behind a stand of rocks, circled and gazed back toward the camp.

"Son of a bitch," he said, staring up in awe as flames and black smoke billowed upward from the burning wagon. "Frank Bannis, you are one lucky *hombre.*" He gave a dark chuckle, watching the riflemen give up their chase and turn to fight the raging fire.

Chapter 12

The Ranger and Mattie Rourke stood atop a cliff looking out past a lower hill line where black smoke drifted along an evening breeze. A few feet behind them lay a set of fresh hoofprints headed down the trail.

"A campfire maybe?" Mattie asked, sounding doubtful. "It is coming from about where the Munny Caves are."

"No," said the Ranger, "I wouldn't think it's a campfire. Not if Dad's people are trying to keep from being seen."

"The posse from Goble?" she asked.

"Could be," Sam replied. He looked all around, toward hills off to their left. "Ragland knows this terrain. The four of them could have made some good time if they didn't run into any of Dad's men along the other trail." He considered it. "We haven't heard any shooting."

"Dad's people don't make mistakes like this," she said, gesturing toward the smoke.

Sam nodded, watching the long drift of smoke curl and roll off across the evening sky.

"One thing's for sure," he said. "If we see it, so does Dee Ragland. If the posse's not already headed there, it soon will be."

The two made their way back to their horses.

Stepping back into their saddles, they turned their horses to the trail, following the fresh set of tracks left by the last of Dad's Redemption Riders to come down the trail toward Munny Caves.

An hour later they slowed their horses to a halt and sat at the bottom of the steep hill trail. Looking out, they gazed across a new stretch of trail winding atop a connected string of natural stone bridgework and barren ridge. Two-thirds of the way across a deep rocky gorge, the trail turned back upward onto a hillside covered with boulders and scrub timber.

"On the other side of these hills is Munny Caves," Mattie said. She looked at Sam. "From here there are lookout spots that can see every move we make down here."

Sam studied the hill line for a moment.

"This is a dangerous stretch," he commented. "I can see why Dad would pick Munny Caves as a hiding place."

"For Dad it has always been a resting place," Mattie said. "It's a good place to lie low for a few days and find out who is on their trail."

"And stop them right here," Sam said. "Or at least find out just how serious the lawmen were. This trail is an ambush waiting to happen."

"Few ever even try to make it past here," Mattie said quietly. She paused, then added, "We can go around, but it'll take a good five or six hours longer."

Still following the trail with his eyes, gauging the distances, Sam realized that while they could be seen from here by any guards atop the ridge-line and lookout cliffs along the hillside, they would remain out of rifle range until they had almost reached the safety and cover of the rocky hillside. He estimated no more than two hundred yards that they would have to ride in the open, in danger of rifle fire. From that point on the trail would then wind into rock cover and stay there until it reached the hilltop.

"We both see the risk. I say we need to go on across," he said quietly. "If they want to know how serious I am, here it is."

Mattie smiled tightly, her rifle propped up on her thigh the same as the Ranger's.

"I was hoping you'd say that," she said. "We've both come too far to start giving up ground."

Sam nodded in agreement.

"Keep a few feet between us when we get out in the open," he said. He pointed to a spot in the near distance where a blackened, lightning-scorched pine stood at the edge of the trail and added, "When you reach the dead tree, put your horse up into a gallop and get on into the rocks as fast as you can."

She gave him a questioning look, but then she gazed along the hilltop in the distance.

"Gun range . . . ," she said.

Sam just looked at her.

She smiled.

"Don't look so surprised, Ranger," she said, nudging her horse forward. "I've done a good job figuring things out for myself for quite some time now."

"I have no doubt of that, ma'am," the Ranger replied, nudging his copper dun along beside her.

As the two rode forward at a walk, Sam continued to study the slim, exposed trail lying ahead of them. Starting ten yards out, nothing stood on either side of them but an almost sheer drop of over four hundred feet down hard and jagged stone.

Here goes, he told himself.

With one hand holding the reins loosely, he gave the dun its head, knowing it was now time to relinquish control and rely on the animal's sure-footedness and instincts for survival to ensure his own. In his other hand he held his Winchester cocked and ready. Stepping the dun out onto the narrow open trail, he heard the click of Mattie's horse's hooves fall back a few feet farther behind him, just as he'd asked her to do.

They rode the horses at a safe and steady walk, tensely yet without incident, for the next twenty minutes, feeling an updraft of coolness from below between gusting passes of a hot sun-dried wind. On the jagged hillside facing them, the Ranger knew that rifle sights closely monitored their every step. Yet the eyes behind those gun sights knew as well as he and the woman, as the distance grew shorter between them and the dead standing pine, so did their chances of making it across the gorge alive.

"Get ready," Sam said over his shoulder as they neared the scorched, broken tree.

Almost as soon as he and the woman collected their horses beneath them and batted their boots to their sides, the first bullet thumped into the trail in front of them. Sam and Mattie put their horses into a hard gallop as the sound of the delayed blast caught up with its bullet. The two horses raced past the spot where the bullet had fallen short by fifteen feet. The Ranger hoped he and Mattie would both be moving targets by the time the rifleman got sighted and ready to fire again.

Without waiting helplessly for the second shot, Sam glanced up, caught a glimpse of gray rifle smoke and fired a quick one-hand shot in its direction. It was a million-to-one shot and the Ranger knew it, but as they raced along, he heard the sharp whine of his bullet ricochet off a rock as he levered a fresh round one-handed. When the rifleman's second shot came, it did not fall short but neither did it hit its target.

The two raced on. Another shot struck the rock trail beside the copper dun's hooves, but the dun didn't waver. Neither did the Ranger. He returned fire, not getting much of an aim, but having the low end of the rising rifle smoke on which to concentrate his fire, and he could pressure the rifleman enough to affect his aim.

Behind him Mattie's horse had closed the gap between them by the time they rode off the narrow exposed trail and onto the other rocky side of the gorge. Another rifle shot pinged off a boulder at head level just as the two ducked into cover and slid their horses to a halt. They both leaped from their saddles, Sam's Winchester smoking in his hand, and he slapped the horses' rumps, sending them farther onto the boulder-strewn hillside.

Another shot rang out, but it was too late; the rifleman had missed his chance. The Ranger moved quickly around the edge of the boulder covering them and fired three shots as fast as he could lever his rifle. Three bullets whined off the rocks at the point of the rising gun smoke.

"Are you all right?" Sam asked Mattie as he levered up another round.

"I'm all right," she said, her face flush with a combination of fear and excitement. "Are you?"

"Yeah, I'm good," Sam replied. They looked each other up and down as if checking for wounds they might have missed.

After a tense second Mattie let go of a tight breath and looked back along the narrow trail.

"We did it," she said, sounding almost surprised.

"Yes, we did," Sam said, keeping an ear tuned to the direction of the rifle fire. He knew that whoever was up there realized they had made it across. Now they had cover, but the word of them being here would soon be out. "We best get the horses and get moving," he said.

"Yes," she said, looking around, "they know we're here and we're not backing off."

As they moved away from the boulder and walked up-trail, they both stopped when they saw their horses standing over a sweat-frothed horse lying at the edge of the trail.

"Oh no," Mattie said, looking at the downed animal, seeing one of its forelegs twisted at a bad angle. The horse rolled pained eyes up at them and whined pitifully.

"Stay back," Sam cautioned, already drawing his Colt as he looked back and forth along the rocky trail. "Somebody must be looking for a horse out here."

Mattie stood watching the trail, rifle in hand, as Sam stepped forward, gathered their horses' reins and pulled the two animals away from the downed horse. He handed Mattie both sets of reins, turned and walked back to the faltered horse, the look on his face showing he didn't like what he had to do.

Mattie waited until Sam held his Colt out at arm's length, pointed down at the hapless animal. She managed to look away at the very second he pulled the trigger and kept looking away until Sam stepped over to her and took the dun's reins from her hand. He started to say something, but before he could a harsh voice called out from across the narrow trail.

"Neither of you move," said Deacon Jamison, standing up suddenly from behind a waist-high rock. "I'll be taking those horses—your guns too." He waged a big Remington at them.

Sam noted the big revolver was not cocked, as it should have been upon making such a demand. Still holding his Colt down his side as if having foreseen such a situation, Sam stepped away from Mattie and raised the Colt an inch, his thumb going over the trigger.

"You're one of the men who robbed the mine payroll, the bank in Goble?" he asked in a mild, almost conversational tone of voice. Mattie stood watching, stunned into silence.

161

"I am," said Jamison. "I told you to drop that gun."

Ignoring his demand, Sam raised the Colt level, not fast but steadily, cocking it on the way.

"I'm Arizona Ranger Sam Burrack," he said in the same mild voice. "You're under arrest for two counts of robbery."

"Are you deaf, Ranger?" Jamison growled. "Did you hear what I told you? I said drop that gun!" But even as he repeated his demand, he saw his mistake had been made, and there would be no correcting it. Whatever edge or surprise he thought he'd taken, the Ranger had just taken it away from him.

Sam saw a desperate look come over the man's face, his eyes. As Jamison tried to throw his thumb over the Remington's hammer to cock it, Sam's Colt bucked once in his hand and sent him flying backward to the ground. The Remington fell from his hand.

"You will forever . . . rot in hell for this, Ranger. . . ." His words fell away in his throat; his eyes glazed over in death and stared straight up at the endless sky. A long breath came from his lips and stopped short.

Sam stepped forward and picked up the Remington. He looked out and up across the hillside in the direction the rifle fire had come from. Mattie watched as he raised the big revolver and fired it twice in the air, then paused and fired again.

Mattie gave him a curious look.

"That'll give them something to think about while we climb this trail," he said. Lowering the Remington, he walked to Mattie and took the dun's reins from her hand.

High up on the rugged hillside, Stan Liles and Dallas Burns made room for a gunman named Manning Thomas as he climbed down using a rope dangling from the trail above them.

"I heard shooting and came running quick as I could," Thomas said, crouching against a short rock, his rifle pulled in close to his chest. Liles cocked his head around and looked up at the edge of ground above them.

"Is anybody else coming, or are you it?" he asked.

"Yeah, I'm *it*," said the rough red-faced gunman. "Everybody else pulled out over an hour ago. What have you got going on down there anyway?"

"A couple of riders wearing trail dusters came flapping their tails out across the gorge, but they never made it up this side," Dallas Burns said with a dark grin.

"You got them both?" asked Thomas.

"No," said Burns. "But we saw Deacon Jamison down there earlier. We heard shooting—sounded like Deacon's Remington. We're thinking he must've lain in wait and stopped their clocks for them."

"How do you know they didn't kill Deacon?" Thomas asked bluntly. "Have you seen him since?"

"No sign of him yet," said Liles, he and Burns gazing out down the rugged hillside.

"Not a glimpse," Dallas Burns put in. "Of course, if Deacon doesn't want to be seen, he ain't going to be. Could be he knows there's more posse coming and he's going to drop them too."

Manning Thomas just stared at the two as if in disbelief for a moment. Then he rose into a crouch and dusted off his trousers and coat.

"Boys, this will never do. See you," he said to the two men. He turned and reached for the rope.

"Wait a minute. Where are you going?" Burns asked.

"Down the trail to see what happened," said Thomas. "I don't want Dad or Barcinder asking me about it, and I don't know who's dead and who ain't."

Burns and Liles looked at each other.

"Hold on. We're coming with you," Liles said, both of them standing in a crouch and moving over to the rope.

"We're talking about an ambush, right?" Burns asked to be clear on the matter.

"Absolutely," said Thomas, "it's the only way to go."

Burns and Liles both breathed easier as they climbed up to the steep path, gathered their horses and rode down the trail toward the gorge. Ten minutes down the hillside, at the sound of slow-walking hooves against the hard ground, they cut off the trail and took cover behind a low stand of rocks.

As a figure walked into sight, leading two horses, Burns reached down and cocked his rifle slow and quiet. Liles did the same.

"Damn," he whispered, "Deacon must've got one of them, but it looks like they've killed him." He nodded at the body lying across the first horse's saddle, wrapped in Deacon Jamison's coat. "Yeah," said Liles, "and this one left his dead pard behind so he can haul Deacon in and show off his kill."

"I hate a show-off son of a bitch," said Thomas. "Let's go." Standing, his rifle aimed, he walked sideways onto the middle of the trail.

Let's go?

"What about the ambush?" Burns whispered in protest even as he and Liles hurried to keep up with him.

"End of the road, mister," Thomas called out to the figure clad in a long duster and low-pulled hat. "Throw your rifle aside. We're having ourselves an Apache-style skinning party."

Jesus . . . ! Burns looked at Liles, wild-eyed.

They watched the tall figure swing the rifle to the side as if to throw it away. But instead of turning it loose, the figure ducked away with it, jerked the reins of the first horse, pulled the animal sidelong to the gunmen, swung the rifle up and fired.

Across the horse's back, the Ranger rose, his big Colt in one hand, the Remington in his other, firing both guns at once.

Mattie's first shot hit Manning Thomas dead center and sent him flailing backward, his feet scrambling to find purchase like a clown on ice. He hit the ground as she quickly levered another round and aimed at the other two outlaws in a mad exchange of gunfire.

The Ranger's first shot had hit Stanley Liles and knocked him to the dirt. Liles' rifle flew from his hand. The Ranger's second shot did the same to Dallas Burns, but while Burns hit the ground dead, Liles managed to struggle up onto one knee, draw a revolver from his holster and attempt to take aim.

Mattie's rifle shot rang out above the sound of Sam's big Colt. Both bullets hit Liles at once. Red mist jetted from his back as the shots lifted him from his knee almost onto his feet before hurling him backward to the dirt.

Mattie stood dry-mouthed in a ringing silence, smoke curling up around her from her rifle barrel. She watched Sam walk forward, the Colt leading him as if he held some small yet deadly animal on a leash.

Stepping sidelong, Mattie picked up the reins to both horses, pulled the Ranger's duster down from across the dun's saddle and carried it to him.

Standing over the dead, reloading his Colt, Sam looked surprised when he saw Mattie hold his duster out toward him. But he thanked her and took it. Holstering the Colt, the Remington shoved down in his belt, he took off Jamison's bloody coat, dropped it to the ground and put on his duster.

"They know we're coming," he said. He looked at the bodies on the ground, then at Mattie. He started to say, "Good work." But something about the look on her face advised him against it. "They'll be ready for any surprises from now on."

Mattie only nodded. Sam took the dun's reins from her hand and noted that it took a second for her to release them.

"If all goes well, when we top the hill, we'll stop and rest awhile before we go on—"

"No, please," she said grimly, turning her eyes to the dead on the ground. "I've got to finish this as quick as I can."

"I understand," he said, realizing the killing had begun to wear her thin.

He swung up into his saddle and waited for her to do the same.

Chapter 13

The Ranger and Mattie rode the rest of the way up the thin trail to Munny Caves with caution, expecting the worst. Yet, as they approached the tall black crevice in the waning evening light, they were relieved to find the place had been abandoned by Orwick and his followers. The three riflemen they'd encountered along the top of the trail must have been the only men left behind to offer them any resistance.

Out in front of the crevice, a fire burned inside a circle of heavy stone. It seemed as if countless fires had burned there for centuries past. Beside the fire stood an elderly Mexican wearing what was left of a frayed and ragged black cape over threadbare peasant clothes. A battered straw sombrero hung in his hand. He held his free hand up in a welcoming gesture.

"Welcome, *señor y señora*," the old man called out. "Feel free to sit by the fire. I will water your horses."

The two rode closer and then stepped down from their saddles. Sam let the man see the badge on his chest.

"You realize I'm pursuing the people who just left here, don't you?" he said.

"Yes, this I do know, Ran-jur," the old man said, "but here there is only me and the dead, and we take no sides in the matters of man." He grinned and gestured a weathered hand at the dugout hovels on the sides of the surrounding hills, remnant signs of life that had once clung to the place for thousands of years.

"How many armed men does Orwick have traveling with him?" Sam asked.

"Even here among the dead, lies and loose talk are cheap and worthless," the old man said, his eyes turning sad with such a revelation. His wrinkled palm turned upward deftly.

Sam pulled a small gold coin from his vest pocket and laid it in his palm.

"How many?" he asked again.

"As they have come and gone, there are over a dozen men," the old man said, "all of them armed. All of them prepared for trouble, as they have been this past year that I have come to know them." He eyed the Ranger up and down as if realizing the trouble Orwick's men had been anticipating now stood before him. "With him also are seven women. These are the older wives that *Señor* Orwick will be replacing."

"How do you know this?" Sam asked, testing him.

"Aw, Ran-jur," the old man said, giving Sam and the woman the sad, wizened trace of a smile, "what man who can afford many wives will not replace them when he decides it is time to do so?"

"Oh, like so many horses, or field cattle?" Mattie said in a clipped tone.

Seeing the resentment in her eyes, the old man shrugged his bony shoulders.

"*Por favor, señora*," he said, again sadly. "Only if you are bitter at rain for falling from the sky, will you ever take solace in despising man for following the path man's nature bequeaths itself."

All right. . . . Sam nodded. The old cliff dweller had to be acknowledged.

"I see you study the ways of the ancients, the nature of man?" Sam said. "But what good does all this do me when I need to hear what's going on right now?"

Again the old man gestured a hand around at the dugouts on the cliff walls, the footpath worn low across a flat stone ledge leading to the black crevice.

"I thought myself a holy man—a *priest,* no less—until I journeyed here and saw this place and communed with those who whisper to me from within these ancient stones."

"Easy, now," the Ranger said. "Ours is not a spiritual quest."

"But still, it is sacred here, Ran-jur," the old man said, not to be swayed, "and its sacredness must be acknowledged. In this holy place you must take what wisdom is handed down to us and decipher from it that which will—"

170

"Okay, that's enough," Sam said, cutting him off. "Tell me something useful, or I'll take back the piece of gold."

The old man looked aghast at the prospect.

"Take back the piece of gold, my small pitiful coin?" he said in disbelief.

"Yep," Sam said, "in about one second, even if I have to turn you upside down and shake it from you—"

"Wait!" the old man said, holding up a stopping hand toward him. "I will tell you this." He pointed to the black crevice. "One of Orwick's men is inside. His *esposa* tends to him."

Sam and Mattie looked at each other.

"All right," Sam said, "lead us to them, *por favor*." He reached into his vest pocket and took out another small gold coin and held it out to him.

"*Sí*, of course," the old man said. "Follow me."

Sam and Mattie walked along close behind the old Mexican cliff dweller, their rifles in hand, through the black front crevice and down into the first chamber of the large cave. Before they were halfway down the narrow, torchlit hallway, they began to hear a man's string of mindless babbling interspersed with the calm, soothing voice of a woman.

Glancing back over his shoulder, the Mexican said, "I'm afraid the *señor* has been beaten into idiocy. He speaks of incidents from his

171

childhood, and from the great civil conflict."

"What happened to him?" Mattie asked.

But before she could receive a reply, the babbling voice echoed off the stone walls.

"Whose dog is that? Whose dog is *that?*" the injured man cried out. His voice sounded as if it were stifled by a mouthful of rocks.

The woman spoke quietly, trying to settle him, but the beaten man would have none of it.

"Will somebody tell me whose dog is *that?*" he demanded even louder. "He's licking the churn! He's licking the churn. . . ."

His voice trailed down beneath the woman's soothing pleas as the three stepped into sight. Upon seeing the Ranger and Mattie, the woman looked away from the man, panicked, ready to bolt. She raised a handful of wet cloth from the man's bloody, welted and split forehead.

"Please," Mattie said, "we're not after you. Don't be afraid."

"You're—you're after Dad, though," the woman said, sounding frightened, distrustful. She looked from Mattie to the Ranger with her head lowered, her face almost out of sight, eyeing his badge in the flicker of torchlight.

"Yes, but not you, ma'am," Sam said, checking her hands, making sure he saw no weapons as the old cliff dweller moved aside and he and Mattie walked closer.

"Is this man your husband?" he asked, hoping

172

to engage her in something other than her fear of them.

"He—" She stopped, seeming to have to think about it for a moment, then said with her head still lowered, "Yes, he is my husband." But she sounded unsure.

"What happened to him?" Mattie asked, quietly, feeling the woman settle down a little. She noted the woman's black eye even with her face half turned away, a strand of long silver-gray hair shrouding her cheek.

The battered man blurted out deliriously, "The same thing that happens to *any man!* Hold that line, boys! Hold her solid! Kill every fornicating cat in the litter! Look at them out there, look at them out there! Oh God, the *craven devils* fornicate before our eyes!"

"*Shhh,* now, Brother Phillip," the woman coaxed, placing the wet cloth back down on his purple, split forehead. "Quiet now, before you start swearing again. You know how Dad feels about swearing."

"Dad? *Dad . . . ?*" The man's eyes rolled around toward Sam in the flickering torchlight.

Sam let out a breath and shook his head.

"I warned you, this one is an idiot, Ran-jur," the old cliff dweller whispered, leaning in close to Sam.

"Yes, you did," Sam replied almost in a whisper. "Who did this to him?"

173

The woman spoke up before the old Mexican could.

"I'm afraid I caused it all," she said, almost in tears.

Mattie gave her a close and curious look as she listened to her continue.

"Dad *unbound* several of us from himself and bound us to any of his brethren he felt were worthy of us." She tilted her chin up in Orwick's defense. "It was a wonderful, God-inspired act. I am ashamed to admit it, but I selfishly rebelled at the idea."

"*Whoa!* There it goes!" Phillip Kendrick blurted out. "Something dropped loose *inside my head!*"

"There, there, Brother Phillip," the woman said, pressing the wet cloth against his forehead. Finally looking directly at Mattie and the Ranger, she shook her head.

"Anyway," she continued, "Brother Phillip struck me. I should say *corrected me* for my own good. One of Dad's secular associates saw it and took offense, and before I could explain that it was my fault, he beat poor Brother Phillip with his pistol barrel—as you can see."

"Oh my goodness," said Mattie, suddenly struck almost breathless by her recognition of the woman. "Isabelle? Isabelle Rourke? Is that you?"

When she heard her maiden name spoken for the first time in what seemed like forever, a strange look came upon Isabelle's face. She stood up slowly, staring at Mattie as if in a stupor.

"Oh no," she said, "my name is Isabelle Orwick, or so it was. Now, I suppose it has become—"

Sam watched, taking it all in, already seeing the resemblance between the two women. *Twins . . . ?* No, but their similarities were not far from it, he decided. Seeing the woman standing, he noted, *Same height, same size and build, near the same age, their hair worn the same way, almost the same shade of gray.*

"Isabelle, *stop it!*" Mattie demanded, her voice sounding like a cold slap in the face. "It's Matilda, your sister! Look at me! Clear your mind and *look at me!*"

"Matilda?" Isabelle said, struggling with it. She paused tensely, then said, *"Mattie?"*

"Yes, Mattie! It's me!" Mattie said, stepping quickly around the prone battered man lying on a blanket on the stone floor.

Sam watched the two embrace tearfully. Glancing at the old Mexican, he saw him shrug his thin shoulders.

"But—but you're dead, Mattie," Isabelle said, holding her sister at arm's length. "You died long ago. . . ."

"No, Isabelle, I didn't die. You were only told that I died. You were lied to, the same way I was lied to. I was told that *you* were dead. It was Dad and his brethren. They lied to us—they used us. The way they are still using you."

Sam eased back a step and looked all around the large cave in the flicker of torchlight. Eyeing the old Mexican, he finally said quietly, "Come on, you mentioned watering the horses. I'll go with you, give these women some time to talk."

While the old cliff dweller watered and grained the horses, the Ranger took the opportunity to look the place over and gauge the number of riders by the abundance of hoofprints and debris left by Dad's group. After a few minutes he concluded the old man had been telling the truth. Over a dozen riders had passed through here within the past couple of days.

Walking back to where the horses stood drinking water from two short oak water buckets, Sam checked the animal over and slid his rifle back into its boot. In his saddlebags he carried two bundles of money stolen from the mine payroll, one he'd taken from the body of Burt Tally, the other he'd taken off the deacon's body earlier that day. Opening the flap, he riffled a hand down through the bundles of cash, then reclosed the flap.

"What was burning here earlier?" he asked as the old man finished with the horses.

"One of their wagons," the old man replied. "I was there among the wagons when the man was beaten senseless. Luckily for the man who gave him the beating, one of the wagons caught fire when he left, so Orwick's men did not go after him."

"Who was the man?" Sam asked.

"His name is Bannis," said the old Mexican.

"Frank Bannis?" Sam asked.

"*Sí*, Frank Bannis," the old man said. "You know him?"

"I've heard of him," Sam replied. "What do you know about Orwick?"

"Not so much," said the old Mexican. "I only knew him for a year, since he started moving all his people to Mexico." His voice dropped secretively. "I only see him one time, when his men did not know I was there."

Sam just looked at him.

"They want no one to see, Ran-jur," he whispered.

"Why do you suppose that is?" Sam asked, trying to get a better understanding of the men he was hunting.

The old Mexican shrugged and spread his upturned palms as if submitting to lack of knowledge.

"Forgive me. I do not know," he said. "Perhaps they did not want the world to know that a man so young could have such power and lead such a large band of followers?"

"So young?" Sam asked.

The old Mexican cliff dweller went on as if he hadn't heard the Ranger's question.

"Perhaps he is ashamed to be a man so young, yet with so many *esposas* who are old enough to be his *madre*."

"His wives are old enough to be his mother?" Sam asked. "Are we talking about the same man here?"

The old Mexican's eyes widened as he turned in a circle, his arms outstretched, a supplicant to the silent ancient ruins surrounding them.

"What . . . ?" he asked, staring wildly from one dark open dugout doorway to the next as if seeing the entities from the past staring back at him. "Yes, yes, I hear you! Yes, of course, I hear them coming!"

But as he turned back to share this revelation with the Ranger, Sam heard the sound too. It was not information offered by unseen entities—it was something offered by the stone walls themselves. It was the sound of horses' hooves, and as he listened, he heard the rumbling sound become clearer as it rolled closer up the hill trail.

"Riders," he said aloud, already gathering the reins to his and Mattie Rourke's horses. As he hurriedly led the horses out of sight, he saw Mattie appear from the crevice and come running toward him, her rifle in hand.

"I heard them too," she offered, seeing the questioning look on Sam's face. She took her horse's reins from him as they rounded a stone edge and stepped out of sight from the trail.

"Wait here and keep me covered if I need it," Sam said, jerking his rifle from its boot. "I have a hunch I won't need it," he added coolly. "It's about time we ran into somebody up here who doesn't want to kill us." No sooner had he said it than he looked around the edge and saw six dusty, sweat-streaked riders come into sight.

In an upsurge of freshly stirred dust, at the head of the six riders, Sam saw Clayton DeShay's horse spin in a circle before settling down and coming to a halt. Off to the side of DeShay, Dee Ragland sat unsteadily in his saddle, an arm clamped around his bloody bandaged middle. Behind the two rode Arlis Fletcher and Morgan Almond. Behind Almond rode two hatless, bloody prisoners on the end of a short lead rope. Their hands had been bound behind their backs; their battered faces were blackened with dried blood. Their eyes were swollen shut. Their heads bobbed limply on their chests.

"Wait here anyway," Sam said to Mattie Rourke. "It looks like their bark's on."

"Careful . . . ," she said, before she could stop herself.

Sam only looked at her. As a precaution, he handed her his rifle. Then he stepped out into sight, his hands raised chest high.

"DeShay," he called out across the stone floor covering the wide area in front of the crevice.

DeShay spun toward the sound of the Ranger's

179

voice, horse and all, his rifle coming up pointed until he recognized Sam and eased in his saddle. Ragland and Fletcher turned their horses as well.

"Easy, fellows, stand down," DeShay said to the other two men. To Sam he called out, "Ranger, we are mighty damned glad to see you!"

Sam lowered his hands and gestured for Mattie to step out beside him. He took his rifle from her slowly and held it in the crook of his arms.

"No more than we are to see you, Sheriff," he said, the two of them walking forward.

"I need to get back to my sister, Ranger," Mattie said, now that she saw everything was all right.

Sam only nodded and walked on as she turned and hurried back toward the caves.

Chapter 14

Sheriff Clayton DeShay stepped down from his saddle and over beside Dee Ragland. The Ranger arrived at the sheriff's side in time to help him lower the wounded scout from his saddle. Moving his horse next to the two prisoners Morgan Almond was leading, Arlis Fletcher raised a boot and gave one of the men a hard kick, sending him to the ground. He raised his boot again, but this time before he could get in his kick, he caught the hard stares of both DeShay and the Ranger.

Almond turned in his saddle with a look of anger on his sweaty face.

"That'll do, Fletcher," said DeShay. "These men won't be mistreated while I'm in charge."

"Let's not forget that these *men*—these lousy *sons a' bitches*—are the reason our tracker is standing there with a bullet stuck in his gut, Sheriff," Fletcher said. "I don't mind keeping them under a heavy hand right up till we swing them from a limb."

The man in the dirt struggled to his feet and tried to stare up at Fletcher through eyes swollen almost shut.

"Do I look like I'm afraid of swinging from a limb to you, you fine-haired bastard?" he said through split, puffy lips. He spit toward Fletcher. Fletcher jumped his horse forward and started to kick him again.

"Damn it, stand down, Fletcher!" DeShay shouted, his rifle coming up pointed at the cold-eyed gunman. "What you're doing is against the law."

As quickly as Fletcher's temper had erupted, it settled. He spread his gloved hands in submission, a bemused look on his face.

"Whatever you say, Sheriff," he said. "You know me, I'm all about law and order." He swung down from his saddle, walked over to the other prisoner and said cordially, "Please, sir, may I help you down from your saddle?"

"Jesus . . . ," DeShay grumbled and shook his head. Turning to Sam, he said, "It's been this way from the get-go with him. I've never wanted to kill a man any worse in my life."

The two helped Ragland over to the shade of a large rock and sat him in the dirt. The old Mexican appeared with a goatskin full of water and gave the wounded scout a drink.

Stooping down beside Ragland, Sam pulled open the wounded man's buckskin shirt, lifted a blood-soaked cloth and looked at the bullet hole.

"Are you able to make it back to Whiskey Bend?" he asked the wounded trail scout.

"You tell me, Ranger," said Ragland. "It didn't go all the way through."

Sam wiped the blood aside enough to see the redness surrounding the wound. He gave a grim look and set the bloody cloth back in place.

"It's got to come out of there," he said.

"Then you do it, Ranger," Ragland said. "If there's no whiskey around, I'll just lie still and cuss you the whole way."

"It could be in there deep," Sam warned.

"Cut it out for me, Ranger," Ragland insisted.

"Let me see this *deep* wound," the old Mexican said, taking on a sudden air of authority.

"He says he used to be a priest," Sam said, seeing Ragland's questioning eyes. "You judge."

But the old Mexican didn't even wait to hear from Ragland. He stooped down and rolled the scout onto his side. Ragland grunted in pain. Sam watched the old Mexican expertly probe a purple lump on Ragland's back.

"It's too deep from the front," the old Mexican said, "but it's not so deep from here." He took the Ranger's hand and guided his finger to the lump on Ragland's back and pushed on it. "There, do you feel it?" he asked.

"Yes, I feel it." Sam nodded, the hard nose of the bullet on his fingertips. The bullet had bored straight and deep, digging into the scout's back. It had been stopped short by Ragland's muscle and sinew.

"Get to cutting, Ranger," Ragland said with resolve. "The sooner, the better."

Almond and Fletcher had led the horses and the two prisoners over beside DeShay for a closer look.

"First let's get you inside the cave," Sam said. "It might be best if this man cuts it out. He seems to know what he's—"

"Huh-uh," said Ragland, cutting him off. "Last time a Mex cut on me it was over a whore in Sonora. I swore it would never happen again."

Ignoring Ragland's remark, the old Mexican stood up and took a step back.

"I have a keg of mescal buried in the rocks," he said. "It will help deaden the pain."

"Mescal. . . . ? A *keg* of it?" Ragland perked up.

"*Sí*, more than enough, so that you will not

know when I do my cutting," the old Mexican said. Only then did he look down at Ragland as if seeking permission. "Shall I go get it?"

Sam started to answer for Ragland, but the wounded scout spoke ahead of him.

"Well, hell yes, *go get it.* We're going to do this thing right from the start, *hombre.*"

The old Mexican left to get the mescal and Sam and Morgan Almond helped Ragland to his feet to move him inside the torchlit caves.

Mattie came out of the black crevice and moved toward them with a grim look on her face. Halfway across the stone walkway, she stopped and waited for the Ranger.

"My sister's husband is dead," she said quietly.

Sam just looked at her.

"When I got back," Mattie said, seeing the look on the Ranger's face, "she told me he just stopped breathing."

DeShay looked back and forth between the two of them.

Sister? Husband . . . ? He turned to Sam. "What's going on here, Ranger?" he asked.

"I must get back to her," Mattie said.

"We'll talk about it later," Sam said to DeShay, stepping in beside Mattie as she turned to hurry back to the cave.

Inside the cave, Isabelle Rourke stood out of the flickering torchlight with her arms folded tightly across her bosom, as if trying to ward off a hard chill. Seeing Mattie return with the Ranger at her side, the two looking down at Phillip Kendrick's limp body, she turned away before speaking to them.

"I didn't kill him," she said, although no one had brought up the possibility. "I stepped away for a moment, and when I returned, this is how I found him."

As she spoke, Sam kneeled down beside the body and closed its gaping mouth. He spread the bloodstained shirt collar open a little and looked at the throat for any signs of strangulation.

"What's he doing?" Isabelle asked her sister. "Doesn't he believe me?"

"Of course he believes you, Isabelle," Mattie said. Then she asked Sam, "Don't you, Ranger?"

Sam closed the shirt collar and stood up, seeing no signs of foul play.

"He took a bad beating," Sam said, looking at not only the long barrel marks on Kendrick's face, but at an assortment of deeper gashes as well—gashes made by the deadly hammering edge of a gun butt. "The shape he was in, there's no point speculating. We'll never know exactly what killed him."

Even as he spoke, Sam noted that one corner of the blanket beneath the body was folded over. He imagined how easy it would have been for a strong hand to hold that blanket edge down over the man's face and nose until the body ceased to struggle.

Stop it. He put the notion aside, hearing DeShay and the others walk into the cave from the narrow stone hallway.

The two prisoners looked at Isabelle through swollen eyes, and down at the body of Phillip Kendrick on the blanket.

"Recognize him?" Sam asked them.

"It's Brother Phillip, one of Dad Orwick's main saints," said one of the prisoners, "or what's left of him."

"It couldn't have happened to a more deserving son of a bitch, far as I'm concerned," said the other. He turned his battered, swollen face to Isabelle. "It's us, ma'am," he said, "Bob Hewitt and Donnie Dobbs."

"Oh my!" said Isabelle. "What in God's name has happened to you two?" she asked.

"In God's name, not a whole lot, ma'am," said Bob Hewitt. He turned a pained and crooked half smile toward the posse men and replied to her. "But otherwise, you might say we ran afoul of the law."

"All of us Redemption Riders did," Donnie Dobbs put in, "except all of Dad's churchmen got away—which is no surprise, since they always do."

Paying no attention to the two prisoners, DeShay gestured toward the body on the ground.

"Fletcher, you and Almond get this one out so we'll have room for Ragland in the torchlight," he said.

Almond started to step forward, but Fletcher stopped him.

"Sure thing, Sheriff," he said. He reached the toe of his boot out and rolled Kendrick's limp body off the blanket. "Done," he said, dusting his hands together.

Sheriff DeShay gave the surly gunman a harsh look.

"You and Almond get out front and stand guard while the Mexican cuts the bullet out of Ragland," he said.

"Anything you say, *Sheriff,*" Fletcher said half mockingly, touching his hat brim toward the seething DeShay, then toward the two women.

"Whatever you need, Sheriff, you holler out," Almond said in earnest.

"Obliged, Almond," said DeShay.

Only moments after Almond and Fletcher left, the Mexican walked in from the stone hallway carrying a cask of mescal under his arm and a large wooden cup for Ragland to drink from. Ragland's face brightened a little as he saw the strong drink arrive, but his expression changed when he saw the Mexican draw a lengthy knife and a pair of long-handled surgical tongs from inside his frayed robe.

"You'll need the Ranger and me to help hold

him down," DeShay said, stepping in close and peeling his coat off.

"No," the Mexican said confidently. Smiling, he set the cask and the cup down beside Ragland. "He will never know when I cut into his back."

Mattie only stood staring, but Isabelle looked stunned at the prospect of what she was about to witness.

"I'm taking the womenfolk and your prisoners out of here," Sam said to DeShay. "We'll get a fire going out front and boil some coffee."

"Obliged," said DeShay.

"Ragland, you're going to be all right, if the mescal doesn't kill you," Sam said.

"Obliged, Ranger," Ragland replied, watching the Mexican pull a wooden plug from the cask and fill the cup. "If the mescal does kill me, I'll just figure I had it coming."

"Let's go," Sam said to the two prisoners, gesturing them ahead of himself and the women toward the long stone tunnel. On their way, Sam made sure they heard him lever a round into his Winchester for good measure.

"You won't have to worry about us, Ranger," Hewitt said over his shoulder. "Donnie and I have had it. All we ever were is decoys and trail guards for Dad Orwick anyway."

"Yeah," said Dobbs, walking along, both of them with their hands tied behind them, "Orwick doesn't give a blue damn for any of us outlaws."

"Or anybody else who's not a part of his church *brethren,*" said Hewitt.

"So, anything we can tell you about him and his disciples that might help us catch a softer bunk when we get to Yuma, feel free to ask us," Dobbs put in. "We can tell you more than Isabelle can. No offense, ma'am," he said over his shoulder to her. "But Dad's kept you in the dark since he left you up at his northern compound."

Isabelle only lowered her head in silence.

"How long have you been riding with Dad?" Sam asked the two men.

"We've both been with him the past seven or eight months," said Hewitt. "But I worked for him five years ago for a while."

"How old a man is he?" Sam asked. Mattie shot him a curious look in the flicker of torchlight along the stone tunnel.

Hewitt gave a shrug, walking along ahead of them.

"I don't know, but he's an old geezer," he said. "Too damned old to have so many young new wives being brought to him—again, no offense, ma'am," he added over his shoulder to Isabelle.

Walking behind the Ranger, Isabelle continued looking down in silence. Beside her, Mattie held one arm around her sister's shoulders.

"How long since either of you've last seen him face-to-face?" Sam asked.

The two outlaws looked at each other through their swollen eyes.

"Hell, come to think of it," Hewitt said, "I haven't seen him since I took up with him this time. Used to be I saw him all the time. Not anymore. Elder Barcinder sent for me the day I got out of jail in Tinus. I haven't seen Dad."

"Neither have I," said Dobbs. "All I know is when they want someone to get shot at while him and his disciples slip away, they send some of us out."

"Decoys and trail guards, huh?" Sam said, wanting to keep them talking.

"Yep, that's all we are," Hewitt said, his inflamed face keeping his voice stifled. As he talked, they walked out of the crevice into the waning sunlight. "And I'll tell you right now, you haven't seen the last of them yet. Anywhere Dad and all his disciples go, there's going to be plenty of trail guards strung out behind him—"

Hewlett's words cut short as a bullet thumped into his chest, sliced through him and erupted out the middle of his back. A second behind the bullet came the explosion of the distant shot. Blood and fine viscera matter stung the Ranger and the women walking behind the hapless outlaw.

"Get back!" Sam shouted, pushing Mattie and Isabelle back into the shelter of the stone tunnel as two more bullets slapped Dobbs backward before he could duck away and take cover.

190

Fifteen yards away, Fletcher and Almond heard the rifle shots and dived behind rocks. They returned fire with nothing to aim at but the rising spirals of smoke on the distant hill line.

"Hold your fire," the Ranger called out to the two posse men, when a moment had passed without any more gunfire from the rocks. "I've got a feeling they've done what they came here to do."

"What? Kill two of their own men?" Fletcher asked in a sarcastic tone.

"That's right," the Ranger said. "They didn't want them talking to us." He hugged close to the edge of the crevice entrance and searched the distant hills. But it was no use. If the men were still up there, they'd changed positions by now.

"What now?" Fletcher asked. "We can't stay stuck down here hiding like rats!"

"You're right. We can't. Cover me while I get to my horse," Sam said. "I'll ride around out of their sights and flush them out."

"You're covered," Fletcher called out. "Get going."

Sam heard DeShay's running footsteps coming up the stone tunnel. Looking at Mattie, he said, "You and your sister stick close to the posse until I get back. Tell DeShay what I'm up to."

"Sam, don't go," Mattie called out. But it was too late. The Ranger had already begun running across the wide bed of stone toward where the horses stood behind a large boulder, out of rifle range. Freeing the dun's reins, he stepped around and tightened the cinch on the saddle.

"Yep, you guessed it," he said to the dun when it turned its muzzle around to him. "Time to go," he added, swinging up into the saddle. He quickly righted the horse and raced away toward a thin trail down the backside of the rocks. In seconds he was out of sight, circling wide and headed toward the hill line, his Winchester in hand.

Chapter 15

Knowing that all signs left behind by Dad Orwick and his people—including hoofprints and wagon tracks—were pointed south toward the border, Sam swung wide of the direction of the shooting. Instead of taking the trail leading up the hillside, he rode around the hill in time to see a rise of dust behind two fleeing horsemen.

The ambushers?

Sure they were, he decided, or at least that was how he had to play it. In a game as deadly as this, choices had to be made fast, and weighed decisions and gut hunches rode hand in hand. *Here goes,* he told himself, instinctively booting the big dun forward at a run. In this desolate land, who else would be riding down from that very same direction?

The copper dun raced across a sandy stretch of flatlands between hill lines, the Ranger barely able to see for the heavy dust drifting behind the riders. Knowing he had little chance of reaching the riders before they took cover in the next set of rocky hills, he considered reining the dun down a little for safety's sake. But the dun showed resistance when he touched back on its reins, testing the animal.

"All right, let's fly," he said to the dun under his breath, letting the reins go slack, giving the animal its way.

Rifle in hand, he leaned low and forward in the saddle, feeling an extra burst of speed. Even though the horse had been racing flat out to begin with, the strong-willed animal actually bellied down a little more now that it knew it was given charge of itself. The Ranger felt his sombrero lift off and fly back from his head and hang in the wind on the rawhide string around his neck.

With nothing to follow but the rider's dust, the Ranger sped forward on the dun for over a mile before noting that the dust had begun thinning. As his vision in front of him cleared a little, he saw one of the riders limping away on foot, his horse thrashing hard on the ground, only its rear hooves kicking up dust. It whinnied long and loud. Far ahead of the limping man, Sam saw the other rider edging upward onto a rocky path along the hillside.

Seeing the injured man turn toward him, stop and throw his rifle up to his shoulder, Sam quickly did the same with his Winchester. Two shots resounded as one, but the limping man's bullet only whistled past the Ranger; Sam's bullet nailed the man hard and flung him to the ground. The man's rifle flew from his hands; a boot spun upward from his foot.

Sam tapped the dun forward, seeing the man fumble with the gun holstered on his hip. On his way past the whinnying horse, he sighted down his rifle barrel. The shot exploded and the suffering horse fell silent as Sam tapped the dun again and rode in closer to the downed man.

"Don't draw that pistol," he warned, stopping the dun and looking down at the man.

The wounded man gave up and let his hand fall to the ground.

"This is supposed to be . . . one of them newfangled holsters that never gets stuck," he said with disgust.

"That's too bad." In the corner of his vision, Sam saw the other rider disappear from sight into the distant hills. He swung down from his saddle, picked up the discarded rifle and walked over to the downed man.

"Are you one of Dad's outlaws, or one of his churchmen?" he asked, tucking the man's rifle in the crook of his arm beside his Winchester.

The man stared up, squinting at the Ranger's badge in the failing evening light.

"How about you go kiss . . . my sister's dirty ass, lawman?" he said haltingly. Blood gushed from the left side of his chest.

"I'm going to guess. *Outlaw?*" Sam said.

"Ha, ha," the man said, humorlessly. He coughed up blood and smeared it across his lips as he tried to wipe it off. "So . . . this is what dying feels like."

"Must be," Sam said. He stooped and drew the pistol from the man's side.

"Damn it to hell," the gunman cursed, seeing how effortlessly his Colt slipped from its holster for the Ranger.

"What's your name?" Sam asked.

"I don't feel required . . . to give it," the man said.

Sam only nodded and tucked the man's empty rifle up under his arm.

"Those were two of your own men you killed back at the caves," he said, checking the man's gun in his hand.

"Yeah, so?" the gunman said. "Dad said shoot Isabelle too if she shows her face. She used to be . . . his wife. I never seen him so fired up."

Sam just stared at him—a real hard case, this one. "So, how many of you outlaws you figure Dad is going to sacrifice to keep his *brethren* safe?"

"As many as it takes, I guess," the gunman said, clutching his chest to save the flow of blood.

"It doesn't bother you," Sam asked, "being put in the gun sights, killing your own, while Dad's churchmen gain the rewards?"

"Huh-uh," the man said. "As you can see, I appear to no longer have a dog in this fight." He attempted a bloody-toothed smile.

Sam took a step back, lifted a canteen by its strap from his saddle horn and walked back. Taking the cap off, he held the canteen down to the dying man. The man accepted the offer and coughed up a red spray as he raised it to his mouth.

"Watch the blood," Sam said.

But the man took a swig first, then held the canteen back and looked at the blood running down the cap.

"Well, excuse . . . the hell out of me," he said wryly. "Where *are* my manners today?" Only then did he wipe a shirtsleeve across his bloody lips. "You just as well . . . leave this here for me," he said slyly, as if he'd won something by bloodying the canteen.

"It's yours," Sam said, "if you tell me what I need to expect from Dad Orwick between here and Gun Valley."

The man looked off to where his horse lay dead in the sand.

"For that kind of cooperation . . . I'd require my gun back too," he said.

"Done," Sam said. He raised the man's gun, dropped five of the six bullets into his palm and put them in his pocket. He closed the gate on the revolver and pitched it down by the man's boots.

"That was too easy, lawman," the gunman said, coughing up a short laugh. "I might have . . . changed my mind."

"I can take it back," Sam said flatly. "Let you watch whatever's eating you tonight for as long as you can stand it."

"You're a cruel . . . son of a bitch at heart," he said. "We would have . . . gotten along well, you and me," he added with mock admiration.

Sam ignored him and asked, "How long will Dad be leaving men behind to guard his back trail? Seems like he would have drawn them back by now. He's bound to be across the border."

"He ain't . . . drawing nobody back this time, lawman. Everything'll turn around at the border —Dad will be the one doing the hunting there."

"Why?" Sam asked.

"I think we both know why," he said with a crafty look.

Sam only stared at him.

"Jesus, you really *don't* know, do you?" the man said in surprise, and coughed.

"I'm through with you," Sam said, stooping, picking up the big revolver. "Tell the wolves I said *enjoy their dinner.*"

"Damn it. . . . Wait, okay," the man said, seeing Sam ready to grab the gun, turn back to the dun and ride away.

Sam stopped and stared down at him.

"Dad knows you killed his boy, Young Ezekiel," the dying man said. "Some of his men found where . . . you hid his body."

The news came as a hard blow to the Ranger's gut, realizing what had happened and who was responsible for it.

"You're lying," he said, not wanting to believe what terrible thought this man had just introduced to him.

The man took on a strange look. "Nobody's ever called me a liar before and been *wrong,* Ranger. But this time, you are."

"Where was he shot?" Sam asked, hoping to hear something that would discount what he was saying, for Mattie's sake.

"Up on a lookout ridge above the water hole—"

"I mean where was he *hit?*" Sam asked, cutting him off.

"Above his left eye," the man said, appearing to gather strength discussing such gruesome matters. "That was some fine shooting. Then you dragged him off . . . out of sight." He gave a weak, bloody grin and seemed to relax in satisfaction.

"I didn't shoot him," Sam said.

"Dad figures you did," he said. "You were on our trail awfully tight." He watched the look on the Ranger's face, and said, "I see that all this is ringing a bell for you. . . ."

"How old was Dad's son?" Sam asked.

"How the hell would I know?" the dying man said. "Why? You want me to tell him . . . *happy birthday* when I see him in hell?"

Sam stood running the ages through his mind. How long had Mattie been away . . . ? How many children did she say she'd borne for Dad Orwick and had to leave behind? Could the dead young ambusher she shot—a boy still in his teens—have been one of hers?

This is bad. . . .

Sam didn't like what was going through his mind. He looked off toward the border, then back down at the man lying in the dirt. He pitched the gun down near the man's hand this time, seeing he was getting too weak to reach very far.

"I'm leaving," he said quietly. "Is there anything else I can do for you?"

"You must mean . . . reading material, or whatnot?" the man said, his voice sounding weaker with each word. He shook his head slowly. "No, I'm just fine here. Got water . . . . Got a bullet in my pistol . . ." He sighed. "You go on now. . . ."

Sam backed away. Still not trusting the man, he kept his eyes on him as he slid the Winchester into its boot and held the man's rifle in his gloved hand. He stepped into his saddle, turned the dun and rode back the way he came, a grim expression on his dust-streaked face. He had much to consider on his ride back to the caves.

He had anticipated Orwick's tactics of striking, then escaping, gaining ground with each surprise attack. It was nothing new; the Apache had been using these tactics for years. Sam knew it took a steady, patient hand to turn this sort of fighting around. He had done well with it up to now, following the riders, anticipating their moves as he went, waiting and weighing his chances, finding out a little bit more about his enemy after each encounter—each and every ambush.

But it wasn't Orwick and his men that bothered the Ranger as he rode back toward the caves. He could handle anything these men threw at him. What troubled him was knowing what Mattie had done the day she'd shot the ambusher. Not just any ambusher, he reminded himself, letting the dun choose its own pace again, this time with no sense of urgency.

After all this poor woman had been through, he knew he couldn't bring himself to tell her that by her own hand she might very well have killed her son.

Evening shadows had grown long and black across the tops of boulders and below the cliffs by the time the Ranger heard the distant sound of the single pistol shot resound on the flatlands behind him. He rode on with the nameless dead man's rifle across his lap, crossed the natural stone bridge and headed upward toward Munny Caves.

As soon as the sun dropped below the far western hill line, he felt the coolness of the gorge rise from the black darkness behind him. Before he reached the flat upper trail stretching toward the last few hundred yards to the caves, he sensed himself being flanked and followed by something risen from that deep abyss. Beneath him the dun grew restless, aggressive, and fought slightly against the Ranger's stay of the reins. On either side of them the Ranger heard the soft brushing sound of padded paws whisk across stone and dirt. With a quick turn of his head, he caught sight of long, ghostly shadows darting in and out and over rocks like streaks of black liquid, growing bolder, edging closer with the encroaching darkness.

Wolves. . . .

He raised the dead man's rifle from across his lap, realizing that by now the strong scent of both the dead man and his horse's blood had drawn in the prowling night hunters and by morning the two would be well on their way back to the elements of the earth.

So be it.

He cocked the rifle across the crook of his left arm and at the next sight of one of the bolder wolves, he pulled the trigger and let go a blast and a streak of fire that sent the animals scurrying away.

For the next thousand yards he rode alone, but then as if they had sunken into the land and magically resurfaced beside him, he saw their outlines reappear, a long line of them sitting as still as stone, eyes glowing red, their ears piqued tall, backlit against the purple sky.

"Not tonight, fellows," he said quietly to them.

And he rode on.

Ten minutes later he caught sight of a single rider moving in and out of the greater darkness, descending the hill trail toward him.

Sam stopped and sidestepped the dun off the trail and sat waiting as the rider drew nearer. When the rider was close enough to hear him, Sam cocked the rifle across his lap and watched the horse come to a sudden halt.

After a tense silence, DeShay's voice said softly, "Ranger, is that you?"

"Yeah, Sheriff," Sam said. "What were you going to do if I said no?"

DeShay let out a breath and nudged his horse toward the edge of the trail.

"Start shooting, I guess," he said. He let the Ranger hear him uncock the big custom Simpson-Barre .45 lying on his lap. "I wasn't counting on any strangers out here making friends tonight." He slid the gun into his holster. "Anyway, we started hearing shooting leading this way the past couple of hours, figured it was you. Everything all right?"

"As good as it's going to get for now," Sam replied. "How about at the caves?"

"Tense," DeShay said. He turned his horse around onto the thin trail.

"How's Ragland?" Sam asked, turning the copper dun beside him.

"Doing all right now," said DeShay. "Everybody's all right. Fletcher got into the mescal and got a little mouthy for a while, but he passed out before I left. He'll be hell on hooves come morning."

"We might all be hell on hooves come morning," said Sam. "I caught up to one of the men who shot the prisoners. He said Dad won't be letting up on sticking his gunmen along the trail to keep us from getting to him."

"Hmmm," DeShay said, considering it. "Must be nobody's ever stuck to his trail this long. It's got him spooked, you figure?"

"Could be," Sam said, not about to reveal why Dad hadn't drawn his men back by now. It was not the sort of information that one lawman could keep from another. But for now he would. "Whatever it's about, I'm not turning back. He's gotten his people across the border now, heading for Valley of the Gun. Once they're there, he'll disappear. It could be months before he sticks his head up."

"You'll ride into Ol' Mex after him?" DeShay asked.

"I will," Sam said.

After a pause DeShay said, "I'll be riding with you, if you'll have me, that is."

"I won't," Sam said flatly.

"What?" DeShay sounded indignant.

"You heard me," Sam said. "You're not that kind of lawman."

Another pause; then DeShay finally relented and said, "Okay, I know I haven't been. But I want to be."

"Everybody wants to be," said the Ranger.

"I know, but I mean it," DeShay said. "I've taken money from Orwick for looking the other way when him and his men rode through Whiskey Bend. To be honest I came after him because I didn't like how he's treated me the past year. Partly I came wanting to catch him. Partly I came wanting him to pay up."

"But something changed your mind after you got out here and got on the hunt," Sam interceded for him.

"It's the truth, Ranger," DeShay said, seeing he was being doubted. "A man puts on a badge, he means to do right. But after a while, sometimes he loses sight of what *doing right* means."

"And now you're back on track," Sam said, still sounding a little skeptical.

"Can't a man change, Ranger?" DeShay said.

"I don't know, Sheriff," Sam said quietly. "You seem to be saying so."

"I'm saying *I have,* Ranger," DeShay insisted.

"And you want to prove it by riding across the border with me and killing a man you used to take money from?"

"It sounds bad when you say it that way," DeShay said.

"It *is* bad when I say it that way," Sam replied. "But there's no other way to say it."

"All I'm asking for is a chance to make myself right," DeShay said. "I'm changed, you'll see."

After a silence, the Ranger said, "You better be *changed* if you ride into Old Mex with me."

The two rode on in silence, toward a flickering firelight dancing in the clearing at Munny Caves.

Chapter 16

As the Ranger and Sheriff DeShay reached Munny Caves and stepped their horses up onto the wide stone clearing out front, they rode past Morgan Almond, who stood guard at the edge of the trail, his rifle cradled in his arm now that he recognized the two in the grainy darkness. The two reined their horses at the hitch rail and stepped down from their saddles. Mattie, also standing guard, walked forward from the shadows, her rifle in arm. Isabelle stayed back near the crevice at the entrance to the caves.

"We heard shooting," Mattie said to the Ranger. "We were getting worried."

"Wolves," Sam said. He only loosened the cinch instead of removing it from the copper dun's back.

Mattie noted he didn't pull the dun's saddle. Rather, he untied his blanket roll from behind it.

"Are you expecting more trouble tonight?" she asked as he took down his rolled blanket and tucked it under his arm.

The old cliff dweller whisked in like a spirit while the two spoke. He took the dun's reins and led the horse away to water and grain it and place it with the other animals.

"Yes, I am," Sam said. Letting the Mexican take the reins, he turned to Mattie and said, "I killed one of Dad's men. Before he died he told me Dad has gone wild. He won't be disappearing on us. Once he gets his wagons and people settled into Valley of the Gun, he's going to turn the tables on us when we're deep across the border."

"Maybe that's better for us," Mattie said, considering it. "Instead of us having to hunt him down, he'll come to us. Usually he rides away and leaves the trouble for his gunmen to settle. That's why nobody ever catches him. We'll get him, Ranger, when he comes for us," she added, her eyes aglow in anticipation. "Once he comes into—"

"What about your sister, Isabelle?" Sam asked,

cutting Mattie off in a slightly sharp tone of voice. He regretted what he was going to have to do.

"Don't you worry. I'll watch over her," Mattie said, noting the change in his voice. "Nothing's going to happen to Isabelle ever again, not so long as I'm alive. She's my older sister by two years, but I always looked out for the both of us . . . the best I could, that is."

Sam only stared at her for a moment. Finally he took a deep breath and proceeded with what had to be done.

"Mattie, you're not going any farther on this hunt," he said firmly. "For your sake and Isabelle's, you're both going to Whiskey Bend come morning. Almond's going to take Ragland back for medical care. He'll take the two of you as well."

"Oh? And somehow that's going to make everything safer for both of us?" she challenged, seeing he had given the matter consideration. "What about all these trail guards, all the ambushing going on?"

"The back trail will be safe enough now that Dad's men are across the border," Sam said. "Sheriff DeShay, Fletcher and I are going on out across the border. We'll do whatever needs to be done when the time comes."

"You won't find Dad's compound without somebody guiding you to it," she said.

"I doubt if we'll have to find his compound,"

Sam said. "According to what the gunman told me, I figure Dad and his men will be coming for us."

He stopped and watched her eyes, hoping he'd said enough. But she only stared at him, revealing nothing.

"It isn't like Dad to turn and fight," she said. "I wonder why he's doing it."

"Who knows?" Sam said, not wanting to go any deeper into the subject lest he have to reveal to her what he'd discovered. "A man like Dad Orwick makes a whole life out of not doing what he's expected to do."

Mattie seemed to consider it for a second. Then she looked back at him with unflinching determination.

"Well, it doesn't matter why. I'm not turning back until he's dead," she said.

"I've given that some thought too," Sam replied. "I'm wondering if he's dead already, maybe has been for a while. If he is, this whole trip is one you didn't need to make."

"Dead, huh-uh," Mattie said. "I'll believe he's dead when I stand with my boot on his chest."

"Whether he's dead or alive," said Sam, "you've taken this vendetta of yours as far as you can take it. The game has changed on you. It's not just your life you're risking now. You've got to think about your sister. And while you're thinking about her, DeShay, Fletcher and I have to think about the both of you."

"Ranger, you know good and well that I can take care of myself as well as any man. If I've come up short in any way, I need you to point it out to me."

"You've done well, Mattie," Sam said, not liking the words he had to say. "But it's my decision, and I say that you have to go back to Whiskey Bend come morning. If Dad Orwick *is* alive, I will bring him down, you have my word on it."

Mattie looked at the determination in his eyes, gauging it against her own.

"I can tell your mind's all made up," she said. "You and DeShay talked it all out on your way back here, and decided to cut me out." Tears of anger and hurt welled up in her eyes. She looked away from Sam to keep him from seeing her face.

"We did talk it all out riding back here," Sam said, determined not to give an inch. "This is what *I* decided. DeShay made it my call, and this is it."

"And nothing I say is going to change your mind, is it?" she said, taking a deep breath.

"No," Sam said, "there's no changing it."

"Then I won't even bother trying tonight," she said calmly, still turned away from him. "Can we talk some more about it first thing in the morning?"

"No," Sam said, "it's done."

"We'll see where we stand in the morning," she said as if she didn't hear him. "Sometimes things feel different after a night's sleep."

Sam let out a breath, watching her walk away. There was nothing more to talk about in the morning. She knew it as well as he did.

Still, something told him the matter was far from being resolved. Sam considered how she'd handled the conversation while he walked to the spot where the Mexican had taken the copper dun to be grained and watered.

Satisfied that the horse was well attended, he walked into the cave, the Mexican by his side, and checked on Dee Ragland. They found the wounded man sleeping comfortably in the flickering torchlight.

A few feet from Ragland, Arlis Fletcher lay facedown snoring in the dirt, his jaw cocked in a way that stirred a puff of dust with each breath.

"This one likes my mescal very much," said the Mexican, picking up the cask from the floor and jiggling it to gauge its contents. "He asked if I would like to remove an old bullet from the calf of his leg for practice."

Sam shook his head, looking down at the gunman. An empty tin cup sat inches from Fletcher's fingertips. His Colt lay near his elbow, as if he'd dropped it before passing out on mescal.

"The sheriff was grateful when he fell on his face and did not get back up." The old Mexican grinned.

"I bet," said Sam.

Stooping, he picked up Fletcher's dust-covered

Colt, shook it off and slipped it into the sleeping gunman's holster. Fletcher's snoring continued undisturbed as Sam turned and walked out of the cave.

"*Buenas noches.* . . . Sleep well, *amigo*," the old Mexican said quietly as Sam disappeared along the dark stone tunnel.

Outside the crevice, Sam kept out of the circle of firelight. Ten yards away in the shadow of a large rock, he wrapped his blanket around him, Mexican peasant–style, sat down with the rifle across his lap and leaned back against the hard stone. He watched the two women come in from the shadows and stoop at the fire's edge for a moment. Isabelle picked up a battered coffeepot from the glowing coals, poured a cup of coffee and held it out to Mattie.

Sam watched the two sit talking with an arm around each other's shoulders. Mattie appeared to have taken Sam's news well enough, but he still didn't trust it. She had been too intent on killing Dad Orwick to be dissuaded so easily.

"*We'll see where we stand in the morning,*" she'd said. Huh-uh, he wasn't buying it.

For many reasons, the Ranger knew he wasn't about to allow himself to sleep very soundly tonight. Even though both his mind and body ached for rest, he managed to keep his eyes open enough to watch the two women closely. When they both stood up and walked away from the firelight and out of sight again, he kept a loose track of time. But, to his relief, he noticed they hadn't been gone long before Mattie walked back into sight, set her cup by the fire, picked up her blanket and dragged it back out of the firelight.

The Ranger let out a breath as he saw her lie down on her side and gaze toward the fire. Maybe if she thought about the situation for a while, she would understand that going back to Whiskey Bend was the best thing for her sister, if nothing else. Sam relaxed his head onto his crossed forearms and allowed himself to doze for a few guarded moments. He didn't care why she agreed to go back. *Just go back,* he thought, drifting off.

Every few minutes throughout the night, he raised his head long enough to see the woman still lying on her blanket, half of it pulled over her body, guarding her from the chilled breath of night. His light sleep was such that had she stood up and walked away, he would have known it. When Morgan Almond walked into the firelight to warm himself for a moment, he knew it.

"You sleep like a watchdog," he heard a voice from the past say inside his head. He drifted on the edge of some ethereal realm, not awake, yet not asleep.

It's an old Comanche trick, he heard himself reply. *Sleep with your eyes open. . . .*

And he continued drifting until he fully opened his eyes and saw the first slim orange-silver line of morning crawling up the eastern side of the earth. Knowing the woman was still sleeping there where she'd been all night, he swept his eyes back and forth across the campsite without raising his head or making any waking movement.

A crackling sound came from the fire when the Mexican stepped into sight and pitched an arm-load of dried brush and downfallen pine into the glowing bed of embers. As the flames stood up from the coals and danced and licked at the wood, Sam saw the woman rise from her blanket, walk to the edge of the fire and rub her hands together over it.

He eyed her up and down in the morning fire, hoping she had resolved things in her mind during the night. But as he started to look away, something demanded him to look back at her. Something was wrong here? Something was missing—*something was not as it should be.* . . .

"Oh no," he said under his breath as realization suddenly swept over him.

Springing to his feet, his eyes on the ankle-high shoes on the woman's feet, Sam raced to the fire, grabbed her by the arm and swung her around to face him. In the turning of a second, he'd already prepared himself for what he discovered.

Isabelle turned her face away from his quickly

and raised a hand as if to shield herself from the kind of man's anger she was used to.

"Please, don't hit me," she pleaded with Sam. "I—I tried to tell her not to."

From the shadows, Morgan Almond came running, rifle in hand, and slid to a stop. He stood watching in surprise.

"Nobody is going to hit you, Isabelle," Sam said. "I should have seen this coming." He turned her loose and she sank down onto her blanket.

"Mattie's gone?" Almond asked quietly. "This is her sister, Isabelle?" He looked down at the woman, the fringed buckskins she wore. She had exchanged clothing with her sister when they had stepped out of the firelight.

"Yes," Sam said. "This is Isabelle. Mattie got me. . . ." He looked off in the direction of the border, knowing she'd had all night to get a good head start on him.

On the blanket Isabelle settled herself and wiped her eyes on the buckskin shirtsleeve.

"She said to tell you she's sorry, Ranger," she said, sniffling. "That she didn't do this to be spiteful—only that she couldn't stop here, after coming this far."

Sam still stared off toward the trail to Mexico.

"She said that, huh?" he murmured almost to himself, realizing there was nothing he could do now to shield her from learning what she might have done. All he could do now was hope to stop her, join her or slow her down enough to keep her from getting herself killed.

"Yes, she said that," Isabelle replied, standing up again, looking closely at the Ranger. "She said that you would understand."

"Yes . . . the trouble is, I do," said Sam quietly, looking around the camp, then back to Isabelle. "Did she tell you to go on to Whiskey Bend with Almond and Ragland and wait for her there?"

"Yes, that's what she told me to do," Isabelle said.

Sam looked at Almond.

"Don't worry, Ranger," said Almond. "I'll see her on to Whiskey Bend. Won't nothing happen to her unless something happens to me first."

"Obliged, Almond," Sam said.

Sheriff DeShay walked in from the shadows, pushing back his hair and putting his hat on.

"What's going on here?" he asked, seeing the Mexican, Morgan Almond, the Ranger and only one of the women standing in the firelight. "Where's Mattie's sister, Isabelle?"

"This *is* Isabelle," Sam said. "Mattie and her traded clothes. Mattie tricked me. She slipped away in the night."

DeShay looked the woman up and down, Mattie's fringed buckskins, her plainsman's hat, right down to the women's shoes on her feet. Not seeing Mattie's boots, he understood. The different footwear triggered recognition.

"Dang, Ranger," he said, "don't feel bad. They

look enough alike, they would've fooled me too."
He shook his head and pushed his hat up on his
forehead. "I take it she wouldn't hear of riding
back to town while we go on into Old Mex?"

"I should have seen it coming," Sam said.
"Maybe I should never have brought it up to
begin with."

He realized that in attempting to help Mattie,
he might have put her into more danger, but it
was something he wouldn't explain to DeShay, at
least not right now.

"She'll be riding on the trail in front of us,
Ranger," DeShay said. "It's a bad place to be."

"I know," Sam said.

"How do you want to play this?" DeShay said.

"I'm riding on ahead," said Sam. "Maybe I can
catch up to her before she runs headlong into
some of Dad's men. Throw some water on
Fletcher and get him woken up. Get Almond,
Ragland and Isabelle here headed to town. You
and Fletcher catch up to me along the trail. I'll
keep watch for you."

"You got it all, Ranger," said DeShay.

Sam started to turn toward where the Mexican
kept the horses, but Isabelle took him by the arm.

"Ranger, please bring her to me safely," she
said with a concerned expression.

"Don't worry about a thing, Isabelle," Sam said.
"Get to Whiskey Bend and wait there. Your
sister's going to be all right. I'll see to that."

216

PART 3

Chapter 17

It had been only shortly after dark when Mattie Rourke slipped out of camp and walked her dapple gray quietly down to the same side trail the Ranger had taken earlier when he'd pursued the riflemen who'd killed the two prisoners. Wearing her long trail duster over Isabelle's blue gingham dress she'd swapped her buckskins for, she had stepped atop her horse, gathered the dress up around her and ridden like the wind throughout the night.

Where deep rock shadows blackened out the trail, she'd slowed the dapple down for safety's sake; when the horse began to slow its pace on its own, she'd stopped long enough to rest the animal. Otherwise, she'd made short work of the trail until the eastern horizon unfolded grudgingly above the coming day.

As she started across a stretch of flatlands, she saw in the purple starlit grayness the black silhouettes of wolves snarling and threatening one another over the night's offering. Beneath her she felt the dapple gray grumble and try to sidestep away from the sound of the wolves. But she reined firm and kept the horse forwarded on the trail.

Drawing tight on the reins with her left hand,

she slipped her rifle from its boot, cocked its hammer and held it ready as she passed the feasting animals twenty yards to her right. The wolves held back and stood protectively over their prey. Mattie made out what she thought might be the carcass of a horse and the body of a man—*the rifleman the Ranger had gone after earlier?* she wondered. She continued on, moving confidently and unhurriedly past them in the pale grainy light.

When she had judged the wolves to be over fifty yards behind her, she whispered to the horse, "Now you can run. . . ."

She batted her boots to the dapple's side and put the horse up into a hard gallop, anxious to put the wolves and their grizzly feast behind her.

At the first streak of silver light to the left, she saw the trail in front of her edge upward back into the rocky hills. This was land she'd traveled before, although it had been years. She knew that somewhere on the upslope of this line of hills lay the border, and at some point below the dapple's hooves she and her horse passed from the United States into Old Mexico.

Now to Valley of the Gun. . . .

Shortly after daylight, the rifle back in its boot, she had crossed the hills and headed back down to the next stretch of flatlands. Two miles into the barren flatlands, a raw morning wind filled with dust and sharp sand launched a passing assault on her and her horse. When she'd outridden most of the wind and the body of it fell away southeast behind her, she stopped the horse and stepped down. Taking off her duster, she shook it out. Looking off to the southwest, she stood holding the duster like some observing matador as she spotted two riders come into sight diagonally across the sandy flatlands.

Her first thought was to climb back atop the dapple gray and head back for the cover of the hills behind her. But the easy gait of the approaching riders caused her no alarm. Watching them draw closer, she folded the duster and stuck it up behind her saddle. Then she slipped the rifle back out of its boot and stood holding it ready in both hands.

"You're close enough," she called out, seeing both men studying her.

"Miss Isabelle?" said the younger of the two men, both of them wearing long dusters of their own. They reined their horses down and sat staring at her from fifty feet away, their faces and clothes as dust-covered as her own.

Hearing her sister's name, she stood frozen and returned their stare, seeing what the men might reveal to her if she kept silent.

"It's me, Frank Bannis," the same rider said. He took off his hat, slapped it against his chest and rubbed a hand over his face, to better disclose himself. "Don't you recognize me?"

"Easy, Frank," said the older man beside him. "I believe she's stunned." He jerked his hat from his head as well, raising a small cloud of dust and said, "Ma'am, it's me, Kerr."

Recalling the name Isabelle had said when she'd told her the details of the story, Mattie nodded slowly and looked the two men up and down.

"Yes, I recognize you, Frank," she said. "You too, Kerr. Please forgive me. I'm afraid I am stunned. I've been riding so long."

Smiling friendly, Bannis laid his hat on his lap and nudged his horse a step forward.

"You *should* remember me—you brained me with a skillet the other day at the wagon camp."

"Knocked him daft as a cockeyed loon, is what you done," said Kerr with a dark chuckle.

All right, *stunned* was the way for her to play this, Mattie told herself. Keep quiet, rely on what little she already knew and let them fill in the rest. They'd thought she was Isabelle without her needing to say a word. She was in a good position here if she kept them thinking it.

"And I'm terribly sorry for that, Frank," she said, lowering the rifle in her hands. "I was afraid you'd kill my husband and in doing so get yourself killed by Dad's churchmen."

"I understand," said Bannis. "May we step down?"

"Yes, of course," said Mattie. "Do you have enough water to spare me a drink?"

"You bet we do," said Bannis. He swung down from his saddle and reached for a canteen hanging by its strap from his saddle horn. "Were you riding to meet me at the dugouts, like you said you would?" He uncapped the canteen and held it out to her.

Mattie took the canteen and drank from it.

"I meant what I said, Frank," Mattie said. "I was worried about hitting you so hard."

"That means a lot to me, Miss Isabelle," Frank said, "you coming to check on me. Fact is, we were riding all the way back to Munny Caves to see about you."

"How is your husband after that terrible head whipping?" Morton Kerr cut in, giving Frank a stern look of reprimand.

"Oh, he's sore, but he'll be all right," Mattie said, realizing the bad spot he would be in if it was learned that the beating he'd given Phillip Kendrick had killed him. She even wondered if the beating really had killed Kendrick, knowing the unstable frame of mind her sister had been in when she and her weakened husband had been left alone in the caves. "He's still back at Munny Caves, recovering nicely. I left him there with the old Mexican cliff dweller—"

"So you could ride on ahead and check on me." Bannis finished her words for her with a warm appreciative smile.

"Yes, that's so," Mattie said, returning the smile.

"And I can't tell you how relieved I am that you're doing so well. I couldn't have forgiven myself had something terrible—"

"Nonsense, ma'am," said Bannis, cutting her off.

Kerr cut in, saying, "I always said he could use a skillet upside his head now and then, just to clear his thinking and settle him down some."

"I couldn't stand the thought of him putting his hands on you, Isabelle," Bannis said.

"Bless you, Frank," said Mattie. "It wasn't as bad as it appeared. Look, you can hardly see it now that the swelling is gone."

"That's real good, Isabelle," Bannis said. "I know I was out of line, beating a man for hitting his own wife. But there's something about it that doesn't sit right with me."

"Even though every law in the land permits it?" Kerr questioned him. "The same as a man's got a right to correct a dog or an unruly field animal?"

"Being the law doesn't make a thing right," Bannis said. "I'm only an outlaw and a long rider, but I know that much."

"You were gallant and wonderful," Mattie said, "and I will never forget you for it."

Bannis smiled and looked embarrassed.

"I wouldn't go so far as to say *gallant and wonderful*," he said quietly.

"Neither would I," said Kerr, giving him a look. Turning to Mattie, he asked, "Where are you headed now, to the new compound in Gun Valley, I reckon?"

New compound . . . ?

She hadn't considered that Dad Orwick might do something like this, move the family compound after such a long period of time.

"Yes, that's right," she said, thinking on her feet. "I do hope I can find it, having never been there."

The two men looked regretful.

"I'm sorry, ma'am," Kerr said. "I forgot that only the new wives would know its whereabouts."

"But I bet you do," Mattie said quickly.

"Yes, ma'am," said Bannis, "but I wonder what my reception will be after beating Kendrick half to death."

"Your reception will be quite all right, Frank," said Mattie. "I'll simply tell Dad or Elder Barcinder that in a jealous rage, Brother Phillip attacked you, and there was nothing for you to do but defend yourself."

Both men looked shocked.

"You—you would lie for me, ma'am?" he said. "I didn't think you saints' wives ever lied or did anything that—"

"We don't," Mattie said, cutting him off. "That's why Dad and Elder Barcinder will have no choice but to believe me." She paused, then added, "After all, Dad will know that you could just as easily have shot Brother Phillips down, yet you chose against it—out of respect for Dad and his saints."

"Ma'am, I don't know what to say," Bannis whispered as if in awe. "I was telling Kerr that no woman has ever reminded me so much of my beloved ma than you." He paused and caught himself. "I mean, not to say that you're old enough to be my ma—just that you've always treated me so kindly when I've been around you."

Mattie managed a maternal smile.

"The fact is, Frank, I am old enough to be your ma. Not by a lot, mind you," she added, pointing a correcting finger.

"No, ma'am," Bannis said, looking relieved.

"Then it's all settled," she said. "You two gentlemen will escort me to the new compound and I'll square things for you."

"Sounds good to us, ma'am," Bannis said. He took back the canteen, capped it and draped it from his saddle horn. He held out a hand to assist her back into her saddle. "There's going to be guards scouting all along the trail, but they'll all recognize you, especially with us riding alongside you."

Kerr stood eyeing the woman curiously as she adjusted herself, hiked her dress up and settled onto the saddle. He watched her take the reins Bannis had gathered and handed up to her.

When both men had mounted and their horses had fallen in a few steps behind the woman, Kerr leaned over and whispered to Bannis,

"Does she look different to you some way?"

"What are you talking about?" Bannis asked as they lagged back a little.

Kerr considered it and then said, "I don't know. She looks different, or acts different, or something."

Bannis glared at him.

"That's right—you *don't know*," he said, "*don't know* what you're talking about, or how hot it's making me if you're trying to say something untoward against this good woman."

"Frank, forget it," said Kerr, a little fearful, remembering the beating Frank had dealt Phillip Kendrick. "I've just been too long away from good folks, I suppose."

"Yeah, that's what I think too," Frank said.

"But listen to me, Frank," Kerr said. "For both our sakes and hers too, don't forget how Dad doesn't want any of his older wives around anymore. That's why she doesn't know where the new compound is. Dad keeps the wives from knowing much about what's going on around them. They don't even know where their own offspring are by the time they're half-grown."

"Yeah, I know all that," said Bannis. He spit in contempt of Dad Orwick. "But if she wants to go there, I'm taking her. If Dad gets too much bark on I'll deal him what I dealt Kendrick. This is a good woman, Morton. I'll see to it she's treated like one."

"Jesus, Frank," Kerr whispered as the two nudged their horses up beside Mattie Rourke. "I've seen you worked up before, but never like this. Did that lick in the head cause you to act this way?"

Bannis ignored him and stared straight ahead. At the edge of the flatlands, he saw three riders pop into sight and ride toward them.

"Here's some of those trail guards now, ma'am," he said to Mattie, sidling up closer to her. "They'll be churchmen most likely. Most of the gunmen like myself will have already taken their cut of things and lit out for a while, the way they always do."

"Won't matter, though, which they are," Kerr put in. "They'll let us on through." They watched as the three riders put their horses into a gallop and rode toward them.

In a large stone, timber and adobe hacienda recently known as Casa Orwick, Elder Barcinder stood at an open window. Beyond the hacienda, smaller but similar homes stood on lower hillsides encompassing the western portion of the Valley of the Gun. Past Barcinder, three upper-ranking churchmen sat in high-backed Spanish-style chairs facing an ornately carved wooden and marble desk. Behind the desk sat Dad Orwick's large thronelike chair. Dad's long trail duster mantled the chair's tall leather back; his wide-brimmed hat lay at the center of his duster.

With his hands studiously folded behind his back, Elder Barcinder walked behind the desk and stood beside the big empty chair facing the three men.

"Brethren," he said, "as you all know it has been a long, hard endeavor, but I am happy and proud to say that upon Dad's arrival last night, this lovely rugged valley that God has bequeathed us is now our home." He smiled and raised his hands in front of him as if offering up two service trays. "Let all of us rejoice."

The three men rose, nodded and clapped their hands. They remained standing until Barcinder's hands turned palms down and pressed them gently back into their chairs.

"Now, then, while Dad is himself occupied with other matters, are there any questions I myself can answer for you?"

"Yes, a question, if I may, Elder Barcinder," a man said, his hand going up slightly to be recognized.

"Certainly, Deacon Sillborn," said Barcinder.

"When will Dad address us himself, the way he always did before?" he asked.

"Soon, my brother," Barcinder replied, his stare boring into Sillborn's eyes. "But for now, my words will have to be enough for you. Dad has a lot on his mind with our migration here, raising funds for our families and our ministry.

The Mexican government places a tremendous financial burden on our living here."

As Barcinder finished speaking, another of the deacons by the name of Millard Romly turned in his chair toward Deacon Sillborn.

"Dad has a lot on his mind with the death of his son Ezekiel," he said. "We need to be patient."

"Well said, Brother Mill," the third deacon put in, clapping his big hands again. "I want to suggest that we put forth a significant effort to capture the man who killed him and stand his head on a stake at the entrance to Gun Valley. Let the world see that our saints will not be slaughtered and abused by Americans. That's the sort of thing we came here to—"

"Enough of that sort of talk, Brother Abell," said Barcinder. "Dad insists that we allow our mercenaries to take care of such matters."

"But we can help, can't we?" said Deacon Abell.

"Of course, if the opportunity presents itself," said Barcinder. "Otherwise, we have plenty to do here. Dad had me appoint Uncle Henry Jumpe to this matter. I'm sure Uncle Henry will handle the problem to our satisfaction. He is, after all, a former investigator for Allen Pinkerton."

"This job will require a cold-blooded killer. I'm talking about catching the man who did it and sinking his head on a stake," said Deacon Abell. "Are we certain Uncle Henry Jumpe is capable of doing that?"

As Deacon Abell spoke, the door to the office creaked open. In the doorway stood a stocky man whose shoulders almost touched the doorframe on either side. Barcinder gave a sweep of a hand toward the squarely built man wearing a black swallow-tailed coat over a black pin-striped vest. A black bowler hat sat level atop his large head above thick muttonchop sideburns.

"Here is Uncle Henry now, Deacon Abell," Barcinder said in a level tone. "Feel free to ask him yourself if he's capable."

The stocky Henry Jumpe walked into the room straight and steady, yet his peg leg made a hard bumping sound with each step.

"Am I capable of what, sir?" Jumpe asked in a low but thunderous voice. He stopped uncomfortably close to where Deacon Abell sat and stared down at him, his thick hands hanging clawlike at his sides.

"We were—that is, I, sir," Abell stammered, "would like details on Young Ezekiel's killer—?"

Almost before Abell had finished speaking, Uncle Henry said, "The man who killed him is an Arizona Ranger named Sam Burrack." He looked back and forth at the seated men. "I spotted him with my telescope on the ridge where poor Ezekiel's body was later found. From what I know about this Ranger, it's my belief that he is on our trail. That being the case, I'll either kill or capture him the minute he sticks his head up in Gun Valley."

Deacon Abell cleared his throat nervously.

"Very well, then," he said. "In that case—"

"But that wasn't what I heard you asking," Uncle Henry said gruffly. Taking a step even closer, the crotch of his trousers almost in the frightened deacon's face, he stared down. "I heard you asking if I was capable of sinking his head on a stake. And I am, sir," he added, "if that's to be the way of things. Allow me to show you how I would do it."

"Plea-please, no—" Abell groveled.

Ignoring Abell's plea, Jumpe snatched an imaginary handful of hair right in front of the deacon's face, and said. "I would grab him like this while he's still alive." His hand went behind his back beneath the swallow-tailed coat and came back around with a vicious swing of a glistening bowie knife. The deacon's eyes filled wide with terror as the big sharp edge of the blade stopped short right against the side of his neck.

The other deacons gasped. Barcinder gave a cruel smile. Abell's face turned the color of dried bone. The blood vessels in his eyes appeared to swell twice their size as his eyes bulged, horrified.

Lowering the knife, Henry Jumpe took a step back, looked at the other men with a shrug and said, "Of course, if I took more than one swing, I would simply swing harder the second time." He gave a broad grin, still looking back and forth. "Any other questions?"

A tense silence set in for a moment until Barcinder stepped forward and smiled.

"In that case, Deacons," he said, "you are all three excused." He gestured a hand down at the floor beneath Deacon Abell's chair and added quietly, "Please watch where you step on your way out."

When the men had left, Barcinder turned to Henry Jumpe and said in a lowered voice, "If the Ranger comes here, you deal with him straight-away."

"What did I just say?" said Jumpe with a cool gaze.

"Once a man has been soundly accused, nobody wants to find out he's innocent." He smiled. "Isn't that the way of human nature?"

"I don't know nothing about human nature," said Jumpe. "I just know that anytime I need money, there's somebody needs killing or catching."

"Exactly." Barcinder beamed. "Now go *catch* the Ranger. Keep him alive if you can, for Dad's own pleasure."

"Dead, alive." Jumpe shrugged. "It's all the same to me."

Chapter 18

Pushing hard along the hill trails, the Ranger followed the hoofprints left by Mattie's dapple gray onto the flatlands and stopped where two new sets of prints joined them. The Ranger was well aware that she had traded clothes with her sister not only to fool him, but also to make her way through whatever guards and gunmen Dad Orwick had protecting his lair.

Did she realize how dangerous this game could get if anything went wrong?

Sam studied the hoofprints, seeing no indication of a struggle. Yes, he decided, of course she knew the risks. Mattie was nobody's fool. She was headstrong, self-reliant and self-possessed—not about to be dissuaded from what she'd set out to do. But he'd seen no signs of foolishness in her.

The life she'd been forced to lead had not dampened or killed her spirit. Rather, over the passing of time, Dad Orwick's dominance and abuse had only served to strengthen her resolve. As his eyes followed the three sets of tracks off across the flatlands, Sam realized that Orwick had—with every bite of the whip across the young child's back—forged in the child that which one day would return and destroy him.

And so it goes. . . .

Sam nudged the copper dun forward along the three sets of tracks. Within only yards of where Mattie and the two riders had met, three new sets of tracks had come from the other side of the flatlands and confronted them. Still, no signs of struggle or disagreement, Sam noted.

"Whatever you're telling them, Mattie, keep it up," he murmured to himself.

For the next seven miles, Sam followed the tracks across the flatlands, onto a thinner trail leading up among rocks and scrub cedar around the side of a steep stony ridge. As the copper dun made its way up the narrow winding trail, the Ranger looked down at the six sets of hooves that had now tightened and formed into twos.

Looking up and all around along the boulders and overreaching cliffs towering above him, the Ranger took off his sombrero and laid it on his lap. With the reins in his left hand, he loosened his dusty bandanna, shook it out and wiped his forehead. When he draped the bandanna back around his neck, he left his sombrero off, hooked its strap around his saddle horn and rode on.

Twenty yards farther up the trail, he saw the three gunmen appear suddenly, sitting atop their horses in the middle of the trail facing him. One rider held an aimed rifle to his shoulder; the other two held cocked and aimed revolvers at arm's length.

"Arizona Ranger," the rifleman said, noting the badge on Sam's chest. To his two companions he said, "Brethren, this day has truly blessed us abundantly."

Sam sat still as stone atop the cooper dun, staring at the three men, summing up them and their horses. The horses stepped restlessly in place and had to be checked down firmly— handsome, well cared-for animals, Sam noted, but not trail hardened, he'd bet.

The man with the rifle appeared the eldest, the more experienced, yet still not as at-ease as a man who made his living with a gun. The other two were younger, around Sam's age, but neither with the bearing of men who could face bullets being shot at them and keep the kind of cool, level head needed for killing.

"Lift the rifle with your left hand and toss it aside," the rifleman said.

Sam lifted the cocked Winchester with his left hand, but he held it suspended for a moment.

"How much farther to the compound?" he asked, much like one man asking another for the time of the day.

For a moment the rifleman appeared as if he was tempted to answer Sam instinctively. But he caught himself and steadied the rifle.

"Never you mind how far," he said evenly. "You'll not be going there. Now toss the rifle away."

But the Ranger only raised the outheld Winchester another inch as if ready to toss it away, but not quite yet.

"I'm following a woman and two other riders headed there," he said. "I don't suppose—?"

"Brother Lowery, Brother Anders!" the man said, getting edgy, cutting Sam off. "If he doesn't toss the rifle away when I count three, shoot him down."

"Shoot him?" said one of the younger men, looking away from his revolver toward the rifleman as he asked.

"Yes, Brother, shoot him! Are you deaf?" the rifleman said.

Getting rattled, Sam gauged, watching him.

"One!" the rifleman called out with determination.

"All right, stop," Sam said. "I'm tossing it. See?" He raised the cocked rifle and pitched it away, in a manner that caused it to stand straight up and strike the hard ground butt first. The hammer fell; a blue-orange blast of fire exploded from its barrel.

All three men flinched in surprise; their horses almost bolted. The riders tightened their hold on the spooked animals as the Ranger flipped his sombrero aside with the tip of his big Colt lying cocked in his hand beneath it.

Jerking the dun's head to his left, quarterwise, the Ranger fired, once, twice, three times, seeing the rifle and the revolvers fly from the men's hands and the men fly from their saddles. He saw two of the horses rear and bolt away, breaking from the trail, racing and sliding down the steep hillside. The third frightened animal turned tail, bucking and kicking, and ran away, following the hill trail out of sight.

Sam nudged the copper dun forward through a cloud of smoke, stopped and looked down, his Colt still cocked and ready. On the ground one of the younger men held a bloody hand up toward him.

"Please, don't shoot no more," he said. "I'm dead here."

Sam stepped down from the copper dun and unhooked his canteen strap from his saddle horn out of habit. He looked at the two men sprawled dead in the dirt and stepped over to the one who lay panting and clutching his bloody chest.

"One of Dad's brethren saints, I take it?" Sam said, stooping down beside him. He uncapped the canteen and offered it to him.

"Yes . . . that's right," the man said. "I—I didn't die in vain. I'll be rewarded . . . for this, you know." He shook his head toward the canteen.

Sam noted desperation in his trembling voice.

"I hope so," he said. He ran his fingers back through his damp hair and looked around. "Who're the two men riding with the woman?" he asked.

"Two of Dad's gunmen . . . escorting Miss Isabelle to the new compound," the man said in a strained voice.

"Isabelle," Sam said.

"Yes . . . one of Dad's older wives," he said. "But she's . . . not anymore."

"Because Dad has replaced all of his wives with some younger women," Sam said.

"He had . . . good cause to do so, Ranger," the wounded man said, defending his leader's actions. "Some of them . . . were too close akin. A man has to be careful of that . . . with so many wives."

Sam didn't understand, but he nodded anyway.

"How many of Dad's gunmen are going to be waiting for me at the new compound?" he asked.

"Most of the gunmen . . . have drawn out and gone," the man said. "But Dad's saints will kill you . . . for what you did, killing Dad's son."

"I didn't kill that boy," Sam said.

"Dad was told you're to blame . . . so you'll die for it," the man said.

"Blame . . . ?" said Sam. "If anybody's to *blame,* it's Orwick. He should have taught his son, if he shoots at people there's a possibility people will shoot back."

"His son Ezekiel lived for a cause . . . ordained by God," the dying man said. "What cause do you . . . live or die for?"

Sam didn't bother answering. He looked at the man's revolver lying a few feet away.

"I shot one of Dad's outlaws, night before last. It was almost the same as this. He asked me for a gun with a bullet in it so he could spare himself being eaten by wolves."

"So," the man said, "are you asking . . . if I want a gun for that same reason—to end my own life?"

Sam stared at him and said, "Night *will* come. So will the wolves. If you're still alive, lying here . . ." He let his words trail, knowing the man got the grim picture.

"Keep the gun. I will not condemn my soul to hell . . . committing murder on myself."

"You'd rather watch the wolves rip out your belly?" Sam said, offering it as harshly as he could.

"If that's God's will," the man said, clutching his stomach with both hands now against the spreading circle of blood. "If you shoot me . . . it's a different matter," he added.

Sam saw the pleading in his eyes.

"You would have me commit the sin, but the sin is beneath you?" he said, picking up the gun from the ground.

The man just stared at him.

Sam said, "I saved you from sinning when I shot you before you could shoot me."

"You're a murderer anyway," the man said. "Your soul has . . . never been cleansed by forgiveness. Mine has."

"Good point," Sam said, dismissing the matter.

He turned to the dun and stepped up into his saddle.

"Wait," the man said. "You can't just leave me here . . . like this."

"What do you want me to do?" Sam asked, staring down intently at him.

The man only looked on, clenching his jaw.

"It's your call," Sam said. "Make it, or I ride away."

"I—I can't," the man said, shaking his head. "Don't you see I can't?"

"Yes, I see," Sam said. He nudged the dun along the trail. But in a few yards he stopped and took a deep breath. He looked back at the wounded man who sat trembling, staring out across the rocky land. The sun had made its turn in the sky and leaned to the west.

No, he couldn't leave him here like this, Sam told himself.

The man never heard the gunshot; he only felt the sudden impact of it, and only for a split second at that.

The Ranger watched his body flop over onto its side. He sat for a moment in contemplation. Then he pitched the smoking gun away and turned forward in his saddle. Nudging the copper dun, he rode on.

Later in the afternoon he lost the tracks belonging to Mattie and the other two riders' horses crossing a stone plateau above the eastern canyon of the Valley of the Gun. Fortunately, when he'd crossed the plateau and ridden on a few miles through a thick pine forest perched on a long sloping hillside, he picked up a wagon trail marked with fresh wheel prints. He'd followed the wagon trail for three miles when he spotted smoke rising from a partially hidden gully and crept forward on a cliff overhang for a better look.

In the rocky gully he saw a single Conestoga-style wagon sitting with a team of oxen still hitched to it. Around the wagon he saw women and children busily at work, the children chopping and carrying wood from a deadfall pine, the women preparing the evening meal over a large campfire.

Were they Dad's people? Yes, he was certain of it.

But looking all around closely and seeing no sign of Mattie or her dapple gray, Sam eased back from the cliff's edge, rose in a crouch and turned to walk back to the dun, his rifle in hand. Before taking a step he froze in place, seeing the copper dun facing him from the edge of the trail, a young boy holding the horse by its reins. Behind a tall rock, a man clutching a long shotgun stepped into sight and stood close behind the boy.

"This is as far as you're going, lawman," the man said.

Sam looked all around, seeing more men with

shotguns and rifles step into sight half circling him, each of them standing closely flanked by wide-eyed children.

"Do not test us, Ranger," another of the gunmen warned, seeing a look on Sam's face that showed no sign of surrender. This man stood behind a young girl with long blond braids draping down past her thin shoulders. She clutched a rag doll against her chest.

"These are your own children?" Sam asked quietly, appearing surprised that men would do such a thing as put children between the sights of loaded guns.

"Mister, they are the Lord's children, and of course Dad Orwick's," said the gunman standing behind the young boy. "We are only given their charge for a time, until Dad or the Lord sees otherwise fit to call upon them."

"What happens now is a lot up to you, Ranger," said a man holding a pointed rifle, a young boy on his left, a younger girl on his right.

"What's Dad going to say when he finds out you held these children hostages in a gunfight?" he asked, stalling, looking for any way out, any way but *this*.

"Dad knows that we're out here to do his bidding," the man between the two children said. "Anything that happens to these innocent young ones will be your fault, and nobody else's."

My fault? Sam looked back and forth. Recalling

the words and lopsided rationale of the men he'd killed earlier, he realized there was no talking to these people, no reasoning with their blind side, no getting through the layers of their religious madness. It was useless to try.

"Now drop your rifle," another man said. "Let not the blood of the innocent be upon your head."

"And what happens then?" Sam asked, already knowing he had to give up his guns or start the bloodletting. Had he the slightest notion that these men were bluffing, he wouldn't give up his guns. Yet as he looked back and forth, he realized, there was no room here to call even their bluff. Either he would give up his guns or the next moment bullets would be flying. He stood tense, waiting for a reply.

"Once we have your guns, we're taking you to Dad," said the man standing behind the young girl with the blond braids. "It will be Dad's decision—and God's, of course—whatever is to become of you, Ranger. We will have fulfilled our duty to Dad and our church."

"Dad can't ask for more than that, I suppose," Sam said under his breath, lowering his rifle, letting it fall from his hands.

Chapter 19

As Mattie, Frank Bannis and Morton Kerr drew nearer to the new Orwick compound in the long shadows of evening, a band of armed churchmen rode forward out of the rocks on either side of the valley trail and formed a circle surrounding them. At the center of the riders, Uncle Henry sat atop his horse with a rifle perched on his thigh, his peg leg sticking out to the side.

"Uh-oh," Morton Kerr said under his breath, "Uncle Henry's got his peg out." He glanced sidelong at Mattie.

Mattie sat in silence, staring, listening. *Learning as I go,* she told herself.

Kerr caught the blank expression on her face.

Looking all around at the circling riflemen men, Frank Bannis shook his head and gave a sarcastic chuff under his breath.

"Uncle Henry," he called out, "has anybody ever explained the drawbacks of a circular firing squad to these *brethren?*"

"You're real funny, Bannis," Jumpe said in a flat tone. "I believe what these men lack in experience they'll overcome in enthusiasm, especially if I tell them to shoot the tops of your heads off."

"I share your belief in that, Uncle Henry," said

Bannis, his own rifle leveled at Henry Jumpe's belly. "At the same time, let me *share* with you that I never look forward to dying alone." He cocked the rifle and gave a menacing smile.

"Well, then," said Jumpe, seeming to settle down, "now that we've convinced one another we can both pass water the same distance, I'll inquire what you're doing, bringing one of Dad's wives here." He looked Mattie up and down.

Offering only a flat stare, Mattie made it a noticeable point to look Jumpe up and down in return.

"I can speak for myself, Uncle Henry," she said, using the name she'd heard Frank Bannis call him.

"I know you can, Isabelle," Uncle Henry said stiffly, "but I'll suggest you do so sparingly. You've caused enough trouble, getting poor Brother Phillip beaten senseless—"

"She didn't cause that, Jumpe," Bannis said, stopping the man short. "I gave him that beating. Guess why." He stared coldly at Jumpe.

Uncle Henry caught the threat in Bannis' words. He proceeded on, yet now with a more amiable tone.

"I prefer to hear it from you, Isabelle," he said, "Brother Phillip being your new husband."

"Brother Phillip turned out to be a jealous man," Mattie said. "He attacked Mr. Bannis for no reason at all. Mr. Bannis defended himself as any man must do. I stepped in to defend Brother

Phillip, which was right for me to do as his wife, yet wrong to do under the circumstances."

"Oh . . . ?" said Jumpe. "And yet I have never heard any suspicion of Brother Phillip being that sort of man."

"With all respect, Uncle Henry, who would you hear it from?" Mattie said, playing it just right. "Wives do not reveal such things about their husbands. We are taught not to." She stared at him knowingly.

Jumpe considered the matter for a moment.

"Well," he said, "it's something Dad or Elder Barcinder will have to decide on."

Mattie nodded slightly and said, "Any particulars needed, I'll be glad to express to Dad *in person* when I see him. No one else."

Jumpe looked away from her and back at Bannis and Morton Kerr.

"I suppose you'll report what you saw on your pard's behalf?" he said to Kerr.

"Only as much as it's the truth," Kerr said defensively, even though he was lying.

"The truth?" Jumpe looked skeptical.

"Damn right, *the truth*," said Kerr. "I might not be one of the *saints*." He swept a narrowed look of contempt across the armed churchmen. "But I'm not a damned liar either."

"Disappointing, ain't it, Uncle Henry," said Bannis, "if you were counting on getting bathed and dressed up to come to my hanging."

Looking off along the trail behind them, Jumpe spotted a single rider racing toward them, leading a tall rise of dust in his wake.

"I'm not looking forward to seeing you hang, Bannis," said Jumpe. "On the contrary, I was a little bit happy to see you riding in."

"Yeah . . . ?" Bannis just stared at him, curious.

"Most of your pards have drawn their shares and cut out of here—the ones that haven't vanished or gotten themselves killed, that is."

"If they had money coming and didn't show up for it, they're *dead,*" Bannis said with resolve.

He looked off with Jumpe and the others at the coming rider.

"Damn! Wonder what's he feeding that horse to make it run so fast." Kerr chuckled. "I'm lucky I can get a horse to walk a straight line."

"The thing is," said Jumpe, looking back at Bannis, "I could use you and Morton. I've got some lawman to hunt down—"

"Uncle Henry," said one of the churchmen, cutting him off. "This looks important." He gestured toward the speeding rider.

"Brother Stubbens," Uncle Henry said with sarcasm, "feel free to cut right in anytime you think you have something more important to say than I do."

"Forgive me, Uncle Henry," the man said, "but this is one of the brothers from the cliff guard. He must be riding relay."

All eyes turned to the approaching rider until the horse slid down to a walk the last few yards.

Jumpe turned back to Bannis, Mattie and Kerr.

"The three of yas ride on in. Whether or not you can see Dad will be up to Elder Barcinder." He looked at Bannis directly. "We'll talk later about you riding with me, if you get everything settled and cleared up with the powers-that-be."

"I'll get it cleared up," Bannis said confidently.

He touched his hat brim to Uncle Henry. The three collected their horses beneath them. The churchmen opened their circled ranks to allow them forward as the single rider stopped in front of Uncle Henry.

"Jones," Uncle Henry said, recognizing the rider, "I hope you're worth all the dust you've moved around out here."

"Uncle Henry," the rider said, out of breath, "I just had a relay rider come to my lookout cliff a while ago. He said some of our brethren have captured the Ranger."

"My, my," said Jumpe. "That certainly is some good news. Was he riding with a posse?"

"No, he was riding alone," said the relay rider. "They've got him and they're headed this way. They should be arriving here sometime in the night."

Uncle Henry looked off along the far trail, rubbing his chin.

"Sometime tonight . . . ," he said in contemplation.

"Midnight or later, I'd put it," the rider said, taking off his hat and slapping dust from the front of his shirt.

Uncle Henry drew his face back from the stirred cloud of dust. He gave the man a harsh sour look.

"I hope there's not a posse following him, lying back, waiting for a chance to slip in on us," he said, fanning a hand in front of his face.

"I hadn't thought of that," the relay rider said, putting his hat back on. He took an uncapped canteen one of the churchmen held out to him.

"I'm sure you haven't," said Jumpe, eyeing him up and down with the same sour expression. "When you finish watering yourself and throwing dirt in our faces, ride on to the compound, tell Elder Barcinder these men and I are riding out to escort the wagon just in case."

"I'm sorry about the dust, Uncle Henry," said Jones, "but isn't this joyous news?" His dusty face suddenly beamed with a smile; his eyes took on a glazed and blissful shine. "Don't we all just thank God for such a blessing?"

"Amen," said some of the churchmen in unison.

"Amen!" said Jones, uplifting his eyes and his right palm toward heaven.

"Yeah, right. *Amen,*" said Uncle Henry dismissingly. "Now get out of here—save it for church."

• • •

On their way to the compound, Mattie, Bannis and Kerr examined their surroundings at the sound of galloping hooves. After a moment the relay rider raced toward them in the evening gloom. They moved to the side of the trail and watched him streak past them, his horse kicking up fresh dust.

"Son of a . . . ," Bannis growled. He stopped and let his words trail out of courtesy to the woman. Untying a wide bandanna from around his neck, he held it over to Mattie and said, "Ma'am, hold this to your face. It's dusty itself, but it beats nothing."

"And what about you, Frank?" Mattie asked.

"Don't worry about me, ma'am," he said. "Dust never bothers me much."

Mattie smiled at him through the rising dust. Taking the wadded-up bandanna, she held it to her face.

"I insist you call me Isabelle," she said.

"Obliged, ma'am," said Bannis, "but it just isn't fitting, you being a married woman."

"I admire your manners, Frank," she said, breathing through the bandanna.

"Wonder what all that's about," Kerr said, nodding toward the rider who was already fading out of sight into the darkness and the dust.

"Could be most anything, Morton," Bannis commented. "The least thing seems to work these churchmen into a frenzy."

Kerr chuckled and spit, turning forward in his saddle.

"They're worse than a bunch of nervous women-folk," he said.

Bannis cut his eyes to Mattie.

"He meant no offense to you, ma'am," he said.

"No offense taken," Mattie replied, managing a smile. Nudging her horse along between Bannis and Kerr, Mattie let out a tight breath in relief. *So far, so good,* she told herself.

When they reached the upturning trail onto a steep hillside, they stopped as two churchmen stepped their horses out from among the rocks.

"We're here to see Elder Barcinder," Bannis said to the two horsemen, recognizing them both. The two horsemen recognized the three of them in return, brought their horses in on either side of them and gestured them forward up the hillside.

At the top of the hill where the land leveled onto a clearing, the two horsemen drew back and waited until the three had hitched their horses at a rail and stepped down from their saddles. They waited as three riflemen walked down from the porch of a large house built into the hillsides.

"Your guns," one of the men said. "Hang your gun belts over your saddle horns. We'll show you to the house."

Mattie stood silent, watching as Bannis and Kerr unbuckled their gun belts and draped them over their saddle horns. Mattie took note of the fact that they hadn't even looked at her, or bothered to ask if she might have a gun.

Real good. . . .

Following one rifleman up toward the large house, the other two walking behind them, the three stopped outside the front door and waited until another man opened the door from inside and motioned them in. Inside, they followed the man across the floor of the large room and into an office. As the office door shut, Elder Barcinder stood up behind a wide desk and motioned for the three to be seated.

"Frank Bannis," Barcinder said, right to the point, "explain to me why I should not have you hanged for what you did to Brother Phillip Kendrick."

Bannis looked at Mattie, then at Morton Kerr. Turning back to Barcinder, he told him every-thing the same way Mattie had explained it all to Uncle Henry Jumpe. When he'd finished, the three sat in silence while Barcinder lit a thick cigar, blew out a thin stream of gray smoke in contemplation, and sat down in his large leather chair. As he took another deep draw on the cigar, he stared at Mattie.

"Is all this true, Isabelle?" he asked her.

"Every word of it," Mattie replied.

"There will be those here who will still want to see you hanged for laying a hand on one of our brethren," he said to Bannis. To Mattie he said, "When will Dad and I expect to see Brother Phillip and hear what he says about this?"

"Any day now," Mattie said quietly.

"Very well, then," said Barcinder. "We'll wait until he shows up and settle this matter completely. If he tells us the same story as I've heard it here tonight, we'll dismiss the entire matter." He smiled behind his cigar.

Seeing Barcinder was ready to send the three of them away, Mattie spoke up quickly as he rose to his feet.

"I need to see Dad," she said. "I have some personal matters that need discussing."

"Now, Isabelle," said Barcinder, "you know the rules. Once a wife is unbound, there's to be no more contact."

"I understand," Mattie said, "but this is something too important to dismiss."

"Too important to dismiss?" questioned Barcinder. "It would have to be a matter of life and death in order for Dad to bend the rules."

"It is a matter of life and death," Mattie said.

"In that case, you need to first tell me," Barcinder said. "I'll be the judge of whether or not you'll be permitted to present the matter to Dad."

"No," Mattie said, "I won't talk to anyone but Dad himself. All the years we were together, surely he can talk to me."

Barcinder let out a sigh.

"I'll ask him, Isabelle," he said. "That's all I can do." He looked away from her when a quiet knock drew his attention to the office door. "Yes, please come in," he called out.

Two plainly dressed women near Mattie's age walked into the office and stood on either side of her chair.

"You know my wives Anna and Stowie," he said to Mattie. "They'd like you to spend the night at their home down the hill. Tomorrow, after you've rested, I'll have an answer for you from Dad."

Mattie looked back and forth. The two women smiled at her. One laid a hand on her shoulder. Realizing she had little choice in the matter, she stood up and resolved herself.

"All right, then," she said. "A night's sleep sounds like just what I need."

When the three women turned to leave, Bannis and Kerr started to rise also. But Barcinder motioned for them to remain seated. The two looked at each other and relaxed. Bannis caught himself looking toward the door when it shut. Knowing how it would seem if he appeared too attentive to one of the saints' wives, he looked quickly back at Elder Barcinder.

Barcinder smiled and drew on his cigar.

"I'm glad the two of you happened in here this evening," he said. "Some big changes are about to take place. I can use the help of a couple of gunmen like yourselves." He picked up a wooden engraved cigar box from atop his desk, opened it and held it out to them.

Each man took a cigar and looked up at Barcinder as he set the box back on his desk.

"Does this have anything to do with the relay rider who passed us on the way here?" Kerr asked. "Is there a posse headed here you need our help with?"

"No, nothing like that," said Barcinder, "although the rider did come to tell me they've caught the Ranger who killed some of your men."

"Oh?" said Kerr. "So you want us to kill the Ranger?"

As Kerr spoke, Bannis just sat studying Barcinder, listening closely.

"No," Barcinder said, "he's small potatoes." He brushed aside the idea of killing the Ranger. "Besides, Dad wants to take care of the Ranger himself for killing Young Ezekiel."

"The Ranger killed Young Ezekiel?" Kerr said. He shook his head and said, "Well, if it was the Ranger you wanted killed, I'd kill him straight up, *for free—*"

"Morton, shut up," said Bannis without taking his eyes off Barcinder. "He told you it's not the Ranger. I've got a feeling it's somebody much more important."

"I always said you're a smart man, Frank," Barcinder said. Grinning, he struck a large match and held it out to Bannis' cigar.

"Nice of you to say so, Elder Barcinder," Bannis replied. He drew on the cigar until the tip glowed red. "Just tell us when you'd like this killing to take place and how much you're paying us when we get it done." He paused, then asked, "What about Uncle Henry? Is he going to be a problem?"

"On the contrary," Barcinder said, "Jumpe is with me on this all the way."

Kerr looked dumbfounded.

"Who is it we're killing anyway?" he asked.

"He's wanting us to kill Dad Orwick," Bannis said in a lowered tone. "Now shut up, Morton. Let's hear what the good *churchman* here has in mind."

Chapter 20

When Barcinder's two wives escorted Mattie from the house, they walked flanking her like guards until they were on the trail leading downhill from the large house to where they lived in one of the long plank buildings on the valley floor. One of the women carried a small oil lantern to light their way. Walking down the dark trail, Mattie looked back toward the house.

"What about my horse?" she asked.

"Don't worry, Isabelle," said Stowie, a tall, thin woman whose hair hung in a single long braid down her back. "Someone will take the horse to the common barn down here where we're going."

As the three walked on, Anna sidled up close to Mattie and looked all around as if to make sure she wouldn't be overheard.

"If you're unhappy about being unbound and replaced, don't feel alone, dear. So are we," she said almost in a whisper.

"There are seven of us Barcinder wives, and we're every one being replaced as soon as Elder Barcinder brings his new wives down from the territories," Anna said in the same guarded tone. "From what we're able to gather, all the saints' wives are as upset as we are."

Mattie looked both women up and down.

"If everybody is so upset, why doesn't anybody do anything about it?" she asked, even though she knew the question was meaningless.

"You know why, Isabelle," said Stowie. "These are our husbands. The Lord says we have to obey them."

Keep quiet, Mattie warned herself. Nothing had changed here, not in all the ten years since she'd made her getaway.

"One good thing about all of us being replaced," Anna offered, "is that since we've been in Mexico, we've sometimes had a chance to talk to other wives when no one is watching. We've gotten to share information about our children, where they've gone, what wonderful people they've become."

Mattie clenched her jaw as they walked on. She

wasn't going to ask anyone anything, not until after she'd killed Dad Orwick. If there was time afterward, she would ask about her children. But not now. For now, killing Dad was foremost on her mind.

"It's terrible that all of us have lived so close together over the years, yet we've never been allowed to visit and keep in close touch with each other," said Stowie.

"I wouldn't say we haven't been allowed," Anna offered. "Perhaps *not been encouraged* is a better way of putting it." She smiled in the circling glow of lantern light.

Mattie kept her thoughts to herself. These were women who did not realize how much had been taken from them over the course of their lives. If they did, she wouldn't have to tell them to do something about it; they would have done so on their own, the way she'd had to do those many years ago.

When they reached the bottom of the hill a few minutes later and turned off the trail toward a long, plain building, the two women stopped and turned to Mattie.

"We know we shouldn't do this, Isabelle, but would you like to see Dad's new wives?" Anna whispered.

"Yes, I would," Mattie replied. "Are they nearby?"

Anna pointed at another building standing thirty yards away in the pale moonlight.

"They're staying there until the bonding ceremony," Anna whispered. "Stowie, put out the lantern," she said.

In the pale moonlight, the three crept forward hand in hand to the rear of the building and up to a dusty rear window. Looking inside, Mattie made out a long, sparsely furnished room. Small army-style cots lined the wall, a large potbellied stove stood in a far corner, a few small bundles of clothes and personal items were arranged on the floor. Then Mattie looked closer at the five young women gathered around a small table in a corner, two of them sewing, one brushing another's hair.

"My God, they're only babies," she whispered to Stowie and Anna. She became so stricken by the sight of the young women who looked barely in their teens that she turned around and leaned against the building for support.

"Maybe so," Anna whispered, leaning beside her, "but they're the right age to start bringing new babies into the world."

"They're no younger than we were," Stowie whispered. "Dad and his saints like to start them breeding young. Anyway," she sighed softly, "that's the new wives, soon to be bound in spirit to Dad."

"They've replaced you, just as other young women are on their way to replace us," Anna whispered, giving a quiet little giggle. "I can't say I'm sorry."

"Neither can I," said Stowie.

Mattie felt her stomach churn, seeing the young girls inside the building, a building no different from an army barracks or a prison dormitory.

"I want to go on," she said, pushing away from the building.

The two women looked at each other.

"This way," Stowie whispered.

Carrying the blackened lantern, she led the way to their own building. But she and Anna both stopped outside and turned to Mattie.

"The others are looking forward to seeing you, Isabelle," said Stowie, "but before we go in, we want to tell you how much it meant to us, what your sister, Mattie, did years ago, getting away."

Mattie only stared at them. She knew Isabelle must've taken some harsh comments and cold stares from the men—Dad's handpicked *saints*.

Anna cut in, saying, "We know she violated the rules and even broke the sacred covenant our people have with God. But in spite of that, when she ran away, most of us always felt like a little piece of ourselves went with her."

"Of course we couldn't come out and say it," said Stowie. "We even made ill remarks ourselves, just to look right in Dad's eyes." She squeezed Mattie's forearm affectionately. "But wasn't there something grand and joyous in her gaining her freedom?"

"Wherever she is, do you suppose she would feel good knowing that?" Anna asked.

Mattie felt her eyes well up with tears. She held them back as best she could.

"Oh my goodness, yes, gals," she whispered. "I just know she would." In spite of her effort, she felt a single tear spill down her cheek.

"Gals . . . ?" Stowie smiled. "Gracious me, Isabelle, I don't believe I've been called a *gal* since as far back as I can remember."

"Well, you are *gals,*" Mattie said, collecting herself. "We all are. We've had a lot of things taken from us—but we're still all *gals* at heart."

"Old *gals* now," Stowie said with a tired smile.

"It's too bad we haven't talked like this over the years," Anna said.

"They would never have allowed it," Mattie said with a bitter twist to her voice. Then she asked, "Do you have any idea where you'll go when the new wives are bounded?"

The two looked at each other.

"No." Anna shrugged. "I once overheard Elder Barcinder tell another of the saints that it is a shame the women are not treated as well as their riding stock and field beasts. He said the animals were dealt with more humanely than we."

"At least Elder Barcinder has our best interests in mind," Stowie said.

"Yes, he's all heart," Mattie said wryly.

"What will you do, Isabelle?" Anna asked.

Mattie remained silent for a moment, but finally couldn't help herself.

"I'm leaving the first chance I get," she said.

"You mean going to where Brother Phillip sends you?" Anna asked.

"No," Mattie said, "I'm leaving on my own. You're welcome to join me if you like. Only keep quiet about it. Meanwhile I need to look around the compound some without you saying anything. Can I count on you?"

"We're not supposed to keep secrets from our husband, Isabelle. You know that," Stowie said, on the verge of chastising her.

"He won't be our husband much longer, Stowie," Anna said. She looked at Mattie and saw the apprehension in her eyes. "Don't worry. We won't say anything about your comings and goings. But I don't think we can just up and leave with you."

"Why not?" Mattie asked. "There'll be nothing to hold you here. All you'll have to do is slip away and go."

"You make it sound easy," Anna said, "but it's not."

"Not unless someone tells us it's all right," said Stowie.

Mattie just took a deep breath and nodded, understanding their thinking on the matter.

"If you decide to change your mind, you better do so quickly," she said. "When it's time to go, I'm gone."

The two turned with her toward the door to the building.

"Now you sound like your sister, Matilda, all those years ago," Anna said. "Had we gone with her back then, God forbid, there's no telling where we'd be today."

In the middle of the night, the wagon rolled into the center of the torchlit compound with armed churchmen surrounding it. From the edge of the darkness, Frank Bannis and Morton Kerr stepped forward and watched as Uncle Henry Jumpe and two of his men dragged the Ranger to the rear of the wagon and threw him to the ground. One of the men—a large fellow with a red-gray beard, two purpling swollen eyes and a red swollen nose—saw the Ranger land on the hard ground with a grunt.

"There, lawman," he said, "that serves you right for laying hands on one of us."

The Ranger wobbled to his feet and stood with his hands tied in front of him. His left eye was puffed and red. Once standing, he steadied himself and looked all around, like a man who had no plans for staying there long. He looked on as a churchman unhitched his copper dun from behind the wagon and led the spirited horse away toward a long common barn.

"The Ranger must've nailed the big fellow in the nose before they tied his hands," Kerr offered to Bannis, who stood beside him.

"Not so," said a young outlaw named Riley

Dart, overhearing him. Dart had met the church-men and Uncle Henry along the trail. "His hands were tied when he got him," he said in a lowered voice. "The big fellow backhanded him for no reason, but the Ranger was having none of it. He grabbed the big fellow by both ears and head-butted him three times hard as he could before the other *brethren* pulled him away."

"Jesus," said Kerr, "that had to hurt."

"Yep, I bet it did," said Dart. He grinned. "But it was fun as hell to watch."

"What are you doing here, Dart?" Bannis asked.

"I came looking for you, Bannis," Dart said, "like you said I should if I needed work."

"You're about three weeks late, Dart," Bannis said.

"Funny, that's exactly how long I was stuck in jail over in Sonora," Dart said with a smile. "I guess if everything's all done here, I'll just ride on and see what's past the next hill line."

Bannis and Kerr looked at each other.

"Stick around, Dart," Bannis said. "We might have something you'll want to help us out with. I can't imagine you'd mind shooting holes in somebody, would you? For pay, that is?"

"I'm up for shooting holes in somebody, pay or not, Frank," the young outlaw said, "as long as I don't have to answer to these religious sons a' bitches."

Bannis grinned at Kerr knowingly.

"No problem there," he said to Dart.

As the churchmen stepped down and dragged the Ranger off toward a small timber and iron-clad building, Bannis gave Kerr and Riley Dart a nod and the three outlaws followed along behind them.

From back in the shadows, Elder Barcinder stood watching as Uncle Henry Jumpe walked over, his peg leg thumping with each step, and stopped in front of him.

"There's the Ranger, signed, sealed and delivered to you," Jumpe said, a thick hand resting on the big pistol holstered and tied down on his hip. "It looks like everything's starting to go our way on this thing."

"Indeed it does," said Barcinder.

"Are you going to tell Dad we caught him tonight?" Jumpe asked, glancing up toward the largest house on the dark hillside, where a trimmed lantern was glowing low in a second-story window.

"Tonight?" said Barcinder. "Oh no, I don't think so tonight." He gave a thin, twisted little smile and held his hands folded behind his back. "Dad left orders not to be disturbed."

"I see," said Uncle Henry. "Then I take it he must be busy breaking in one of his new wives tonight?" He glanced again up toward the large house.

"The Lord's work must go on," Elder Barcinder

said with the same twisted smile. In a lowered tone he added, "He has several new wives to choose from—each one of them as sweet as a handful of peaches."

Jumpe shook his head slowly and wiped a hand across his brow just envisioning the scene.

"Whew," he said. "Times like these, I'd say the Lord's work is plumb enviable."

"Yes, it is," said Barcinder. He stepped forward, closer to Uncle Henry. "But keep in mind, the Lord helps those who help themselves. Once we do what God has commanded me to do and take this ministry over, you'll be ordained as one of my saints, and be required to take on wives of your own." He stared into Jumpe's eyes. "Can you live with that?"

"I can, Elder Barcinder," Jumpe said. "I can also live with taking charge of these outlaws and keeping them in line when we set out to raise money to support ourselves." He paused, then added, "That is, if you don't mind me taking over that responsibility."

"Mind?" said Barcinder. "No, Uncle Henry. I won't mind. In fact, if I never have to lay eyes on another of these robbing, murdering heathens, it will suit me fine."

Chapter 21

Sheriff DeShay and Arlis Fletcher had followed the copper dun's prints to a spot on a bald ridge where something seemed to have gone afoul for the Ranger. Cautious, the two had followed the trail down until they sighted wagon tracks, which appeared to make a wide swing and head off toward the Valley of the Gun. Without speculating aloud, they shared the silent feeling that the Ranger had been taken prisoner by Orwick's men.

Fletcher, still suffering the aftereffects of too much strong mescal, sat slumped to one side in his saddle, an open canteen of tepid water in his hand. Finally he stated what they both knew.

"They got him, Sheriff," he said quietly, looking down, shaking his aching head. "What do you want to do now?"

Sheriff DeShay looked all around in the dark moonlight. Gazing back over his shoulder for an extra moment, he finally turned forward in his saddle and crossed his wrists on the saddle horn.

"I'm going on," he said.

"That's foolish," said Fletcher.

"You asked," said DeShay.

"Yeah, I asked," said Fletcher, "but I've got to call it how I see it."

"You can turn back here," Sheriff DeShay said. "You don't owe me a thing."

"You're damned right I don't," said Fletcher with a slight chuckle under his breath. "And I most especially don't owe the Ranger nothing."

"I'm obliged for your help as long as it lasted, Fletcher," DeShay said. He nudged his horse a step forward.

"Whoa, hold on," said the hungover gunman, sounding suddenly irritated. "What the hell is that supposed to mean—*obliged, as long as it lasted?*"

DeShay stopped his horse and stared at him.

"It means just what it sounds like," he said. "I'm *obliged* for your help. Now go on home."

"Huh-uh," said Fletcher, "you're not getting by with that, saying I haven't done my part."

"Damn it, Fletcher, what the hell is wrong with you?" said DeShay. "I'm trying to say *thanks*. I'm not trying to stick glass in your biscuits."

Fletcher sat staring sullenly at him.

"I just don't want bad said about me later on," Fletcher replied. As he spoke, he almost fell off his horse. But he managed to right himself in his saddle.

"Jesus, look at you, Fletcher," said DeShay. "I don't know if you can make it back home, let alone ride on with me. Are you all right?"

"Damn right, I'm all right," said Fletcher. "I

could ride on if I wanted to. I just don't want to."

"All right, I understand, Arlis," said DeShay. "*Adios*, then." He nudged his horse forward, this time up into a gallop.

Fletcher sat slumped and watched the sheriff ride off into the purple darkness for a moment.

"Damn it," he said aloud to himself, "I've been gut-shot with bad mescal and I know it." He kicked his horse forward behind DeShay and called out, "Wait up, Sheriff. You ain't leaving without me! I've still a hand in this game."

Catching up to DeShay, the gunman swung his horse in close and gave him a scorching look.

"I've never run out and left a job half-finished in my life," he said harshly, "and I won't be accused of it."

DeShay looked him up and down, then turned his head quickly and stared back along the trail behind them.

"Why do you keep doing that?" Fletcher asked, clutching a hand to his growling midsection.

"Doing what?" DeShay asked.

"Looking back like you think somebody's following us," said Fletcher.

DeShay listened closely back along the moonlit trail before answering.

"Because it sounds like somebody's following us," he finally said, his voice lowered. "It sounds like they're coming at a hard gallop and they're getting closer by the minute."

With his hand still gripping his sick stomach, Fletcher listened too.

"You're right, Sheriff," he said. "I say we stop right here and shoot it out with whoever rides up on us."

"No," DeShay said firmly, "we might kill ourselves an innocent person." He lifted a coiled rope from his saddle horn. "I've got a better idea. Let's lift whoever it is from the saddle and see why they're following us."

"I'm with you," said Fletcher.

With a dark chuckle, he took one end of the rope from the sheriff's hand. DeShay let the rope uncoil as the gunman stepped his horse across the trail. Reaching out from his saddle, he wrapped two turns of the rope chest high around a young scrub pine standing near a tall pile of rocks. When he finished tying the rope, he stepped his horse behind the rocks, drew his rifle from its boot and sat waiting.

Across the trail, DeShay secured the other end of the rope in the same manner around a chest-high stand of cactus, then backed his horse away into the darkness as the sound of a single set of hooves pounded closer.

While they waited, DeShay began having second thoughts about what they were going to do. What if it was Morgan Almond or someone else on their side—someone attempting to catch up with them for any number of reasons?

No, this is a bad idea, he told himself.

At the last second, he started to shout out in the night and warn whoever was riding hard on the dark trail. But his change of heart came too late. Before he could get out a word of warning, the pounding hooves sped past him and kept going as a loud *twang* like that of some giant upright bass resounded above the trail. The rope, drawn tight between the cactus and the pine, had the effect of launching the rider from a sling-shot. DeShay heard something *whoosh* backward twenty feet through the air and land with a solid rolling thud.

The sheriff winced at the sound, knowing it was a person landing unexpectedly on the hard, rocky dirt. Farther along the trail the pounding hooves trimmed down to a walk, then stopped. DeShay heard a long agonizing groan and dropped from his saddle, rushing out onto the trail, the big custom pistol cocked in hand. From across the trail, Fletcher did the same.

"Holy *Gawd!*" said Fletcher, the two of them staring down at Lightning Wade Hornady sprawled in the dirt, making a rasping sound as he tried to squeeze air back into his lungs. In the moonlight, they could see where the chest of his duster and shirt had been ripped apart and flung back over his shoulders, torn loose from the tops of his sleeves. Oddly, his hat brim had been ripped off the crown by the taut rope. The tall crown hung down his bare chest by the hat string around his neck, like some strange graining bag. The bandage that had covered his chest wound had been ripped off by the rope. Blood ran down his ribs.

"Let's get him up from there," said DeShay.

Between the two of them, they managed to pull Hornady to his feet as his breath started coming back to him in short gasps. As they walked the dazed outlaw back and forth, DeShay reached down and pulled a big revolver from Hornady's waist and looked at it.

"I could almost feel sorry for you, Lightning, if I didn't know you had every intention of killing us."

"What . . . did you hit . . . me with?" Hornady managed to say.

"Nothing," said DeShay. "We set a skunk trap and you jumped right in it."

"I'll . . . kill you," Hornady said in a squeaking voice.

Both DeShay and Fletcher shook him hard.

"Don't start threatening us, Lightning," DeShay warned. "You're in no shape."

"Are . . . you going to . . . kill me?" Hornady asked, starting to breathe a little better.

"Not if you play your cards right," said DeShay. "We think Dad Orwick's got the Ranger. You're going to guide us to Orwick's compound, get us in past the trail guards."

"I'm not . . . going to do it," said Hornady. "To hell with the Ranger."

DeShay reached up and gave him a sharp rap on the side of his head with Hornady's own long-barreled custom revolver.

"We're not asking—we're telling," he said.

"Jesus, all right," Hornady said in surprise, cupping the side of his head. "I thought you and Dad . . . were on good terms . . . not you and the Ranger."

"Things change," said DeShay. He gave the outlaw a shove to the side of the trail. "You're riding between the two of us and getting us inside the Valley of the Gun. Make one false move, you'll get yourself killed by your own gun." He turned the big custom Simpson-Barre in his hand.

"I'm bleeding," said Hornady. "I'm hurt . . . bad." He gestured at his bare chest, his hat crown hanging by its string.

"You sure are," DeShay said flatly. He raised the brimless hat crown and shoved it atop Hornady's head. "Straighten your duster down over you. Let's get going."

Fletcher cut in, saying, "Give me a minute, Sheriff. I need to walk off into the brush." He held a hand clutched to his belly.

"What's wrong . . . with that one?" Hornady asked as Fletcher hurried away off the trail.

"Bad mescal," said DeShay.

"Oh. . . ." Hornady understood. "If he got it from . . . the old hermit at Munny Caves . . . God help him."

"Yep," said Sheriff DeShay, "that's where he got it."

A little while later the three were mounted and headed farther out along the trail running into the valley. When they reached a large rock shelf standing a hundred feet above one side of the trail, a flickering torch appeared above them and waved back and forth slowly. DeShay and Fletcher sidled up tight against Hornady on either side.

"Halt and be recognized down there," a trail guard called out to them.

"Here's your chance to show us how pretty you can sing," DeShay said to Hornady almost in a whisper. He jammed the big custom revolver into the gunman's ribs.

"Who's down there on the trail?" the voice called out again, sounding impatient.

"It's me, Lightning Wade," Hornady shouted up in reply to the young-sounding voice.

"Lightning Wade, who . . . ?" the voice inquired.

"Damn it to hell," Hornady growled under his breath. "It's Lightning Wade *Hornady,*" he shouted up as loud as his injured chest would allow him to. "I'm riding in to see Dad. He knows I'm coming."

"Who's that with you, Lightning?" another, older-sounding voice called down to them in a gruff tone.

Recognizing the voice, DeShay called out before Hornady could answer.

"It's me, Sheriff DeShay from Whiskey Bend," he said boldly. "The man with me is my new deputy, Arlis Fletcher."

The ridgeline above them fell silent.

"Sit tight right where you are," the gruff voice said. "We're coming down."

"Jesus, Sheriff," Hornady said in a lowered tone. "Why didn't you keep your mouth shut? I could have told them anything."

"Like as not they'll know me from town," said DeShay.

"Like as not you've got us killed if they don't," said Hornady.

Fletcher and DeShay both stared at him.

"You don't get it, do you, Lightning?" DeShay said.

"Get what?" said Hornady as the two trail guards walked down from around a rock, rifles in their hands.

"I'll tell you later," DeShay whispered to Hornady, keeping the revolver out of sight but still aimed at him.

"Howdy, Dale," DeShay said to the older trail guard, recognizing him from riding through Whiskey Bend.

"Sorry, Sheriff. I figured that was really you, but I needed to come down and make sure," said Dale Fenders, one of the few outlaws who lived full-time with Orwick's Redemption Riders.

"I understand," said DeShay, giving Hornady a look.

"Did Dad send for you, Sheriff?" Fenders asked.

"No, but he'll be happy to see me," DeShay said confidently. "Ride in with me if it'll make you feel better."

"Naw," said Fenders, "I feel good enough."

Next to Fenders, the younger outlaw took note of the brimless hat stuck down atop Hornady's head and stifled a little chuckle.

"What kind of hat is that, Lightning?" he asked. "Something straight from Chicago, I'll bet."

Hornady looked humiliated, but stayed straight and tall in his saddle.

"Yeah, straight from Chicago," he said wryly.

"Well, you fellows can ride right along," Fenders said, having eyed each of them up and down and noticed nothing unusual. "We'll see you again when you ride out."

"Obliged, Dale," said DeShay. As he spoke, he turned the custom revolver around beside his thigh and gave a glance toward Fletcher, seeing the gunman ready to raise a big Colt jammed out of sight back beneath his rump and start firing.

The two trail guards started to turn and walk

away, but the younger one stopped and looked closer at Hornady's chest.

"Are you bleeding there, Lightning?" he asked, taking a step closer to Hornady's horse.

"Walk away, Brother Toby," Hornady said stiffly, seeing what was about to happen. "Walk away now."

But the young man only stopped and grinned dumbly.

"It sure looks to me like you are," he said.

At that moment, for no reason in particular, the torn front of Hornady's duster fell down past his shoulders, exposing his chest.

Fender didn't know what he was looking at, but he knew something wasn't right. He jumped back quickly, raising his cocked rifle.

"It's a trick, Toby!" he shouted, getting off one wild shot.

Before Brother Toby could get his rifle up, two streaks of blue-orange fire erupted from the barrel of Fletcher's Colt, spun him in place and flung him dead on the ground.

DeShay fired the big custom Simpson-Barre three times, rapidly fanning the hammers. The gun made a distinctly different sound from the Colt, but the outcome was equally deadly. Dale Fenders flew backward, his rifle flipping from his hands. He landed flat on his back, his dead eyes staring up in shock at the purple starlit heavens.

At the sound of the shooting, Hornady's horse

fidgeted, but with his free hand, DeShay reached over and grabbed it by the bridle. The custom revolver pointed at Hornady's belly.

"Don't shoot, Sheriff!" Hornady said. "I wasn't trying to get away."

DeShay settled and swung the smoking revolver away from pointing at its owner. He looked at Fletcher, who raised his smoking Colt and twirled it on his trigger finger. Smoke left a wide silvery circle behind the twirling gun barrel.

"They're going to know you're coming now, Sheriff," Hornady said.

"I expect they will," DeShay said. "But I saw no good in getting the Ranger freed and coming racing back into these men's rifle fire."

"Yeah, with Orwick's men licking at our backs," said Fletcher.

"Sounds like you're feeling better, Arlis," said DeShay.

Fletcher gave a dark grin.

"I always feel better when I've killed somebody," he said, stopping the twirling Colt, the barrel pointed upward in his hand.

Chapter 22

Sam listened to the sound of gunfire in the distance, recognizing the distinct metal after-ring of the big Simpson-Barre. Across the room, Uncle Henry Jumpe and Elder Barcinder turned to each other with thin knowing smiles.

"It's about time we heard from our friend Lightning Wade," Uncle Henry said. "I wonder what he's shooting at."

"I expect he'll be here sometime tonight," said Barcinder. "You can ask him in person."

Sam knew that he had heard the sound of Hornady's custom revolver, but he also knew it wasn't Lightning Wade who had been firing it.

"You men carry on," Barcinder said to the two young churchmen guarding the Ranger. "Dad will deal with him first thing come morning."

"Yes, Elder Barcinder," said one of the guards. They both appeared to be at attention as the elder and Uncle Henry turned and left. The two young men, Lyndel Rowe and Hiram Smith, relaxed now that the church leader was gone.

They had shoved the Ranger into the small timber building moments earlier. Now they stood back looking down at him as he struggled up onto his knees in the darkness. The only light in the building came from the moon shining through an iron-barred window.

"Look at him, Hiram," Lyndel said under his breath. "They are all the same. They have no God, no beliefs. They're no better than the dumb brutes in the field."

"And this one, a man of the law," said Hiram with disdain.

"Huh, what law?" Lyndel chuffed.

"They are all heathens, men without souls, Lyndel," Hiram replied, also under his breath. "Thank God Dad has shown all of us the right path."

"Yes, thank God," Lyndel agreed.

"Anyway," said Hiram, "I wouldn't want to be in this one's boots once Brother Caylin gets his nose set and his black eyes attended to."

"He's going to beat him senseless," Lyndel said, shaking his head slowly.

Sam looked up at them, his hands tied together in front of him with a few inches of slack rope between his wrists.

"Can I get some water?" he asked quietly. His eyes had already made a sweep around the room.

The only thing he'd spotted that might be of any help to him was a rusty spoon, half-covered with dirt, underneath a wall timber. As he asked for water, he stood in a crouch and moved over a few feet to the wall. He sat down and leaned back, a few inches from where the rusty spoon lay.

"What do you say, Hiram?" Lyndel asked his guard partner. "Should I get him some water?"

"No," said Hiram Smith, "we brought him here. We're watching him. That's all we were told to do."

"Yes, but still, *water . . . ?*" said Lyndel Rowe. "What harm is there in that? I don't mind going and getting him some."

"Do what suits you," Hiram said. "I'm going to sit right outside the front door, where we're supposed to be."

The two turned and left. Before the door closed behind them, Sam snatched the small metal spoon from the dirt. He felt along the bottom edge of the wall in the thin, grainy light and found a flat, thick foundation stone. Keeping as quiet as he could, he began rubbing the metal edge of the spoon back and forth, sharpening it.

He stopped rubbing when the door opened and Lyndel Rowe walked back in and held a dipper of water down to him.

Sam drank the dipper empty and handed it back to the guard.

"Obliged," he said quietly. He leaned back against the wall and watched as the guard turned and left.

As soon as the guard had closed the door behind himself, Sam went back to rubbing the edge of the spoon handle against the stone. He needed the edge to sharpen enough to cut the rope wrapped twice around his wrists. After a few minutes, he held the spoon by its bowl and tested the sharpness of the handle's edge against his thumb.

It would have to do, he told himself.

With a twist of his wrist he turned the spoon and started sawing the edge back and forth on the bite of the rope. But he stopped before cutting through the first wrap when he heard the thick nasal tone of the big churchman who had made the mistake of backhanding him earlier on the trail.

"We're not supposed to let anyone in there, Brother Caylin," Sam heard one of the guards say on the other side of the thick door.

"I promise you, Young Brother Lyndel, I won't be a minute," said the thick gruff voice. "Before Dad has him hanged, I owe this man a good bloodletting. Look at what he did to me."

"Go on, let him in, Lyndel," said Hiram Smith. "It'll be fun to watch."

Sam heard the door latch lift on the outside.

"I don't want to watch," Lyndel said. "I'll wait out here."

"Boy, I do," Hiram said, sounding excited at the prospect.

Sam pushed himself up the rough timber wall to his feet and stood waiting, the spoon tucked away between his bound hands.

When the door opened, the flickering glow of a small lantern entered the room. Hiram Smith stood holding the lantern up as the huge, broad-shouldered man stepped inside, rolling up his shirtsleeves.

Lyndel Rowe backed out the door and closed it.

"Well, well, Ranger," Brother Caylin said to Sam, a nasty grin spread beneath his badly engorged nose, his black swollen eyes. "I was just telling these young men, before Dad hangs you I want a piece or two of you myself." He swung his right hand behind his back and pulled out a long skinning knife.

Sam only stared, his back against the wall.

"Oh no, Brother Caylin!" said Hiram, his eyes going wide. "You never said anything about cutting him—"

"Shut up," said Caylin. "I'm saying it now. For what he did to me, he's got a bad cutting coming."

Lyndel backed away, holding the lantern.

Sam held his ground against the wall, his hands tied in front of him. "Are you sure you want to do this?" he asked quietly, his feet planted firmly apart as the big man loomed in closer, the knife blade drawn sidelong, ready to make a swing.

"Oh yes, you bet I do, Ranger," said Caylin. He crouched, moving in closer, as if at any second the Ranger would bolt and try to make a run for it. "I've thought of nothing except doing this ever since you—"

That's close enough, Sam told himself.

He sprang forward from the wall with the quickness of a mountain cat, stopping Brother

284

Caylin's words short. The big churchman, his arms spread wide, moved too slowly to protect his face. All he could do was let out a torturous scream. So did Hiram Smith, who stood back watching in horror, seeing the Ranger make a hard lunging stab, handle in his right hand, and bury the bowl of the spoon deep into Caylin's left eye socket, rounding it deep just beneath the eyeball itself.

Caylin's knife flew backward from his hand and bounced off the wall, landing at Hiram's feet. Sam jammed the spoon deeper into the bleeding eye socket before turning it loose. The big man staggered in place, shaking. His screams resounded long and loud.

As Caylin screamed in agony, Sam grabbed the handle of an empty waste bucket sitting on the floor. He made a long, vicious swing, both bound hands on the handle, and shattered it to bits alongside Brother Caylin's thick jaw. The big man crashed down face-first. Luckily he landed on the right side of his face, the spoon handle sticking from his left bleeding eye.

Hiram's first move was to throw his rifle up to his shoulder. Yet, seeing how things were going, instead of firing he hurriedly backed out the door and slammed it shut before Sam could cross the room to get his hands on him. Outside, Lyndel latched the door quickly as more churchmen came running from every direction.

Inside the building, in the darkness, Sam snatched up the skinning knife and dropped onto his knees beside the downed man. Searching the man's pockets and along his waist belt, he found no gun.

"Ranger, give it up," Uncle Henry Jumpe's voice called out as his big fist pounded on the thick door. "You're not going anywhere. We've got more rifles trained on this building than you can count."

"Your good *brethren* here will lose his eye if he doesn't get some help," Sam called out. "He could die from it."

Sam heard voices speaking back and forth. Then he heard Jumpe say angrily, "A *rusty spoon?* How in the world did he get his hands on a rusty spoon?"

"I've got his knife," Sam said. "I'll gut him if you try rushing in here."

"Good, you do that, Ranger," said Jumpe. "Before you do, I've got somebody who wants to talk to him before you kill him."

"Anybody you send through that door is dead," Sam called out. He was bluffing, trying to stall, buy some time until DeShay and Fletcher showed up—if they'd been behind the gunfire he'd heard to begin with. All right, he admitted to himself, getting out of here alive looked pretty slim. . . . He backed to the wall and slid down into a crouch. He reversed the big knife in his hand and cut the rope off his wrists.

A moment passed; he stared at the front door as it opened slowly and a frightened-looking woman slipped inside holding a glowing lantern. She clutched a small boy to her side, his arms around her waist.

"Mr. Ranger, don't murder us, I'm begging you," the woman said in a trembling voice. "I'm Iris, one of Brother Caylin's wives. This is his oldest boy, Young Caylin. You've got to let us drag poor Caylin out of here." She nudged the boy as if giving him his cue.

"Mr. Ranger," he said, "please don't kill my pa."

Sam just looked at them, realizing that these churchmen of Dad Orwick's had found far more uses for their wives and children than fieldwork and carrying firewood.

"All right, out there," Sam called out past the door, "you win. Come get him out of here." He sat back and let the knife fall from his hands.

As the building filled with armed churchmen, their rifles and shotguns pointed at the Ranger, Sam rose to his feet and held his hands chest high. Three men hurriedly dragged Brother Caylin out the door, his wife and son right behind him, the spoon handle sticking straight up from his bleed-ing eye.

Barcinder stood in front of Sam, flanked by two riflemen and Uncle Henry Jumpe.

"I had hoped we could make it through this night without incident, Ranger," Barcinder said.

"But all this disturbance has interrupted Dad's evening." He glanced at Uncle Henry and the two riflemen. "Take him up the hill. Dad wants to see him tonight."

Jumpe gave a dark chuckle.

"Somebody bring a rope," he said. "We'll be needing one as soon as Dad's finished with him."

With a lasso tightened around him, pinning his arms to his sides, the Ranger was marched up the pathway leading to Dad Orwick's, a rifleman flanking him on either side. Uncle Henry Jumpe walked in front of him, leading him by the rope. A dozen armed churchmen followed, as did Frank Bannis, Morton Kerr and Riley Dart. The three outlaws lagged back a few feet.

"We get inside, fade off to the right. There's a side door there. When Barcinder gives a sign, we bust in, kill Dad and anybody standing close to him."

"Whoooiee," said Dart, excited, "this is the kind of stuff I was born to do."

"This is what Barcinder said to do?" Kerr asked.

"Are you going to start questioning what I say, Morton?" said Bannis.

"No," said Kerr, "it's just that we're taking an awful big chance with all these armed church-men—"

"Forget it, Morton," said Bannis, cutting him off. "The ones who don't run will likely shoot one another once we make our move." He looked at Kerr as they walked along and added, "And, yes, it is what Barcinder said to do, except he figured on us doing this tomorrow. The Ranger fouled things up spooning the big fellow's eye. So now we do it tonight instead."

They walked on behind the churchmen until they reached a stone-lined path leading around the right side of the large house. There they split away from the others without being seen and stopped at a large side door. Kerr and Dart's eyes widened as they saw Bannis pull out a large key and slide it into the door lock.

"Where'd you get that?" Kerr asked in a whisper.

"Take a wild guess," said Bannis.

"Elder Barcinder is slick enough he thinks of everything, I reckon," Kerr whispered.

"You reckoned right," Bannis whispered.

He turned the key and shoved the door open slowly into a pitch-blackness broken only by a slanted intake of purple moonlight.

Dart started to close the door behind them, but Bannis stopped him.

"Leave it open some," he said to him over his shoulder, "else we might crack our heads if we have to get out of here in a hurry."

"Good thinking," Kerr whispered.

As the three walked deeper into the large, dark house, Mattie Rourke slipped from the nearby brush up to the opened door and eased inside, the rifle she'd taken from her saddle boot in the common barn pressed to her bosom.

Hearing the footsteps of the three men moving stealthily through the house ahead of her, Mattie turned into a dark hallway where she noticed a thin line of lamplight seeping beneath a closed door.

Dad's bedroom? Could she be that lucky—catch him here on his way to meet with Barcinder and the men all the way on the other side of the large house?

She eased down the hallway to the door and turned the knob silently. Inside the room, she closed the door just as silently and stepped over to the foot of the large feather bed. Seeing someone under the covers, she raised the rifle to her shoulder and cocked it.

"Who's—who's there?" asked a frightened young woman who sat up in the bed, pulling a blanket up across her bare breasts. "Dad, is that you?" she said sleepily, her eyes not yet registering who stood there in the grainy flicker of lamplight.

Mattie let out a tight breath and lowered the rifle.

"No, it's not Dad," she said, moving around to the side of the bed. She realized this was one of Dad's new wives—*children, victims,* she thought, correcting herself. "You keep quiet, dear," she said. As she spoke, she felt moved to reach out and cup a hand to the young girl's cheek. The girl was barely in her teens, hair the color of fresh cream, eyes the palest of blues, even in the dim light.

Feeling Mattie's hand on her cheek, the young girl dutifully held the blanket open a little for her and said, "Are we supposed to . . . you know?"

Mattie took her hand from the girl's cheek and eased the blanket back in place.

"No, dear, we're not supposed to do anything," Mattie whispered.

"Then what?" the girl asked.

"You get yourself dressed, child," Mattie said. "When you hear a commotion across the house, you slip out of here and go."

"Go where?" the girl asked in a whisper.

"Anywhere," Mattie said. "You'll be free to do whatever suits you."

"In that case, can I stay?" the girl asked.

"Stay?" Mattie just looked at her. "You want to stay here?"

"Yes," the girl said. "I'm bound to Dad as of tonight. I'm now one of his wives. I don't want to leave."

"What about your freedom?" Mattie asked. "Do you want to give that up?"

"Oh, goodness, yes," the girl said. "Dad's scouts found me and bought me from an orphan train four months ago. I've been fed and groomed and given clothes, and even shoes!" Her eyes glistened; she shook her head. "So, no, ma'am, I've seen all the freedom I ever want to see."

Mattie felt her eyes well up a little at the girl's words.

"You can't mean that, child," she whispered. "Look what he's done to you." She thought of the whip scars on her back, and what she would have given for this same opportunity had someone offered it to her years ago.

"Oh, but I do mean it," the girl said, childlike. "Dad has done nothing new to me. I've had men, both heathen and religious, do the same thing to me since I was ten. It always hurt, and I was always sick afterward. With Dad it's different." Her expression softened.

Mattie only stared and shook her head slowly. She felt a tightness crawl in the scar tissue on her back.

"It still hurts some," said the girl, "but at least Dad has bound me to his spirit, for eternity, in heaven. Think about that. . . ." She appeared to drift off to a peaceful place for a moment. "I'm bound not only to him, but to all of his wives—a nice big family, all my own. Don't you see?"

Mattie felt herself start to raise the rifle slowly, with the same dread of purpose she'd sensed in the Ranger when she'd watched him put the lame horse out of its suffering. Yet she stopped herself and took her right hand off the stock, lest she carry out some misplaced act of self-determined pity before she could stop herself.

"Yes, I see," she said. She let the rifle slump in her hand and backed away toward the door. "Lie there quietly awhile, dear. Somebody will come and look after you."

Chapter 23

A guard ushered the two riflemen, Uncle Henry Jumpe and the Ranger into the large house and closed the front door behind them, shutting out the other armed churchmen. Standing in a candlelit foyer, Sam looked all around while the riflemen flanked him. Jumpe pulled a gold watch from his pocket, checked the time and put the watch away.

"Interrupting a man who's bonding himself a new wife this time of night, Ranger, you'll be lucky if hanging is all you get." Uncle Henry ended his words with a cruel smirk.

"Bonding is not something to make jokes about, Uncle Henry," one of the rifle guards repri-manded.

Jumpe's dark grin vanished, replaced by an ugly scowl.

"For your information, *Brother* Shelby, that was no joke. I take this religion as serious as the rest of you." He lifted his chin. "As a matter of fact, I'm becoming a bound brother myself. My spirit will be as *bound* as the rest of you."

"Oh, really?" said the other rifleman.

"Yes, really," said Jumpe. "So you might want to start watching your mouth regarding me. I don't plan on remaining one of you knotheads at the low end of the trough."

"You'll be a convert," Brother Shelby said, "whereas I was born to it."

"So?" said Jumpe. "All that means is you're more apt to be an inbreed. Us converts bring in new blood to this bunch."

Shelby withered under Jumpe's fierce stare. Sam looked down at the floor, noting the round indentation Jumpe's peg leg left in the plush red carpet.

"Look sharp now, Brethren," Jumpe said at the sound of a door opening and closing at the end of a deep stone-tiled hallway. Sam looked down the hallway, seeing how it stepped down, one terraced level to the next, into the steep hillside wed to the rear of the house.

"Where's the woman who rode here ahead of me?" Sam asked, hoping someone would answer without thinking first.

"You mean Isabelle?" said Brother Shelby, doing just as Sam hoped he would. "She went to stay with Barcinder's wives, last I heard—"

"Shut up, Brother Shelby," Jumpe said, cutting him off. "Now you're even sounding like one of the inbreeds we're trying to weed out."

"I am *not* one of the inbreeds, Uncle Henry," Brother Shelby said with a sullen look. "And if I were I'd be proud of it. God has a plan and purpose for inbreeds too."

"Yeah, yeah, I've heard all that *everybody's-good-for-something* malarkey before," Jumpe said. Under his breath he murmured, "Good for panther food and sandbagging a dam." He dismissed the matter as the echo of Barcinder's footsteps barked along the stone hallway tiles.

Sam had heard what he'd wanted to hear. Somewhere around the compound Mattie Rourke was still on her mission. Between her and DeShay, there was a chance he might yet ride out of here alive. A slim chance, he thought, but slim was better than none at all.

"I hope that's not arguing I hear," Elder Barcinder said, walking up and stopping, his hands on his hips. He carried a long-barreled Remington revolver stuck down in a red waist sash.

"Not really, Elder," said Jumpe, "just the good Brother Shelby here trying to convince me he has as much *purpose* in life as an inbreed as anybody else does."

"I did *not* say that," Shelby cut in with a harsh snap. "I am *not* an inbreed."

"Words to that effect," Jumpe said gruffly, with a shrug.

"No, they weren't," Shelby insisted, not letting it go. "Dad knows I'm not an inbreed. He knows who fathered me."

"Quiet, Brother." Barcinder settled the unstrung rifleman with a raised hand. "Dad has quite enough on his mind this night without us adding to his aggravation."

Peculiar, Sam thought, recounting the conversation he'd just heard. He studied the floor and shook his head slowly.

"You there, Ranger. Look at me," Barcinder demanded, staring at Sam coldly. "I hope you're prepared to meet the very saint whose righteous kingdom you've sought to destroy."

Righteous kingdom?

Sam only returned Barcinder's scorching stare. There was no arguing or reasoning with these people. He wasn't going to waste his breath—he would need it to get away from them, and get away from them he would, he assured himself, eyeing the big Remington at Barcinder's waist.

Odds were against him right now, but once they were all inside the room at the end of the hall where Dad Orwick would be within his reach, he would find a way to turn this into *his* game. In a room of men where gun handles stuck up from waist sashes and holsters, and rifles were as plentiful as walking canes among the infirmed, if he couldn't get his hands on some kind of shooting gear, well . . . that would be his own fault.

Seeing that the Ranger was not going to offer a reply to Barcinder, Uncle Henry Jumpe let out a dark little chuckle and gave a tug on the rope looped around Sam's abdomen.

"Let's go, Ranger," he said.

Leading Sam on the rope, Jumpe and the two riflemen followed Elder Barcinder down the long terraced hallway to a thick wooden door. On either side of the door, the hallway split and moved away in opposite directions deeper into the hillside. Flickering torches lined the chiseled stone walls.

When the door opened, the Ranger followed Jumpe across a room with walls of chiseled stone. Facing a smaller black-shadowed grotto, Jumpe pressed the Ranger down into a tall wooden chair.

"Mind your manners, Ranger," he warned. As he spoke, the two guards took position, one on either side of the tall wooden chair.

"I'll try," Sam said. He glanced back and forth at the two riflemen. Then he turned straight ahead.

Looking into the black chiseled-out cavern facing him like the locked jaw of some yawning giant, Sam saw Barcinder step into the blackness with a burning candle and set the candle tin on a wide table. Only as the candle flame sliced into the darkness did Sam see the shadowed figure standing in a hooded robe, looking out at him. On the edge of the table sat a large canvas bank bag. The money stolen from Goble's bank, Sam deduced.

"Ranger Burrack, I won't waste words," said the hooded figure. "You killed my son. Now it's time I wield the wrath of the Lord upon you."

"I didn't kill your son, Dad," Sam said. "If you're talking about the boy lying dead above the water hole, you killed him when you sent him off robbing and murdering with your outlaw mercenaries. You should have kept him home, where he could have learned to hide behind all the women and children, like the rest of your *saints*."

Dad Orwick ignored the insult. Sam felt the riflemen on either side of him stiffen at his remark.

"I sent him off, only for a while, to learn the ways of the heathen's world, and how to support the Lord's work here in *our* world. Before I could bring him back to me, you slew him, shot him down as if he were a maddened dog."

"No, I didn't shoot him, Dad," Sam said coolly. "I found him dead and dragged him off the trail into the rocks. I thought for a while that the person riding with me shot him." He paused and looked around at Barcinder, then Jumpe, and continued. "But now I know I was wrong. I can prove who killed your son. It was someone right here in this room."

"He's lying, Dad," Jumpe cut in. "Say the word,

we'll hang him tonight, this minute! Or I can put a bullet in his head!"

Orwick stared out at Jumpe, his face shadowed by the hood.

"We didn't bring you in here to prove anything, Ranger," Orwick said, overlooking Jumpe. "We know the truth. You killed him. We didn't bring you here to hear your side of anything. We brought you here to charge and punish you. We don't live by your laws or your reasoning, or your principles. God provides our moral reasoning and our law as He sees fit. We only follow."

"Then I've got nothing for you, Dad," Sam said. "I won't waste time saying how you've taken your own twisted morals and laws and justified them by calling them God's." He had already laid out his plan for what move to make when the time was right. For now he wanted to play this out.

"If you've gone so far that you no longer even have the human *curiosity* for the truth, let alone the spiritual need for it, then have your fool move this rope up around my neck and let's get on with it. You can wax righteous the rest of your life, but you'll die never knowing who pulled that trigger."

The cavern fell silent; Dad Orwick stared into the candle's flame.

"Yes," he finally said in a whisper, "raise the rope around his neck, and let's get on with it."

Sam braced himself, ready to make his strike, first to his left, then his right, then straight ahead.

Here goes, he thought, seeing Jumpe step up in front of him, ready to loosen the rope and raise it to his neck.

"Wait," Dad Orwick said, just as Sam started to lift his left foot from the stone floor.

Sam stopped. He managed to check himself down and take a deep breath.

Easy, he told himself. *This situation's getting better every minute.* He glanced back and forth, seeing the boot toes of the riflemen on either side of him. Then he tried to look up at Dad Orwick's face, still hidden inside his hood. Behind Orwick he saw a broad-shouldered trail duster draped on the tall chairback. In the center of the chairback he saw a wide-brimmed hat. Yet something about Dad Orwick didn't seem right. He wasn't sure what. . . .

"Wait?" said Uncle Henry, speaking to Barcinder in a lowered voice, not about to speak that way to Dad himself.

Elder Barcinder raised a hand to calm Jumpe, Barcinder himself not worried about a thing. After all, he had gunmen poised to do his bidding. He gave Jumpe a secretive nod. Everything was all right. He folded his hands behind his back and gazed up at Orwick.

"Dad," he said quietly, "would you like us to take the Ranger back to the stockade building for now, perhaps bring him back later?"

"No," said Orwick, "I want to hear what he has

to say. If I don't like it, I can have his tongue cut out and nailed to the outhouse door." He looked from Barcinder to the Ranger. "Share this truth you have with me, Ranger. Who in this room killed my son, and what proof do you have?"

Sam had Orwick's attention. He was certain Uncle Henry Jumpe had killed the young man, but he would have to time this conversation just right in order to prove it. With his forearms held to his sides by the rope, he pointed at Jumpe.

"There's the man who killed your son, Dad," the Ranger said. "I saw him ride away while your son's body was still warm."

"That's a lie!" shouted Jumpe, who had stepped away from Sam a moment earlier. Now he moved back in close, his hand wrapped around the revolver holstered on his hip. He fumed, "You, Ranger, are a blackguard, a liar and a poltroon!"

"I saw you there," the Ranger insisted, lying.

"You never saw me there. I was never there!" Jumpe bellowed. He started to draw the gun.

"Take your hand off that gun, Uncle Henry," Orwick said in a firm tone. He saw something unsettling in the way Jumpe was reacting to the Ranger's calm allegation. "Better yet, bring the gun up here and give it to me," he added.

"Dad!" said Jumpe. "You can't believe this man! I was not there, nowhere near there!"

"Take the gun from him, Elder Barcinder," Orwick said.

Barcinder stepped over quickly and jerked the revolver from Jumpe's holster. Jumpe stood with a look of disbelief on his face.

"Dad, please!" said Jumpe, as Barcinder stepped over and laid the gun on the table beside the burning candle.

"Shut up, Uncle Henry," Orwick demanded. He looked back at Sam and said, "Go on, Ranger . . . tell me more of your *truth*. Keep in mind you're still the enemy here, no matter what."

Sam stared at him, his hands gripping the chair arms.

"The truth is, I was lying, Dad," he said. "I didn't see him there."

"You see!" said Jumpe. "He *was* lying! Let me kill him, Dad. Put a stop to all this!"

"I had to lie to get to the truth. I had to tell you he was there to get him to deny it," Sam said. "Now that he's denied it, I'll prove he *was* there. Once I prove he was there, he can't deny it again."

"Ha, you're crazy as hell, Ranger," said Jumpe. "I was not there, and you *cannot* prove otherwise."

"Don't use that language here in this place, Uncle Henry!" shouted Orwick. "Or it will be *your* tongue nailed to an outhouse door."

"I'm sorry, Dad. Please forgive me," said Jumpe, trying to calm himself. "This blasted Ranger has me at my boiling point."

You haven't heard anything yet. . . .

The Ranger reached out slowly, loosened the rope with both hands and lifted it over his shoulders. It fell to the floor at his feet.

"I saw his peg leg print all over the ground," Sam said as he reached inside his vest pocket. "But I know telling you that is a waste of time without you seeing proof for yourself."

Orwick, Barcinder and Jumpe watched intently.

From his vest pocket, Sam fished out the small silver wheel with broken remnants of the horsehair watch fob attached to it. He pitched it up toward Dad Orwick. It landed on the table and started to roll, but Orwick clamped a hand down in it. Then he raised his hand and looked at it closely, recognizing it right away. He lifted his head and stared at Jumpe from inside the dark hood. Jumpe fidgeted in place.

"I found *this* near your son's body," Sam said, "lying in the dirt where it fell. That *is* the truth, so help me God."

"It's yours, Jumpe," said Orwick in a flat, dry tone. "I've seen it thousands of times." He picked up the big revolver and cocked it adamantly.

Barcinder had edged up closer. He craned his neck, took a close look and nodded in agreement.

"It's his, no doubt about it, Dad," he said quietly. Noting the big gun in Dad's hand, ready to fire, Barcinder figured it was time he put some distance between himself and Jumpe, at least for the moment. "Now that I see this, some other things I've suspected him of are starting to fall into place."

"Oh?" Dad said, without taking his eyes off Uncle Henry Jumpe.

"I have reason to believe his plans were to first kill Young Ezekiel. Then kill you and take over. All he has talked about lately is becoming one of our saints, taking his own wives, overseeing our mercenaries, getting his hands on our money, is what I'm thinking."

Jumpe stared, dumbfounded. *What the hell . . . ?*

"Uncle Henry, you dirty rotten son of a *you-know-what!*" said Orwick.

Son of a you-know-what?

Sam stared at Orwick. *Unbelievable.*

"Wait, Dad!" Jumpe shouted. "Barcinder's lying too!"

But Orwick didn't wait. The big pistol began to buck in his hand. Bullets flew. The first shot nailed Jumpe in his chest, spun him around and slammed him backward into the guard on Sam's right. The second shot whistled past the Ranger's shoulder.

Sam, knowing he was still the enemy, raised his bootheel as he had planned to earlier and drove it down on the boot toe of Brother Shelby on his left.

Brother Shelby bellowed in pain and jack-knifed forward; Sam grabbed the rifle from his hands, stood up just as Jumpe's body fell to the stone floor and slammed the rifle butt full force into the other guard's face. Another bullet sliced through the air as the guard flew backward, knocked out cold.

Sam swung the guard's rifle toward Dad Orwick, but only caught a glimpse of him as Orwick vanished, candlelight and all, into the blackness behind the smaller cave. The glow of the candle diminished as his boots resounded down a long stone tunnel. Sam raised his rifle for a shot, but had to swing the barrel toward Barcinder, who stood to the side of a smaller cave, the pistol raised from his waist, firing repeatedly in blazes of blue-orange flame.

"Men! Help me!" Barcinder shouted as he fired.

The rifle bucked in Sam's hands. Barcinder flew backward into the darkness. As Sam levered a fresh round into the rifle chamber, a small door carved into the stone wall swung open on the right side of the room. Sam flung himself behind the large chair as bullets barked toward him from the guns of Frank Bannis, Morton Kerr and Riley Dart.

Sam got off three shots as the outlaws scrambled for cover, seeing both Barcinder and Uncle Henry Jumpe lying dead on the floor.

"Frank, we're jackpotted!" Dart shouted, not knowing how many guns they were facing. He ducked behind a large stone embedded in the wall beneath a burning torch.

"By God, I'm not!" shouted Kerr. He made a

stand in the open on the stone floor, his Colt blazing toward the Ranger. Brother Shelby, who had fallen to the floor holding his toes, rose into a crouch and tried to make a dash for cover. But a shot from Kerr's Colt stopped him cold. He hit the floor, a large Smith & Wesson sliding from a belly holster and skittering across the stones.

Sam took aim on Kerr, and in doing so caught a glimpse of Mattie Rourke as she ran in through the open side door. She didn't even slow down as she raced through the darkened grotto and vanished into the tunnel. Still on Orwick's trail, Sam realized. Kerr's shots ricocheted and whined, making long streaks of sparks in a black world of stone. Sam lifted himself from behind the thick bullet-riddled chair and sent a bullet slicing through Kerr's chest. The gunman fell out of sight.

From behind the large table where Orwick had stood, Frank Bannis fired three quick shots at the Ranger, the bullets kicking up more splinters from the tall-backed wooden chair. Sam ducked, then came up and pulled the rifle's trigger on an empty chamber. Bannis heard the empty rifle click, and came running.

Out of bullets. . . .

Pitching the rifle aside, Sam grabbed Shelby's Smith & Wesson and fired two shots into Bannis' chest. The outlaw fell to his knees and wobbled there, his gun gone, his bloody hands clutched to

306

his ribs. Hearing gunshots from deep inside the tunnel, Sam rose into a crouch and ran across the room in their direction, knowing Mattie was in there.

Frank Bannis watched him disappear into the tunnel.

"Isabelle," he said as loud as he could, although it amounted to not much more than a strained whisper. Then he fell forward onto the cold stone floor.

Chapter 24

On his way across the body-strewn room, the Ranger jerked a burning torch from its stand on the wall. Then he picked up the rifle Frank Bannis had left lying on the floor behind the large table and ran on as two more shots echoed from deeper down the tunnel.

"Mattie. Mattie, it's me, Sam," he called out loudly, knowing how quickly she would pull a trigger. "Don't shoot. I'm on my way."

From thirty yards deeper down the descending tunnel, Mattie's voice echoed back along the stone walls.

"I'm down here, Ranger," she said. "I've got him pinned. He's going nowhere but Hades." She lay pressed against the stone wall in a chiseled-out indention, her torch burning low on the floor beside her. The flames illuminated ancient drawings of stick figures, one group chasing another with what looked like clubs and rocks in an ancient endless battle, their rewards unrevealed.

A few yards away, Dad Orwick lay behind a rounded pine timber that time had turned stonelike, to the color of sand. He peeped up over the timber at the Ranger's words, his hood still hiding his face.

"Mattie . . . did he say?" he called out, his extinguished candle standing in the dark at his side.

"Yes! I'm Mattie Rourke!" she ranted in reply. "Remember me, Dad? Remember everything you did to me? You beat me into submission, forced yourself on me, mounted and bred me like I was a beast in season—me and my poor sister, Isabelle! Your wife who you've now thrown aside?"

A silent pause fell over the darkness.

"Oh my dear God," Orwick said finally.

Mattie levered a round angrily into her rifle chamber and fired a wild shot in the direction of his voice.

"You have no *dear God,* you pig!" she shouted as the bullet whined off the petrified timber in a streak of orange. "You never did have! All you ever had were fools who followed you. But they can't help you now, Dad. I am the *past,* come back to kill you!"

The Ranger heard her ranting as he drew closer. He slid to a halt and ducked against the wall at the sound of the rifle shot. He held his burning torch low, out at arm's length at his side. He heard Orwick's voice across the cavern he found widened before him.

"Mattie," Orwick said. "You were never my wife. Neither was Isabelle. You've made a mistake coming here."

"You can't talk your way out of this, Dad!" she shouted. Another rifle shot rang out. "We were your first wives, Isabelle and I. Now you've replaced her with more scared, hungry children."

"You two were *never* my wives, Mattie! I had to turn Isabelle away for younger wives. She's my *mother!*" he shouted louder, to be heard above Mattie's ranting.

The Ranger froze at Orwick's words, the torch flickering at his side.

Silence fell again. This time it hung in place for what seemed like a long time, as if the darkness had run out of air and now had to struggle for breath and regain its essence.

"Oh, dear God," Mattie said finally. A realization came over her. Then the silence returned, taking another moment to harness its sanity. "Ezekiel . . . ? Ezekiel Orwick?" she said in a hushed tone.

"Yes, I'm Ezekiel, your nephew," Orwick said. "Only now *I am* Dad Orwick in the flesh. Dad went to glory last year. He sits at God's right hand. Both his name and his ministry are rightfully bequeathed to me, his firstborn. It has all been sealed and bound by the hand of God, through his most holy Council of Angels."

Mattie fell silent again; the Ranger left his torch on the ground and inched over closer to where Mattie's torch lay burning in the dirt.

"Aunt Matilda?" Orwick called out. "Can you see now why I had to unbind Mother Isabelle—even a couple of my older half sisters who God had instructed Dad to take as wives years earlier?"

"Yes," Mattie said quietly. "Stand and let me see you."

"You won't shoot?" said Orwick.

"No," Mattie said, "I won't shoot. Not if you're my nephew Ezekiel."

The dark figure rose from behind the rounded timber and pushed the hood back from his face. Mattie looked at him, recognizing him from his childhood, seeing the family resemblance. She sighed.

"What became of my children, Ezekiel?" she asked.

He shook his head and spread his hands slightly.

"We were never told," he said. "You must remember how things were done back then. People were kept in the dark about most things." He added in a deep sincere tone, "That's

310

something I'm going to change, once I get things the way I want them. No more hiding the truth, misleading people."

"Does anyone know you're not *the* Dad Orwick yet?" Mattie asked.

"Not yet," he said, "other than my closest saints. But they'll be told, when I decide the time is right—when I know they can accept it."

From the cover of darkness, the Ranger cut in.

"I hate to interrupt a family reunion," he said, "but like you said, we're still enemies, you and I, remember?"

Orwick half crouched, gun still in hand, and looked around in the darkness.

"Ranger? I believe you now," he said. "I know it wasn't you who killed Young Ezekiel. Is there any way we can square things between us? Now that I'm Dad, I want to get along with the lawmen across the border the way Dad himself always managed to do."

"Not a chance," Sam said. He edged along the wall in the darkness, the Smith & Wesson up, cocked and ready. "You rob banks and kill people. You're leaving here today with your hands behind your head, or your bootheels dragging dirt. You decide which suits you."

"The Goble's bank money is on the table out there. Take it back," said Orwick.

"I plan to," Sam replied.

Before Orwick could say anything more, Mattie

suddenly blurted out, "Young Ezekiel is the boy I shot at the water hole?"

"What, you shot my son?" Orwick shouted.

Sam saw him turn back in the direction of Mattie's torchlight, still crouched, still ready to fire.

"Oh my God! I didn't mean to," Mattie said standing, stepping out of the indentation into the small circle of flickering fire. "I didn't know. . . ." She held her rifle, but Sam felt doubtful she would use it right now.

"Mattie, stop, look out!" he shouted, seeing Orwick taking aim at her.

Without waiting another second on her, Sam fired. His shot hit Orwick dead center of his long robe and sent him staggering backward a step, still aiming at Mattie. Sam fired again, and this time Mattie swung the rifle into play and fired with him. Both of their shots hit Orwick, knocking him backward to the stone floor. His gun fell in front of the timber. The two stood ready to fire again, seeing a bloody hand reach over the rounded timber and feel around weakly for a moment. Then the fingertips fell limp to the ancient dirt.

Stepping over to where Mattie stood, Sam reached out and took the smoking rifle from her hands.

"Are you all right?" he asked.

"I shot my nephew—Isabelle's son. I shot her son, and her grandson," she said. She shook her head. "Vengeance has betrayed and misused me, Ranger."

"Vengeance betrays and misuses us all, Mattie," Sam said quietly. He stuck the Smith & Wesson down into his waist.

"How will I ever tell poor Isabelle?" she said.

Sam took a breath and looked at Orwick's body lying on the stone floor.

"You didn't kill her grandson. Jumpe did," Sam said. He nodded toward Orwick's body. "As for this one, was it your bullet or mine that killed him? Who can say?" He paused. "Some folks who wouldn't tell her about this at all," he said.

"I—I don't know that I can be one of those folks," Mattie replied. She stared at Orwick's body. "Would it be wrong not to tell her I shot him, Ranger?" she said.

"I'm not the one to ask, Mattie," Sam said. "That's something you'll have to settle with someone who knows more than I do."

"You mean God," she said.

Sam didn't reply. Instead, he turned toward the tunnel. But before taking a step, he saw another flickering torch moving fast toward them. He stepped back and pulled Mattie around behind him.

Suddenly, in the tunnel opening, Brother Caylin stood tall and broad-shouldered, a thick club in his right hand, a burning torch in his left.

"There you are," he growled at the Ranger,

stepping forward. A thick white bandage covered the left side of his face. The spoon handle still stuck out from his eye socket. A circle of blood on the white bandage surrounded the protruding spoon. "Before they remove this from my eye, Arizona Ranger Sam Burrack, I'm going to beat you to death as bad as I can! Then I'll be able to lie down and let them do what they need to do."

A club . . .

Sam stood still, staring at him, the rifle leveled at him waist high.

"I'm holding a rifle aimed at you," Sam said, wondering if maybe the big man didn't see it.

"I know it. I've got one good eye, still enough to see how to properly bash your brains out," he said, moving closer a step at a time.

All right. . . .

Without raising the cocked rifle, Sam squeezed the trigger. The bullet hammered the big man in the chest, sliced through and out his back in a red mist of blood. The big man grunted, staggered, but righted himself and kept walking. Sam fired again. The second bullet hit him two inches below the first. More blood misted behind him. He kept coming, staggering more, but with the club and torch still raised chest high.

That does it. . . .

Sam raised the rifle to his shoulder and took aim. This time when he pulled the trigger, the bullet hit Brother Caylin in the center of his forehead. He tumbled backward and fell dead on the floor.

Sam stepped forward and looked down at him; a cloud of rifle smoke gathered overhead on the cave ceiling. Out of habit, he toed the thick club away from the man's hand.

Bare hands . . . then a knife . . . now a club, Sam reflected. He shook his head and looked at Mattie.

"Did this man not own a firearm?" he said quietly.

"I don't know," Mattie said. "There's so many people here I never knew, never seen before."

Sam shook his head again. He considered some of the people he'd encountered, Brother Caylin, Brother Shelby, Elder Barcinder, Isabelle . . . and Ezekiel Orwick himself.

"I have to say, Mattie, these people are the strangest folks I've ever come across. What makes them all act this way?" he asked.

Mattie stood silent for a moment, until he turned and looked at her questioningly.

"What way?" she asked.

Seeing she was serious, Sam said, "Never mind." He picked up the burning torch Caylin had dropped, and the two walked into the long tunnel back the way they came. On the way past Orwick's desk, Sam picked up the canvas bag, checked it and saw the pile of stolen bank money inside. With the bag in his free hand, they walked on.

Outside the large house, at the bottom of the stone pathway in the center of the compound, Sheriff DeShay and Arlis Fletcher sat atop their horses, their rifles covering the few remaining churchmen who had not vanished when they rode in. The churchmen sat bunched together on the ground, their rifles and shotguns in a pile off to the side. DeShay and Fletcher kept watchful eyes moving around the wide valley and up toward Orwick's house on the rocky hillside.

Behind DeShay, Lightning Wade Hornady lay draped over his horse's back, a long, thick string of black blood hanging from a gaping hole in his head, bobbing slowly toward the ground. A skinny cat sat licking at the black puddle of blood in the dirt.

"Here they come now," Fletcher said, seeing the Ranger and Mattie Rourke walking down the path, looking back and forth, appearing surprised to see no fighting going on, just the sheriff and his posse man watching over the churchmen as if they were a small herd of sheep.

DeShay raised his free hand to let Sam know everything was all right.

"I see you got the bank's money," he called out.

"Looks like I've got it all," Sam said, "some of the payroll money too."

"That's welcome news," DeShay said. As Sam and Mattie stepped down the last few feet of hillside, DeShay turned his horse quarterwise to the Ranger.

"Can you believe this?" he said. "We rode right in here without a shot fired. A lot of them cut out at the sight of Hornady's brains dripping out of his head. But mostly the rest just carried their guns over and gave them up. Said they didn't know what Dad wanted them to do, so they weren't going to do a damned thing."

"Pardon me, Sheriff," a churchman said from the ground, his hands chest high. "Nobody used *that* word when you arrived."

"Oh? What word?" DeShay asked.

"You know," the man said. *"D-a-m-n-e-d,"* he spelled out.

Sam and DeShay just gave each other a bemused look.

Fletcher slumped in his saddle, shook his lowered head and said in disgust, "I don't know —is there any difference in *saying* than there is in *spelling?* Don't it both mean the same thing?"

"Easy, Arlis," said DeShay. "It's these folks' religion. They've got the right to it."

"Yeah," said Fletcher, "pay me no mind. I'm still sick from unripe mescal."

Sam and Mattie looked at Fletcher.

"It's true. He's got the worst mescal sickness I've ever seen," the sheriff said. "He's puked up stuff would kill a lizard."

Sam turned and looked at Wade Hornady's body.

"How'd he get here? What happened to him?" he asked, eyeing the torn duster hanging down from the dead man's shoulders, the brimless hat hanging by its string.

"He came following us at a full run," DeShay said. "We set a rope line between a pine and a cactus. What a jolt he took."

Sam winced.

"But that's not what killed him," said DeShay. He gave a nod toward Fletcher. "Arlis, my *new deputy* here, couldn't stand him commenting on his mescal sickness, even though, I have to say, Lightning was more than sympathetic, having drunk the old Mexican's brew himself, to the same result."

"Tell on me, why don't you, Sheriff?" Fletcher said with a half-angry scowl.

"The Ranger don't care," DeShay said. "You're my deputy now."

Fletcher stared at Hornady's body and said, "He just wouldn't shut up about it, on and on . . . how sick it made him, how sorry he felt for me, *yak, yak, yak.* When a man's sick on mescal he don't want to hear all that. I either had to kill him or kill myself. So there he is."

DeShay eyed the Ranger, seeing how he would take Fletcher's act. "He had it coming, Ranger," he put in quietly.

Without reply, Sam gave an understanding nod and looked at one of the churchmen on the ground.